SLASHES IN THE SNOW: A BAUM SQUAD NOVEL

M NEVER

Slashes in the Snow: A Baum Squad novel
Copyright © M. NEVER 2019
All rights reserved

Names, characters and incidents depicted in this book are products of the author's imagination, or are used fictitiously. Any resemblance to actual events, locales, organizations, or persons, living or dead, is entirely coincidental and beyond the intent of the author or the publisher. No part of this book may be reproduced or shared by any electronic or mechanical means, including but not limited to printing, file sharing, and email, without prior written permission from author M. Never.

Cover Design By:
Marisa Shor, Cover Me, Darling

Editing By:
Candice Royer

Proofreading By:
Insight Editing Services
Elaine York, Terri Fantauzzi

Cover Photo By:
Wander Aguiar

❦ Created with Vellum

SLASHES IN THE SNOW: A BAUM SQUAD NOVEL

FOREWORD

"We were together . . . I forget the rest." — Walt Whitman

1

Kira

THIS MAY BE the worst fucking idea I've ever had.

I stand static in the doorway of the most intimidating establishment I have ever stepped foot in. I'm an outcast, and every eye pinned on me knows it. Every steely, sharp, probing pupil glaring in my direction.

I take a deep breath and talk myself out of running for my life. If I leave now, I may not have much of a life left to run for.

I take a tentative step forward, and the worn wooden floorboard creaks beneath my foot.

Ohhhh, you can do this. Just walk. Just walk. One foot in front of the other. Right, left, right, left.

I balance on a tightrope as I make my way up to the bar. It's old, wooden, and weathered, much like the bartender behind it. His grey beard is longer than my hair, and half his face is puckered with scars. Holy fuck, he's scary. And by the way he's staring at me, he's not finding any entertainment in my presence.

"What can I get you, princess?" His voice is raspy as I stand before him, a million tiny stabs of judgment tearing my body apart from the captivated audience around me.

"I'm looking for Ky Parish," I announce, placing my hands on the bar's sticky edge. *Ick.*

The old man's grey, wiry eyebrows shoot up, and a low hush ripples over the patrons. I glance around at the rugged faces sitting at the few tables sprinkled around the room and those paused from shooting pool. If I didn't have everyone's attention before, I definitely do now.

A moment later, two large men with thick beards and leather vests flank me. They're not as old as the bartender, but definitely just as intimidating.

"What kind of business you got with him?" The guy on my right leans on the sticky wooden top. He's way younger than the bartender. Late twenties max, with long, copper-colored hair pulled up in a messy bun, and a pair of the brightest green eyes I have ever seen.

"It's personal." I clear my throat.

"Personal?" he snorts.

"Yes." I square my shoulders, trying to make my five-foot-four frame look as large as possible.

Agent Orange smiles down at me. It's a condescending, humor-filled expression that makes me prickly.

"No one gets an audience with the Prez unless they got one of three things. Drugs, money, or pussy. Which one you offering?"

I cock my head and stare up at the leather-clad monster. "None of the above."

"Then you ain't got no business with him."

"Yes, I do," I argue. "I need to see him."

"We hear lots of women say that," the dark-haired man on my left snickers as he lifts the hem of my pleated skirt. I smack his hand away and take a step back. There's a wave of laughter in the room at my expense. *Assholes.* Every one of them.

Panty Peeker is just as tall as Agent Orange, not as broad, but still menacing, nonetheless. *Yup, this was definitely the worst fucking idea I've ever had. Thank you, desperation.*

I continue to backpedal to the door, Agent Orange, Panty Peeker, and a few other men trailing in my direction.

"Since the Prez is preoccupied, you could always *talk* to one of us," Agent Orange offers salaciously.

"I'll pass," I sneer, still backing up. It feels like the walls are closing in on me. Everyone in the bar is staring at the little preppy princess who has no business being here. My heart hammers in my ears as I'm stalked like an animal. Only a few more steps and I'll be out the front door. As soon as my foot hits the rickety porch, I'm going to make a run for it.

"Where you going so fast, hot stuff? We were just getting to know each other." The door is blocked by two more men, and I know I'm fucked.

Fucked. Fucked. Fucked.

"I'm not interested in getting to know any of you," I assert, even though I'm scared out of my mind. I know someone like me doesn't belong in a place like this, and all the men surrounding me know it, too.

"We're interested in getting to know you." One of them fondles the end of my blonde hair.

"Yeah, give us a chance." Another places a hand on my shoulder.

"You got pretty legs." Yet another eyes me up like a piece of sugary candy. I smack each advance away, panic clawing at my throat like a terrified cat up a tree.

"Get away from me," I hiss.

My order falls on deaf ears though. I'm no one to men like these. Ruthless, fearless, savage. I'm a new, shiny toy, and it's clear they want to play.

I become claustrophobic as the circle tightens around me and hands touch me from every direction. Just before I scream in terror, a deep voice bellows, *"Enough."*

I jump sky high as the men scatter around me.

Holy fuck.

I take one more panicked step back and hit the wall. There's nowhere left to go. I wipe my watery eyes and try to calm my hammering heart as the apparition stares me down. He appeared literally out of thin air. I stare back, straight into his arresting blue eyes. They're on fire, burning with indignation. I've only heard stories of the infamous Ky Parish. Tales of a man who was fearless, loyal, and a tad bit reckless. A man who survived the travesties of war as a Marine and emerged a hero. I don't know how biased these stories are since the man telling them was Ky's father, but they all sounded sincere. Gerard Parish, my stepfather, is incredibly proud of his son, which is why I'm here. Everything I've been told about the man led me to believe he's someone I could turn to, possibly even trust. But the person standing before me is a stark contrast to the image I had in my head. He looks . . . *pissed*. No humanity in his eyes, just hatred. Hatred directed right at me. I don't understand where the feeling stems from. I've never met him before. He has no reason to dislike me. *Does he?*

"You know who I am?" I ask meekly. I wanted to have this conversation in private, but it doesn't look like that's going to happen.

"I believe I do." His voice is low, raspy. Sort of sexy. I shouldn't even be thinking that. But I can't help it. The only time I've ever seen Ky was in his boot camp graduation picture Gerard keeps in his wallet. And that person — the cute boy with immense life twinkling in his eyes and a suppressed smirk that concealed trouble — and the one standing in front of me are starkly different. The person in front of me is stormy, hard, and intimidating. Hot as fuck, and definitely not a boy, but a man. A man who's seen a lot of this world and wears his scars predominantly on his face. Namely across his left eye where a long, angry slash stands out.

"What the fuck are you doing in my bar?" Ky cuts right to the quick.

"I needed to speak to you." I try to keep my voice even.

"About what?" He crosses his arms and glares. "My dad?"

"No." I notice all the attention this conversation is garnishing. "Is there somewhere private we can go and talk?"

Ky's lips twist up sinisterly, and I shiver. "Sure, out-fucking-side. You can wait . . . forever." He all but kicks me out of the bar. "Beat it. I'm not interested in anything my deserter father or one of his princess pussies has to say."

I jerk my head back from the blatant insult. I knew Ky Parish was rough around the edges. I didn't know he was a complete and total dickhead.

"I need your help," I whisper, pleading.

"I don't give a crap what you or your family needs." His tone rumbles with animosity. "Now — Get. The. Fuck. Out." He punches every word.

I feel my eyes round and my lip pout. This was not what I was expecting. I don't really know what I was expecting when I came face to face with Ky Parish, but a repeated backhand of insults was definitely not it. I know Ky and Gerard are not on the best terms, but I didn't realize it was this bad, or that he had such ill will toward my mother and me.

I stand up straight, the wall helping me stay horizontal. "You know, I've heard Gerard call you a lot of things. Fucking jerk-off was never one of them." I sidestep to the right, and I'm out the front door. Dashing to my little red BMW parked on the gravel lot, I try to slam the driver's side door as fast I can, but my arm is nearly ripped out of its socket as it hitches on something. I look up to find a dark figure blocking out the sun, holding my car door hostage.

Fuck. I pissed him off. Not the objective for today's visit.

"What exactly has my father told you about me?" he demands.

"Why do you care? I believe your exact words just were, and I quote, 'I don't give a crap about you or your family,'" I spit.

"You're mistaken. What I said is, 'I don't give a crap about what you or your family needs,'" he corrects. "If you're going to quote someone, at least make it accurate."

I bristle. Is he being serious right now?

"Can I go, please?" I yank on the door handle. "This was a huge fucking mistake. I see that now."

The door doesn't budge though. He clearly isn't letting me leave that easily.

"Not until you tell me exactly why you're here. Is my dad okay?"

"He's fine." I fight against his stronghold on the door. I just want to go. Disappear and forget I was ever here. I'd like Ky Parish to do exactly the same. "He's in Paris with my mother."

Ky scoffs, "Of course he is. Living the highlife with his high-profile fucking princess."

"Huge fan of my family, I see," I rip on him as I continually tug.

"Huge is a bit of an exaggeration." Ky moves slightly, and I go flying across the front seat as the force of my fight slingshots me back, the door slamming closed with an absurdly loud crash.

Fucker.

I punch the engine on, but he reopens the door before I can pull away.

"Why did you come here?" he leans over me and asks with all seriousness. I get a perfect look at him. All the hard yet soft lines of his face. The golden five o' clock shadow that matches the messy mop on top of his head. And his eyes. Damn those arresting eyes. They're almost turquoise from the way the light is hitting them.

I have to remind myself to breathe. Ky Parish has to be one of the most striking men I have ever encountered, slash across his face and all.

"I need help," I answer honestly, lost in the taxing moment. Lost from the proximity of our faces and the strange attraction to this man. This man I don't even know, who's technically my stepbrother, even though we are more strangers than siblings.

"What kind of help?" he entertains me.

I swallow hard. "I think someone is following me. Maybe . . . stalking me?"

"You don't sound sure."

"Because I'm not sure." Ky regards me like I'm crazy. At the moment, I feel exactly that.

"You aren't sure if someone is stalking you?"

"No. Yes. I don't know," I scramble. "I just know weird things have been happening."

"Like what?"

"I feel like someone is watching me. When I'm sleeping. When I leave the house. It's just a creepy feeling."

"Why come to me? Why not just go to the police?" Ky straightens up, folding his muscled arms across his chest. All the colorful tattoos peeking out from the hem of his short sleeves bulge and ripple as if animated for a short second. The serpent around his forearm eyeing me makes me inwardly shudder. I despise snakes.

"I went to the police. But I have no hard evidence. Just a feeling. They can't do anything about that."

I know it sounds insane, but it's true. Someone is watching me. I feel it every time I walk into my house. It's freaking me out. And I'm scared. Scared to be alone. Scared to sleep. Scared to walk in and out of my own home from fear of the unknown. Someone, I'm convinced, is fucking with my head.

"Why aren't you in Paris?"

"With my mom and Gerard? I'm supposed to go at the end of the month. After finals. I'm in grad school."

"I see," he muses. "So, what is it that you want from me?"

"I'm not sure, honestly. Help?"

"What kind of help? A bodyguard?"

I shrug. "Maybe. I don't know. I'm just . . . just . . ."

"Just what?" Ky presses. The weight of his stare feels like a thousand pounds of sand being poured on top of me. I suffocate under it.

"Scared, okay," I exasperate. "I'm scared." I hate admitting that, but it's the truth.

Ky continues to gaze down at me in all his menacing glory. I wish I knew what he was thinking. He's more stoic than a Roman statue.

"I'm nobody's bodyguard, Snow."

Snow?

"Please," the word springs from my mouth. "I have money. I can pay you."

Ky actually laughs. "I don't need your money."

"Then there must be something. Something I can trade or give you?"

His humor dies, and the cold, calculating man from earlier reappears.

Ky is skin-tinglingly silent for way too long. I wait on pins and needles for a response, and finally, he gives me one. "You don't have a goddamn thing I need." With that, he slams my car door shut. Conversation over. I watch him head back into the bar, boots kicking up dirt as he strides away. He walks with so much confidence and authority. So much hostility, too.

My last resort disappears into the bar called The Lion's Den, which is aptly named since it feels like I just narrowly escaped from one.

2

Ky

"Scared, okay . . . I'm scared."

Those fucking words. I can't get them out of my head. Or her. I can't get her out of my fucking head either. Those wide, earnest eyes, long blonde hair more beautiful than spun gold, and her body. Goddamn, just as perfect as fucking perfect could be. I'd never laid eyes on anyone so angelic. Almost like a living work of art. A doll or Disney princess come to life.

Snow White, I dubbed her in my head — purer than the freshly fallen snow. A wide-eyed doe in a lair of wolves. And if anyone was going to devour her, it was going to be me. The Alpha.

Kira Kendrick clearly had no idea what she was walking into. It was written all over her gorgeous face.

My estranged father's stepdaughter. My stepsister, if you really want to get down to the nitty-gritty. She's no more family to me than a field mouse in the basement, though.

I haven't spoken to Gerard "Gambit" Parish in over two years. Ever since he walked away from me and our club for a woman no one knew. He just turned on a dime one day, renouncing his presidency and all ties to the Baum Squad Mafia. An MC club my great-grandfather, Alfred Baum, helped found. This club is a family tradition, and he just turned his back on it, and me, for an expensive piece of fucking ass.

My father became a stranger virtually overnight, leaving me to fend for myself and take care of a club way before my time. But I did it. I stepped up and kept it going. Filling his shoes better than I thought I was even capable of. This club is my life, the members my brothers. I could never do what he did. Just walk away. What kind of leader, friend, father, does that? Not me. Not ever. Not for no one.

"You gonna bet, Slash, or just sit there with your thumb up your ass?" Bone heckles me from across the poker table.

"Leave him alone. The Prez has got a lot on his mind." Vet takes it upon himself to speak for me.

"Hell yeah, he does, and those thoughts are in the form of a hot, blonde piece of ass that strolled into the Den today. Did you see how short that skirt was? She looked like a damn virginal tennis player."

"Fuckable from every angle," Breaker adds.

"Enough." I slam down the poker chip. Everyone jumps, including me. Where the fuck did that outburst come from? I've heard these guys talk like this my whole life. It never bothered me before, but the idea that any of these motherfuckers wanted to put their hands on Kira makes me a stark-raving lunatic. *What gives?* I couldn't give two shits about that girl. She doesn't even deserve to share the same oxygen as me.

"Testy, testy," Fender mocks. "None of us would ever touch your girl."

"She's not my fucking girl," I hiss. "Don't be fucking ridiculous."

"Oh, no? You've been walking into walls and daydreaming since she left. I think someone's gotta crush."

"The only thing I'm going to crush is your face if you don't shut the fuck up. She dragged in bad memories as soon as she walked through the door. That's what's bugging me. I should've just let you guys have her."

"That's not your style, Prez. We all knew it. We were just having a bit of fun." Vet shuffles the cards like a pro. These poker games are a weekly tradition. Run by my father in the past, and now by me.

"What'd she want anyway?" The cards fly from one of his hands to the other like an accordion.

I hesitate to answer. "Help."

"And you said . . . no?" He deals.

"You know who the fuck she is. I hate him and anyone associated with him."

The table goes silent.

"That's doesn't sound like you, Prez." Fender clears his throat.

"Yeah, well, when it comes to my dad, I don't exactly act like myself." I take a look around. My stack of chips is significantly smaller than everyone else's. My head isn't in this game. Usually by now, I'd be kicking all their asses. When your father is a big-time card shark, you learn a few things. He didn't get the nickname Gambit for nothing. The man knows how to hustle a table, and he made sure his son did, too.

At the moment, I'm not hustling shit. I'm losing my shirt to a bunch of amateurs.

I'm transparent to the six men seated around me — Hunter "Hawkeye" Stevenson, Trevor "Bone" Youse, Damon "Breaker" — as in "Heartbreaker" — Davis, Levi "Fender" Michelson, Quinn "Vet" Johnson, and Hayden "Tempest" Jones.

We've all been friends for far too long, and they know me all too well. They were there when my father walked away. They helped me pick up the pieces when I fell apart, took the brunt of my anger when I couldn't handle my emotions, and rode beside me until I couldn't keep my eyes open any longer. They're so much more than just friends. They're family — the only family I have left.

"Your father aside, you know I can I track her down like this." Hawk snaps his fingers. "Just say the word, Prez."

"Not interested. My decision is made."

A painful knot forms in my stomach from my response.

I hate myself for feeling this way. But fuck that girl, fuck her family, fuck her problems, and fuck my father.

Even if I wanted to help her, my pride won't allow it. The grudge is too big, the blood is too bad. Getting involved with her is asking for all kinds of trouble. Breaking down doors that should stay locked. Ripping open old wounds that have been soldered closed.

My father was my hero. My best friend. And he abandoned me.

Broke me.

I can't forgive him. I won't. Even if my conscience is eating me alive.

Kira needs my help. I saw the desperation in her eyes. But she's too close to all my pain. All my resentment.

Getting caught up with her would be like slitting my wrists open and watching all my pain ooze out.

Nope. Forget that shit.

"Full house." Big Red slams his cards down obnoxiously. "I. Win." He leans over and rakes up the hefty pile of red, white, and blue chips while several of the others groan. That's his third win tonight. Cocksucker.

"I'm out." I slap my cards down. My heart just isn't in it. A stiff drink and some wet pussy is more up my alley. Less brain power needed.

I saunter out of the back room of the bar, all eyes on me as I walk up to Popeye, our resident bartender. I think he's as old as the damn building. He knew my grandfather and was one of the founding members of the club.

"What'll it be, Prez?" he croaks, sizing me up with his one good eye. The other is concealed under a patch.

"Wild Turkey straight up, old man."

He nods and reaches for the bottle. Watching him as he pours a hefty glass of my favorite bourbon, I feel the burn already. I take a large swig once he hands me the drink, and all the shitty parts of the day wash away with a river of alcohol. In no time, I'm surrounded by my brothers and several club whores in short leather skirts and low-cut shirts. None of them as remotely pretty or enticing as my Snow.

I choke a little bit on the bourbon from the erroneous thought. *My Snow?* What the fuck? This bitch needs to get out of my head. *Now.*

One head nod at the redhead rubbing up against me, and she

knows exactly what I want. I drain the last of my drink and head toward the back room of the bar. It's empty now, and even if it wasn't, I'd kick everyone the fuck out. My bar, my rules.

I push the redhead to her knees and lean against the door. *This is what I need.* My fucking mind blown.

She unbuttons my jeans and sets my cock free. It's a little limp, but it's nothing a little tongue action can't fix.

She goes to town, jerking me off while sucking my rapidly growing erection.

Perfect.

I drop my head back and let her have me, thrusting into her hot mouth as she works me over.

"That's it, baby, swallow me. Swallow me fucking whole." I grip her hair and close my eyes, but as soon as I do, an angelic face and pleading eyes shine in the darkness. I shiver, snapping out of my lust-filled haze. The redhead stops.

"You okay, baby?" She bats her big green eyes at me.

I inhale sharply, collecting myself. "Yeah." Callously, I thrust my pelvis back in her face. "Don't stop. Not for anything. Not until I come."

"Yes, sir." She grabs me again.

A command from the President is immediately obeyed. By anyone and everyone.

The redhead goes back to work, sucking and licking and jerking and swallowing, but I just can't get into it. No matter how hard I try, my hormones are rearing, but my head is somewhere else. With someone else. I hate myself for that. For being attracted to *her*, for wondering about *her*, for wanting *her*.

Fuck.

"Harder, faster." I pull on the redhead's hair. Not that I really care to know it, but I didn't even ask for her fucking name. I just want her to erase the images in my mind. To be a fucking distraction.

She does as I command, taking me in as deep as she can. I'm not gentle. I punch my cock into her mouth all while holding her hair firmly in my hands. She whines and gags, but my temperamental orgasm is just slightly out of reach. I feel it; it's right there, teasing me, so damn close. Just not fucking close enough. I start to sweat, ordering my body to succumb, but it won't. It wants someone else. It's demanding someone else. A deity among men. An angel walking the earth. A woman as pure as the freshly fallen snow.

Cocksucking motherfucker.

I reluctantly close my eyes again and picture her. And the moment I do, the hindrance is lifted. I pretend it's her mouth around my cock, worshiping my erection, coaxing me to come. I see her pink cheeks and swollen lips wrapped around my girth, her blonde hair trapped between my fingers. Something snaps inside me. A feeling I've never encountered before. My heart is beating with the force of Thor's hammer, and my arousal is meeting each thump with equal vigor. I don't know what's happening to me. My body is taking over my mind and telling me it wants *her* and only fucking her.

I come like a stick of dynamite upon the realization, a fast crack and explosive aftermath.

The redhead gags as I hold her head in place and unleash like a broken fire hydrant right down her throat.

We both slump once I release her, the girl sucking in air like she was just suffocating. I know I was.

Thoughts of *her* steal my breath.

I'm in trouble. So much fucking trouble.

My mind says stay away, but my body wants to hunt, and my desire wants to feed.

I'm ravenous. Not at all sated from this little interlude. If anything, I need more.

A hunger that's completely brand new has been born inside me. A hunger I don't understand but can't ignore. It's burning through me like a California wildfire.

Every organ, every cell, every molecule is on fire, and there's only one person who can extinguish the flames.

Her.

Only fucking *her*.

3

Kira

Night classes are the worst.

I didn't used to mind them so much, but lately they're terrifying. Walking across campus, alone, in the dark. Racing to my car, alone, in a nearly deserted parking lot. Pulling up to my house, alone, fearful someone is inside.

See the pattern?

I've never been such a scaredy-cat before, but ever since I've had this sinking feeling someone is watching me, following me, I've been jumping out of my own skin over the smallest things.

Tonight is no different. I pull up to a dark mansion, when I swear I left every light in the house on. It's things like this that've been messing with my head. Small, almost unnoticeable nuances, popping up everywhere. Like they're stalking me. The cops can't help because there is no solid evidence, only my word. I don't want to bother my mother and Gerard while they're away for the global launch of Glam's new makeup line, especially if it's just my paranoia getting the best of me. Although, deep down, I don't believe it is. I just can't prove otherwise.

Ky seemed to be my best, last option. And that idea flew right out the window. He seriously hates my family, although I'm not entirely sure why. Gerard never really shares many details about Ky, just that he's a war vet and extremely proud of him. He didn't come to their wedding. He's never spent a holiday with us, and I just kind of thought we weren't his scene. After our encounter today, I get the blaring feeling there is more to the story than Gerard let's on. The only thing I'm left to do now is ride out the rest of the semester and then hop on a plane directly after my last final. Maybe then I will finally feel some kind of security. Being away from California, safe and sound with the people I love the most. My mom and Gerard.

They bought this mammoth of a mansion shortly after they got married. My mother and I lived comfortably in a beach condo for years in Malibu, just the two of us. Then she met Gerard. It was a whirlwind of a romance. They were dating, then in love, then bam! Married. I couldn't fault her for the quickness of it all. My mom deserves love. My father treated her like crap for as long as I can remember, and then when they divorced, he became downright malicious, hitting her below the belt every chance he got. He even tried to sue for full custody of me, claiming my mother was unfit, a workaholic, and a high-functioning drug user. All false. Well, maybe all but the workaholic part. But she was building a business from the ground up. I watched her commitment, her diligence, all her sacrifice, and he tried to take everything.

He would play both sides of the coin while they were married, pushing her to work all while putting down her small cosmetics company every chance he got, and then when it became a global sensation, he tried to take all the credit and consume all the profits. Luckily, my mother was smarter than him. She documented everything. Secretly recorded him verbally abusing her. Took photographs of her bruises when he was physical. Could prove his promiscuity. My dad didn't have a leg to stand on, but that didn't stop him from trying to make our lives a living hell. It was pretty rough for a long time, but once we were out from under his thumb, the freedom was phenomenal.

Freedom. That's what I need. Freedom from the fucking crazy that has plagued my life.

I turn the shower on and rip my clothes off as the bathroom fills with steam.

I'm washing off the whole bad experience with Ky Parish and then hibernating under my covers for the rest of my life. Okay, that's a bit dramatic. Maybe just for the rest of the night.

4

Ky

I PULL up to the obnoxiously pretentious mansion settled on a hillside in the Malibu Hills. We're so close to the ocean I can hear the waves crashing in the dark.

I can't fucking believe I'm here. I can't fucking believe I'm actually doing this. Just looking at the front door makes me drip with disdain. I can't believe my father actually lives in a place like this. It's a far cry from the modest, one-bedroom condo he left behind. Or the dated, drafty bar I inherited when he walked away. The Lion's Den may be two studs short of a shithole, but it will always be my home away from home. It will always be the place I feel most myself. Most at ease. Surrounded by the people I trust the most. The name is appropriate. It is a den — a den of solace and of protection. I still can't believe Kira strolled right in. The girl has got some balls, I'll give her that, even if my guys nearly scared the holy living shit out of her. She left with her pride shaken but intact. It's more than I can say for others who dared to enter the den.

I collect my bearings, banish all the rage into the pit of my stomach, and dismount my bike. Here goes all the shit.

I ring the doorbell and wait, blowing hostile air out of my mouth. I ring the bell again, still waiting, punching my fist against my hand. *Come fucking on.* I bang on the door this time, straight up annoyed. *I know you're here, Snow. Your little red Matchbox is parked in the drive.*

To hell with all fucks. I try the door handle. To my surprise, it's unlocked. I see myself in.

"Kira?" I voice, but the house is so quiet that her name echoes. Walking slowly through the extreme beach house outfitted in all white, I absorb my surroundings. The place is absurdly rich, and pristine, and so unlike my father's taste. This has to be the makings of her, his new wife, and her decorous daughter.

I continue through the house, making my way to the stairs. I creep up the staircase, on the lookout for any sign of life. Jesus, it feels like I'm climbing forever before I make it to the second floor. That's when I hear it, the running water carrying faintly down the hallway. I should probably stop right here and wait for her to come out, but where's the fun in that?

My interest, and *ahem*, my excitement piques, as the thought of a quick glimpse of Kira's naked body proves a high probability.

I follow the sound, passing several rooms until I find the one that's hers. I walk in, not a creak under my boot alerting my presence, and poke around her room. It's as white and pristine as the rest of the house, with a huge, ornate, king-sized bed situated right between two gigantic sets of French doors that lead out to a sweeping terrace overlooking the pool and the vast Pacific.

Fucking hell. These people don't need for nothin'. A spark of anger ignites inside me. All this shit. All the overindulgence, the lavishness, the flagrancy. No wonder Kira just waltzed into my bar without a second thought. She's probably never been denied a thing in her life.

I'm curious if she cried on the way home after I kicked her out on her ass. It shouldn't, but the thought scratches at a depraved part of my soul. The idea of her suffering tickles me on an all-too-dark level.

I shake off the wicked feelings, not wanting to fall back down that black, disturbing rabbit hole. The place I found myself after my father abandoned me and everything he's ever known.

I crack my knuckles and my neck, the stress tightening my tendons. That's when I notice the silence. The shower has been turned off. Like the creeper I have suddenly been reduced to, I stalk across her dark room and peek through the crack in the door to her bathroom. I'm consumed by what I see. A dripping wet Kira, skin perfect and tan, hair long and thick and sun-washed blonde, and body like a goddess blessed straight from the heavens. I grab my crotch in pain. If I thought I wanted her before, I more than fucking want her now. More than fucking yearn or desire or crave. I fucking ache for this woman. The lust brought forth by just the sight of her. It's inhuman, ungodly, a demonic possession. I've met her all of once, and she has a hold on me like none other before her. Salivating as she rubs herself dry, I squeeze my cock to alleviate the pulse that is struggling to take hold of my entire body. When Kira slides the towel down her torso to pat between her legs, all hell breaks loose in my pants.

"Fuck," I murmur, fighting back the flare of arousal. That's when she notices me. Her eyes fly to the door as she wraps the towel around her naked form. There is visible fear on her face. If I doubted her act at all this afternoon, I definitely don't now. I know fear. I understand it. It has breathed down my neck, danced in my eyes, and taken hold of my heart.

"Who's there?" She freezes on the spot. I say nothing. I know I should make my presence known, but being caught a creeper? Not my MO. I've never had to creep on a woman a day in my life. It's not a trait I want to adopt now.

Kira suddenly moves, grabbing something off the vanity, and rushes the door. Her little body doesn't have enough force to barricade through me and the door, so she ends up propelled back on her ass. I open the door and stalk in, finding my very alluring Snow in a very compromising position.

"Were you going to attack me with a hair brush?" I laugh. The idea is utterly preposterous and utterly adorable.

"It's solid steel." She works quickly to cover up her half-naked body.

"You don't have to on my account." I stare down at her like the starving wolf I am.

"What the fuck are you doing here, Ky? How did you even get in?" Kira stands, clutching the cream-colored towel to her chest.

"Door was open." I thumb behind me.

"What door?"

"Um, the front door."

"No." Kira shakes her head feverishly. "That's impossible." She pushes past me like a cute little raging bull. "I locked the door," she insists as I follow her down the hallway. "I put on the alarm." She continues down the stairs in a flurry to the entryway. "I'm not crazy." She punches a few buttons furiously on the keypad.

"You sort of sound a little crazy," I feel compelled to comment.

"I swear I'm not." Her voice is small, and scared, and distant. She doesn't turn around to face me. She just stands in front of the alarm pad with her arms wrapped around herself. "What are you doing here, Ky? You made it very clear earlier today you want nothing to do with me or this family."

Kira sounds a little more assertive now. Maybe she's not as fragile as she looks.

"I might have reconsidered." I clear my throat. I can't say I love the idea of being here, but Kira has piqued my interest. And if it means there's the slightest chance I can dive between those sexy thighs, I'll hang around a bit.

Kira finally turns to look at me. And god, she is so fucking beautiful. So natural, so pure. So tempting.

"Please don't waste my fucking time, Ky." She tries to brush past me, but I stop her, clutching her arms in a stronghold.

"Let's get one thing straight. I don't waste time. Not mine or yours or anyone else's. You came to me for help. I'm here to listen."

"Why the sudden change of heart?" She's skeptical.

I guess I would be too after the way I kicked her to the curb earlier.

"You're hot."

Her face contorts with an exasperated expression. *What?* It's the truth. I never proclaimed to be noble. I'm here for purely selfish reasons.

"I really don't have the time or patience or sanity for this. You can see yourself out." She tries to wriggle out of my grasp. *Like hell.*

"I'm not going anywhere," I stand my ground.

Kira glowers up at me unbelievably annoyed. "If you're just here to jerk off like a peeping fucking Tom, go outside and get it over with. I'll pretend I don't know you're there."

I stop my jaw from dropping. *Well, hello, Ms. Smart Mouth.* You may look as pure as fucking snow, but there is definitely some punch under that pretty exterior.

I lean in close, deliberately encroaching on her personal space. "Snow," I murmur, "if I'm going to come, the only place it's going to be is inside you." It's definitely a promise.

A heavy silence falls upon us as Kira's big brown eyes sharpen.

Scary. *Not.* She's more like an adorable little kitten showing her claws. Think she'd slap me if I pet her? Probably, but it'd be so worth it if I did.

"Get out, Ky," she fumes.

"Not a chance," I refuse. "I'm your problem now."

"That's a perfect way to describe yourself."

"I've been called worse." I shrug.

"I can imagine," she sneers.

This back-and-forth game is fun, especially seeing how easy it is to get under her skin. *Effect ya, do I, Snow?*

"Seriously, Ky." She yanks herself out of my hold. "If you're not here to help me, just leave." Her voice is crackly now. "You can slither out the same way you slithered in." She turns and heads for the stairs, but I snatch her arm.

"I don't slither," I clarify. "And I'm not leaving."

Kira inhales a deep breath and shivers slightly under my hold.

The way her head is hung, her damp hair covers half her face. And I hate it. I want to see her. All of her. All the sharp slants of her cheekbones, and the plump pinkness of her lips. I want her to see me and see no one else.

"I don't have anyone else to turn to, and I'm scared," she repeats what she told me earlier, defeat echoing in her tone. "If you don't want to help me, that's fine, just don't make things worse."

I take her chin and force her to look at me. Her dark-amber eyes are glassy with tears.

Shit, Snow, you're killin' me.

"It's a bad habit I have, makin' things worse."

"Gerard doesn't think so."

"What the hell does he know?" I bark right in her face. His opinion means jackshit, and if he were standing here right now, I'd spit on him.

I suck in a collective breath. My father is a sensitive subject. As sensitive as igniter fluid near a chemical fire. He's the last thing I want to think or worry about. It's Kira who needs my full attention. "Let's talk, Snow." I tug on her arm. Once I concentrate on it, I realize just how delicate and soft her skin is beneath my fingertips.

Kira is hesitant to move, or speak, or even breathe apparently. My little outburst must have spooked her.

"Don't be scared. You came to me for help, so let's see if I can help you."

I can tell she's calculating her decision. She doesn't trust me. Not one bit. Maybe that's a good thing, for the both of us.

It will force her to keep her distance, and remind me to keep mine.

For now.

"I don't know who I can trust. I'm starting to even doubt myself."

I'm torn in so many directions when I look at this woman. My attraction to her is wild. My resentment toward her fierce, and my curiosity is slowly raking me over hot coals because I want to know more. I want to know more about her, about her life with my estranged father, and why she thinks someone is following her. A smart man would just walk away and never look back. Actually, a smart man would seduce the fuck out of the vulnerable woman standing half-naked in front of him, get his rocks off, and then ghost.

Consequences be damned.

But I'm too glutton for punishment to do that. I'm also afraid if I have her once, I'll want her again. And again, and again.

"Let's talk." I remove my hands from her, giving her all the space she needs. All the space both of us need.

"I should put on some clothes." She tightens the towel around her.

"I'm cool with what you're wearing."

Kira shakes her head. "Sit at the kitchen table. I'll be right back."

"Is that that long glass thing that looks like it seats twenty?"

"That would be the one." She nods, heading out of the room.

I meander through the first floor. It's one big, white, palatial floorplan, and I take a seat right at the head of the table. I slink down into the colorless, modern chair that is surprisingly more comfortable than it looks. I gaze down the length of the table, and anger sneaks up on me. How many times has he sat here? How many breakfasts and dinners has he shared with his new, shiny family? Or with high-profile, LA snobs he used to talk all kinds of shit about?

I clench my fists over and over until the blood turns my knuckles red. I hate this place. I fucking hate him.

"Drink?" Kira suddenly shoves a beer bottle in my face.

"Yes." I grab it straight away, pop the top, and take a swig before she even has a chance to sit. I read the label as the familiar tang passes over my taste buds. I guess some things don't change. Same piss, different establishment.

Kira takes a sip of her beer meekly. No, not meekly, politely. I have to recognize the difference. The women I'm used to don't have such ... *etiquette.*

"I didn't take you for a Miller girl." I chug down the beer, attempting to extinguish the rage burning like fire at the back of my throat.

"I have one every once in a while. I started drinking them on poker night." Kira lifts one knee to her chest, and that's when I take notice of her outfit. Ultra-short shorts and belly shirt to match. Why did she even bother to change out of the towel? It covered more.

"Poker night?" I repeat, distracted as I steal a glance at her run-on thighs. She's definitely not wearing underwear. Nope, definitely not.

"Yeah, Gerard started it." She smiles as she takes another sip of beer. "Him, my mom, and me. We were so terrible at first." She laughs. "But Gerard is a good teacher."

"That he fucking is." I pour the amber liquid straight down my throat, resisting the urge to put my fist right through the fucking glass table. I remember all the poker nights we used to have. He started teaching me at the ripe old age of two. It was our thing, always. Even into adulthood. He had the whole club playing, and it was always us hustling everyone else. You can do that when you're the Prez. The money never mattered all that much. It usually went back into the pot for the next game. It was us against everyone else that mattered. That made it fun. That bonded us.

Even when I was deployed and crawling around the shittiest parts of the world, it was my dad who instilled the heart I needed to carry on. To find my bravery. My upbringing made me strong. Made me resilient. Made me clever. My upbringing is what kept me alive, and still keeps me alive. And whom do I owe that upbringing to? The man I despise. It tears me apart day by fucking day. Eats away at my soul. Even as I try to ignore it. Secrets, lies, and betrayal don't sit well with me. Those three things are dangerous, and for a man in my position, they mean a trifecta of deception. Possibly even death.

Honor is all I have. What I can survive on. And when the person you trust most, idolize even, betrays you, it's hard to come back from. Hard to forgive. Hard to move past. And staring at Kira, sitting in this house, I am constantly reminded of that betrayal. Hatred sneaks up on me around every corner. Considering it now, I don't know if I can do this. Do anything she asks. I'll become a buried landmine just waiting to explode.

Kira peels at the bottle's label quietly, and the soft sound brings me back to her. Our eyes meet, hers dark and soulful, mine raw and callous.

"You wanted to talk," she opens up a line of communication.

"That I did." I lean forward and prepare to deliver the unfortunate news.

"You being here makes me feel safe." Kira drops a bomb out of nowhere. I bite back my bad news. "Despite the fact that you don't like me. And you were being a creeper earlier."

"Who says I don't like you? And I wasn't creeping." I defend myself, even though I'm completely in the wrong. I was totally creeping.

She shoots me a cynical look. She's no dummy. She knows exactly what's up.

"I won't deny I'm not a fan of the people who live in this house." I'm honest, if nothing else.

"*I* live in this house," she points out.

"Yeah, but you're hot, so I can overlook it."

"That's the only reason you're here? Because I'm *hot?*"

"Do I need a better reason?"

"I guess not," she sighs.

"Who do you think is following you?"

"Stalking me." She corrects.

"Okay, who do you think is stalking you?"

"I have no idea. I just know someone is. I can feel it."

"Feel it?" I'm skeptical. "You want me to go off a feeling?"

Kira nods.

"And what do you propose I do?"

Kira shrugs demurely. She has abandoned words apparently.

"Stay here with me?" she finally offers.

"What, like a bodyguard?"

She nods again quickly. The idea even seems a little off-color to her.

"Snow," I grunt. "I have a club to run. I can't just up—"

"It will only be for a month," she interrupts my pathetic attempt at an excuse. "Then I leave. School will be over, and I'll be on a plane to Paris to meet my mom and Gerard." *Leave? A plane to Paris?* Why does that aggravate me like an annoying itch? "Then you'll never have to think about me again." Kira drops her head. She's so sweet. So fragile sometimes. "I just don't want to be alone."

Fucking hell. I'm soft for this woman when I sure as shit shouldn't be.

"One month?" I test the timeframe on my tongue.

"One month, then I'm gone," Kira promises.

I deliberate, trying not to imagine the taste of anything else on my tongue. But Kira is just too damn tempting. If there is even the slightest chance I can slip between those sweet thighs of hers, it's worth the thirty days of agony being in this house. It'll be like an episode of *Big Brother*. Expect the unexpected, and try like hell to sleep with your housemate. Or, step-sister in this seriously messed-up case.

The head in my pants is clearly spearheading the decision here.

"So, I'm like suction-cupped to your ass for a whole month?" Not that it would be completely terrible or anything.

"Maybe not suction-cupped, but you could take me to class and possibly sleep here at night?" She bites her fingernail.

"Sleepovers?" I'm intrigued.

"There are several spare rooms. You can have your pick," she's quick to clarify.

"What if I want to stay in your room?" I lean forward suggestively, resting my forearms on the table.

"The floor is hard, but I'll give you a pillow and blanket."

I laugh. At least the girl's got jokes. "This place is like Fort Knox. You really need me to stay here?"

"Yes. Nighttime is the worst. I haven't slept in days, and you've experienced first-hand how reliable the alarm system is. I had a tech out here two weeks ago, and nothing has gotten better. If anything, it malfunctions even worse. The whole house is wired, so if one thing isn't working right, nothing works right. And I swear, someone is lurking around outside. Sometimes I think they even get in the house." She shivers, clearly spooked. "I find little things out of place, like a shirt I swear I put away, or the smell of my perfume lingering in my room when I know I didn't spray any."

"A faulty alarm, and Casper the Friendly Ghost. I think I can handle it."

"It's not a joke, Ky. There is someone out there watching me," Kira is convinced.

"And now I'm here watching you. If they know what's good for them, they'll fuck off right now. Do you have any idea who it may be? An ex-boyfriend? An ex-coworker? Someone at school, maybe?"

"I can't think of anyone, except . . . *my dad.*"

"Your dad? Explain."

"He's just been an asshole my whole life. He loves to play mind games and fuck around. I haven't spoken to him in three years. Not after Gerard kicked him out of the house on my twenty-first birthday. He's a total control freak, and he lost complete control over me that day. I don't know, maybe he knows my mom and Gerard are out of town and is using this as an opportunity for something twisted?"

"That is quite a conspiracy theory." I crack my knuckles.

"You don't believe me." She's offended.

"I didn't say that."

"Your tone implies otherwise."

"I'm just taking it all in so I can devise a plan of action."

"I thought we had a plan of action?"

"No, we have a jumping-off point, but I believe it's better to be proactive than careless. If there *is* someone out there, I want to get my hands on them before they get their hands on you."

The thought of someone else's hands on Kira has me suddenly enraged. *What. The. Fuck?*

"Can I have another?" I hold up the empty beer bottle. I need to cool my fucking jets.

"Sure, they're in the fridge." Kira doesn't move a muscle.

"I guess I'm not a house guest anymore." I push myself up to stand.

"I'm just not anyone's waitress."

I peer down at her before resting my hands on the glass tabletop. Bringing my face obnoxiously close to hers, I whisper, "Snow, by the end of this month, you *will* be waiting on me, buck naked. And you'll love every second of it."

"A man can dream," she hisses back.

"The best dreams happen when you're awake," I slingshot back like the cocky fucker I am.

"I need to sleep," she ignores my response masterfully. "I have an early study group in the morning. There's plenty of beer in the fridge and your choice of spare bedrooms upstairs." Kira sneaks off her chair in a ninja-like move. *Impressive.* "Don't get too drunk; I'll need a ride."

"Study groups were not part of the deal," I argue.

"They were classified under schooling."

"Oh, is that right?" I scoff.

"Yes, that's right." She struts off, and I shut the fuck up, drooling over her sweet, tight, heart-shaped ass.

Soon, I'm alone and thirsty for more than just beer.

Left with little to do besides twiddle my fucking thumbs, I open the fridge and grab another. I stare at the contents inside. Everything neatly placed, organized, and utterly irritating. *Perfect, perfect, perfect,* I gripe to myself as I push around bottles and plastic containers and condiments until the inside of the fridge is in complete disarray. I smile. *Perfection.* One hot mess. I slam the door closed, pop open the beer bottle, and strut to the enormous, white, U-shaped, fancy-schmancy couch in the living quarters. You can't even call it a room.

Propping my feet up, boots and all, onto the white coffee table, I turn on the TV, get comfortable, and prepare to catch up on *Sports Center*. That's when I see it, a picture frame on the glossy-white piece of furniture under the television with three smiling faces. The new, happy family.

It disgusts me. It's almost hard to believe the man in that picture is the same man who raised me. He looks mostly the same, except his salt-and-pepper beard is kept a little neater and his dark hair is trimmed with a bit more style. And the expression on his face, it's so content he's even showing teeth. I'm not sure I've ever seen my father smile in such a way.

A rapid boil of emotions bubbles beneath my skin. I chug the beer, unable to stop glaring at the picture.

I think I'm totally fucked. No, I know I'm totally fucked. I have no idea how I'm going to survive a month without smashing half this house to pieces.

5

Kira

I WAKE up refreshed for the first time in nearly two weeks. Just knowing Ky was in the house set my tensions at ease. I fell asleep as soon as my head hit the pillow. It was glorious.

Now I'm up, showered, and ready to conquer Thursday.

I bound down the stairs, the house bright with sunlight.

Not everyone is appreciating it, though. I find Ky passed out on the couch, a pillow over his face, his leg slung over the back, and nearly a dozen beer bottles scattered all over the coffee table. The *white* coffee table now littered with water stains.

"Hey." I hit Ky's boot. "Wake up, Sleeping Beauty, we have to go."

He protests with an irritated groan, hugging the pillow tighter to his face.

"Ky, I'm going to be late." I shake his leg harder this time.

"Then leave. No one is stopping you."

I jerk my head back. Is he being fucking serious right now?

"*Ky.*" I use all my might to roll him off the couch and onto the floor. He falls with a thud, then a "What the fuck!"

"I said get up. I'm going to be late."

He glares up at me from the floor, his blue irises shining in the bright sunlight, and his scar pronounced across his left eye. Even with the bedhead and ticked-off expression, he's gloriously sexy, not to mention dangerously intimidating.

"You better watch it, Snow. I'm not some fucking boytoy you can boss around." He pushes himself up onto his feet, clearly in no rush to go anywhere. He yawns, stretching his arms over his head like a lazy housecat. I try not to, but I sneak a peek of his inked abs.

"You can look." Ky catches me. "You can even touch if you want." He pulls his T-shirt all the way up, exposing his ripped, tattooed torso. He's obnoxiously proud of his midsection. *Spare me.*

I just roll my eyes and walk away, grabbing my book bag from one of the bar stools at the kitchen island.

"No touching, then?" he calls.

"Nope," I confirm and walk straight out of the front door. I am seriously second-guessing my decision to ask for his help. My wellbeing seems to be the last thing on his mind — fucking me the first. I keep trying to fit the puzzle pieces together. The person inside acts nothing like the way Gerard described him. Don't misunderstand, I wasn't banking on a knight in shining armor or anything, but I was at least expecting a civilized human being. No such luck. Maybe that's what I get for enlisting the help of a man I know nothing about who lives in a world completely foreign to me.

I know what he sees — poor, entitled, little rich girl who can't fend for herself. Who's a damsel in distress. I must look so pathetic to him, but little does he know how much my mother and I have suffered through to get where we are. More money does not mean less problems. It does not erase emotional suffering, and it does not magically heal the past.

Trust me, I wish it did. I would throw cargo loads away if it could fix all the damage done from my childhood.

No, I'm not a damsel, but I am in distress. And as much as I hate to admit it, I need Ky. Bad attitude and all. If I could survive my abusive father and live through my parents' nasty divorce, I can tolerate Gerard's surly son. My stepbrother. The one who hates me and wants to fuck me all at the same time. As if life could get any stranger.

Of course, Ky keeps me waiting. I'm going to be late. I hate being late.

I pace the front yard, awaiting his . . . appearance. One more minute and I am going to rip him out of the house by his blond, bedhead hair.

The black motorcycle parked on the pebbly drive distracts me. I want to knock it over. I remember all the lessons Gerard taught me about bikes. Number one rule, don't mess with the kickstand. I nudge it a bit with my toe. How pissed would Ky be if I just . . .?

"Snow, back away from the bike," he bites from behind me.

So pissed.

"I needed to do something to occupy my time."

"I can give you a laundry list of things to occupy your time. Messing with my bike is definitely not one of them."

"I don't like to be late." I cross my arms hotly.

"I don't really care." He throws his leg over the seat. "Get on."

"I need a helmet." I'm obstinate just because I can be.

Ky picks up the one dangling on his handlebar. "Problem solved."

I take it reluctantly. "What about your helmet?"

"I don't need one." He starts the bike, pulls out a pair of dark black sunglasses from a little secret compartment, and waits.

I'm no stranger to motorcycles. Gerard has a freakin' collection in the garage, and I've ridden every one of them with him. I hop on the back and slide my hands around Ky's waist. I instantly feel the heat of his body as soon my chest presses against his back. I won't lie; I don't hate it.

"Not your first time, huh?" Ky talks trash.

"Nope." I hug him tighter, completely confident. When Gerard came into our lives, so did the motorcycle way. I lost count how many times we've ridden up and down the coast.

"There's a coffee shop on the way. Do you mind if we stop?" I chirp.

"Yes," Ky is blunt.

"C'mon, I need caffeine to be on my A-game." I rub my body against his, sweet and seductively all at the same time. I play dirty, I know.

I can feel the tension in Ky's muscles as he responds to my request. Glancing back at me, he sneers, "Fine. We wouldn't want you flunking out of school on account of caffeine withdrawal."

"That would be bad," I agree.

Ky pops the clutch, and we pull away.

The drive to Pepperdine is a peaceful, scenic drive down the Pacific Coast Highway. The line at Bradlee's, not so much. There is a monster of a wait.

"Are you fucking serious?" Ky rips off his sunglasses. "It's going to take you an hour to get coffee."

"I know." I slide off the bike. "That's why I wanted to leave early, so there was enough time before class." I smile condescendingly.

Ky is not amused. "I can get you the same fucking shit at Starbucks and not lose a year of my life."

"No way. This is one of only three places in all of LA that I can get a lavender latte. A year of your life is worth it."

"Fucking Christ," Ky gripes.

"Not so much a morning person, huh?"

"No. Not when I have to go traipsing all over Cali for a fucking lavender latte." He makes a puke face.

"It's delicious, I promise. I'll get you one."

"Please don't."

I shake my ass all the way into Bradlee's just because I know Ky is watching. I swear, our relationship would be so much more amicable if he wasn't such an ornery prick.

It does take forever to get coffee, and I can spy Ky through the front window becoming more frustrated by the second. He sticks out like a sore thumb, trapped on the curb as hordes of young college students come and go.

When I finally emerge from the coffee shop, Ky looks like he's about to bust a blood vessel. Malibu is so not the biker's scene.

"How exactly are you going to manage that?" he asks as I clutch my coffee and climb back onto the bike.

"I can hold on with one hand. My building is just up the hill. I got skills like that."

Ky snorts. "Dear Jesus, save me. The girl has skills. If you spill one drop of that on me, I'll make you walk."

"No, you won't." I click the helmet back into place one-handed. "See? Skills."

"Did anyone ever tell you you're a cocky little shit?"

"But I'm hot, right?" I echo his earlier statement.

Ky thins his eyes at me but doesn't humor me with a response. I totally get under his skin. He slides his dark Oakleys back onto his face, and we take off.

When we pull up to the entrance of the Graziadio Business School, all eyes are on us. The Harley is flashy and loud, just like the man who's driving it. I don't mind the attention, though. Secretly, I think it's kind of cool, and hopefully it sends a message if anyone is watching. I'm not alone anymore. And this guy is kind of a badass. *Beware.*

"What time do I need to be back?" Ky asks, crossing his arms aloofly, the bike idle.

"I have a four-hour class, then lunch, then another study group this afternoon," I rattle off my schedule as I slide off the bike, hand him the helmet, and sip my latte. All in that order. "So around 5?"

"Around 5?" Ky drawls.

"4:30ish? I'm not exactly sure how long study group will run." I wince cutely, hoping that a little sugar will sweeten his mood.

Ky slips his sunglasses down his nose so only a fraction of his scar and icy-blue eyes peek out. I can't tell if my tactic worked.

"Just give me a half-hour warning, and I'll be here."

"Done." I nod. That seems fair. "I gotta go." I take a step back, but Ky reaches for my arm. "Text me all your dad's info, too. And the names of anyone else you think I should look into."

"I will," I answer, slightly distracted from Ky's touch. It's firm, but not awkward or unwanted. It's almost nice. He doesn't seem to be inclined to pull away either. Instead, he rubs his thumb across my forearm gently. It's a bizarre encounter. One I find myself liking. One that makes my heart beat a little faster and makes my knees feel a little weaker.

"Have a good class." He finally removes his hand.

"I will." I grin subtly, placing my palm right over the place he was touching me. My skin left tingling and warm.

"Later, Snow." Ky twists the throttle, and the bike roars. Then he pulls away, making as loud and flashy of an exit as he did an entrance.

On a scale of one to ten, how wrong is it to crush on your stepbrother?

6

Ky

I TEXT: **My place. One hour.**

Hawk responds: **B there prez.**

I DRY my hair as I walk around my apartment buck naked. I needed a shower, and I needed to jerk off. Both needs have been satisfied. Spending all goddamn night at Kira's with her wearing those tight little shorts, then having her purposely rub up against me all sexy-like on the back of my bike? She was driving me right to the verge of insanity. I have never been more hard up for a woman than I am for her. It's a fucking disease, I tell ya.

I find a pair of clean boxer briefs just as my doorbell rings. Hawk, right on time. The man is never late.

"It's open," I yell and he lets himself in. We greet in my living room him with a hand clasp.

"What's up, Prez? You rang, I'm here."

"Nice to see a friendly face." I drop down onto the leather couch. My place is nowhere near as fancy, or spacious, or sterile as Kira's, but it's home.

"Where'd you disappear to last night? We were all lookin' for you." Hawk claims his own piece of the couch. I've known Hunter "Hawkeye" Smith for nearly twelve years. Back then, he had a hard-on to get into the police academy, but a debilitating knee injury kept him from passing the physical. He stumbled into The Lion's Den one night depressed, thirsty, and hungry for a fight. He definitely found one, too. He got the shit kicked out of him by my father and half his crew, me included. But Hawk had fire. He didn't go down that easily. And after he was all bloodied up and out of gas, my father offered him a beer and a chance to run with the Squad. He liked his spirit. One thing about my father, he's an excellent judge of character. He can tell within five minutes of meeting someone if they're worth your time or not. Hawk was definitely worth our time. He's proven himself loyal over and over again. I would trust him with my life.

He also has some special skills that come in very, very handy.

"I went to see the girl," I divulge.

"The high-priced pussy? The one who came into the club yesterday?" He pushes his glasses up his nose. Don't let the thick, black rims mislead you. Hawk is no nerd, geek, or fool. Crossing him would be like crossing Matt Murdock. Unassuming, but dangerous.

"That'd be the one," I confirm.

"You hit that?"

"No, not exactly. Not like I wouldn't, though."

"You'd be a fucking fool not to."

"She's a little more complicated."

"Complicated how? You catch feelings or something?"

"No. Nothing like that." I blow out a hot breath. "She's Gerard's stepdaughter."

It takes Hawk a second to connect the pieces. "You mean, she's your stepsister?" he quickly realizes.

"Yeah, that. *Stepsister.*" Not my favorite label.

"Well, what'd she want? A family reunion or somethin'?"

"Not exactly. She's convinced someone is watching her. She's totally freaked out, and apparently my father and his new wife are living it up in Paris for some new makeup launch or some shit, and she doesn't want to be alone."

"So she came to you? A man she doesn't even know?" He sounds suspicious.

"Says my father talks highly of me. And that she trusts me." Sounds just as crazy when I say it out loud.

"You sure she is who she says she is?" Good ol' Hawk, always lookin' out.

"Positive," I reply sourly. My feelings are a mixed bag of shit when it comes to Kira.

"So, you're tellin' me all this why? As a confidant?"

"Not so much. I don't care who knows. I'm just gonna be away from the club for a little while, and I need someone to run things in my absence."

"How long is a little while?"

"A month. She'll be done with school, then she'll meet up with her parents" — the word stings like ten-thousand needles stabbing my tongue — "in Paris. Then goodbye, good riddance." I dust my hands clean.

"So, what I'm hearing is you're gonna be spending a lot of time with the high-priced pussy."

"It's lookin' that way."

Hawk considers. "There could be worse ways to spend your time."

"Ya think so, huh? You haven't met her."

"Maybe one day I'll get the pleasure."

"I highly doubt it." The last person I want to bring around my guys is Kira. That combo sounds like a bad deal just waiting to go down. We barely get along, Lord knows what'll happen if we add the six of them to the mix. "I need one more thing." This is where Hawk's very special skills come in. "I need you to look into a guy named Dex Kendrick, current address Beverly Hills."

"Fancy. Who's the douche?"

"Kira's father. And that's a very accurate way to describe him, according to her."

"On it."

Hawk may have never made it to the LAPD, but he is a computer whiz. He works for the city's IT department now and can hack just about anything on a data network. He's an invaluable asset to have in your pocket.

"Anything else, Prez?"

"That's it for now." I drop my head back, resting it on the couch.

"You look wiped, Slash."

"Bro, I am."

"Girl giving you a run for your money?"

"Understatement of the century. She may be hot, but damn, she is a frickin' pain in the ass."

"Ahhh . . ." Hawk punches me in the thigh. "Isn't that how all great love stories begin?"

I gaze at him vacantly. "God, I fucking hope not."

7

Kira

Ky smells so damn good.

He was just as excited to pick me up from school as he was to drop me off, but as soon as I climbed on the back of his bike and wrapped my arms around him, this woodsy, masculine scent overwhelmed me. I shouldn't like sniffing my stepbrother so much, but I do.

Back at home, all is quiet. Even the alarm is behaving. I checked it all day. I can basically control the entire house from an app on my phone. It's like having a cockpit in the palm of my hand. Honestly, though, I don't even know what half these buttons do. Arm, disarm, lock, and unlock is about as far as my knowledgebase can take me.

My nose has been buried in economics books since we got back. I didn't even realize the sun had set until Ky made a ruckus in the kitchen around me.

"I'm makin' a beer run." He jingles his keys in his hand.

Internally, I panic. "Now?"

"Yeah, now. We're out, and the game is going to start soon."

"Well, can I come?"

"Snow, I'm going to be gone for ten minutes. You'll survive."

I want to argue, but he's right. I can handle ten minutes by myself. I'm a big girl, and what can possibly happen in ten minutes?

Ky leaves, and my stomach sinks a bit. I'm trying not to be dramatic, but night is always the worst. I hate the spookiness of the dark, and the shadows outside hiding the unknown.

Since the house is so offset from the highway, and close to the water, only the floodlights and the moon provide any decent kind of light, and trust me when I tell you, it's not all that much. You can't see a thing past the pool. It's just a black abyss rolled out right in front of you.

I go back to studying. Distraction is good. I try to concentrate on the words in front of me, but they're blurry. I'm stressing myself out for no good reason. I take a breath. Ten minutes. Ten stupid minutes by myself. *Kira, don't be such a wimp.*

Back to studying.

I've finally calmed myself down enough to comprehend the words in the book. Sentences and paragraphs are finally making sense. Ah, there, not so bad.

A few quiet moments tick by before a flash of bright light illuminates the room, followed by a sharp, loud crack. I scream. I scream bloody murder and hit the deck, barricading myself behind an island stool.

Not so calm, not so calm. My heart feels like it's going to punch right out of my chest, and I'm having difficulty catching my breath.

Then the rain starts pouring down. It just falls right out of the heavens in heavy sheets.

It barely ever rains in southern California, and thunder and lightning is even more of a phenomenon. A few tears fall from my eyes, induced by the fright. *I'm okay; it's okay,* I talk myself off the ledge. I listen to the sound of the rain showering on the roof. It's such an unusual percussion to me, but beautiful all the same. Lightning flashes once more, brightening the room. I'm surrounded by windows, so it radiates in every direction. The thunder claps loudly again, but I only jump slightly this time. I was prepared. I crawl out from behind the stool and stand. My fear being gradually replaced with curiosity. I've never seen lightning so close to the coast before. The lights flicker as I walk across the kitchen to stand by the windows. A blackout would totally suck, but I'm mesmerized by the rain hitting the glass and the bursts of lightning flitting through the house moment by moment.

I think about Ky, wondering if he made it to the liquor store, or if he got caught in the torrential downpour. Either way, this is definitely going to prolong his return.

The lights finally go out, and I'm struck with a pang of dread. Alone, in the dark. It's never a fun thing.

I stay planted in place. Hopefully, the blackout will be brief. How long can rain this hard last? I start to hear things outside. Bangs, crashes, thumps, all no doubt a result of whipping wind. I jump whenever I hear a new sound or thunder cracks when I'm not expecting it.

There's a slam on the window right in front of me, and I startle like a spooked cat, then lightning flashes, illuminating the dark, and the figure standing right in front of me. A blood-curdling scream escapes from me as I trip backwards over my own feet and hit the ground. My elbow wails in pain as I crawl across the cool flooring in a panic, tears rushing down my face as fast as the rain outside. I struggle to breathe, but am suffocating from the fright, still continuing to scurry to the closest room with a lock. The bathroom. Lightning strikes, and it allows me to see my way. I stand to run, gaining momentum, but I slam into something hard. No, not something, someone. They try to lock me in their arms, but I fight.

"No!" I scream, crying in terror. "Let go!" I kick and punch, adrenaline coursing through my body like a supersonic electric charge.

"Kira!" My name echoes through my fit. "Kira!" He shakes me like a ragdoll. "Calm down, it's me." Ky battles to break through my panic. As crazy as he has driven me over the past couple days, I have never been more thankful to hear his voice. I sob as I melt into him, burying my face into his wet chest.

"There's someone outside. I saw him. He was by the window. He was watching me." I suck in precious air as I incoherently ramble.

"What? Where?" His muscles tense beneath my fingertips.

"In the kitchen. By the back windows. I was watching the storm, and then he was just there."

"Okay, I'll go check it out."

"No, Ky, don't leave me again." I grab onto his shirt desperately.

"I have to go check it out, Kira. That's what I'm here for, no?" I look up at him in the dark, lightning bursting at just the right moment. I see the concern on his face and the intensity in his eyes.

I don't want him to leave, but I also know he has to go.

"I'll lock myself in the bathroom."

"Good idea. Don't open it for anyone but me." He's strict with his instructions.

"Okay—"

"Kira." He clutches my face and points it up toward his. The house illuminates again, and thunder crashes, but suddenly I'm not scared.

"I won't, I promise. Only you."

"Only me, Snow." For the first time ever, my nickname gives me chills.

Ky sends me off into the bathroom, and I lock the door behind me. I can't see a thing, so I feel my way around until I find the vanity, then the toilet. I sit down, wrap my arms around myself, and rock, trying to keep the hysteria at bay. Someone was out there. Someone *is* out there, and they're after me. I shake inconsolably. *I'm not crazy. I'm not crazy. I saw him. I saw him.* I continue to convince myself. *I'm not crazy.* I begin to cry. So many emotions are leaking out, certainty most of all. Validation. Truth, reality, sanity.

"Kira." Ky knocks on the door, and I jump. Jesus, I'm going to have a heart attack by the time this night is through. "Kira, open up."

"Is it safe?" I feel my way to the door.

"As far as I can tell. There's no one out back. I checked the garage and the upstairs, too."

I hesitate before unlocking the door.

"C'mon, Snow, it's all right," he coaxes me.

Slowly and unsurely, I unlock the door and crack it open. I'm blinded by a light. "Where did you get a flashlight?"

"I keep it on my keychain. Comes in handy when I'm hunting stalkers." He flashes me with the mini bright light.

"That isn't funny." I put my hand in front of my eyes.

"You okay?"

"I'm freakin' terrified." I abandon the bathroom.

"You're not alone." Ky tucks me protectively under his arm.

"You're soaked."

"That's what happens when you play in the rain." He walks us over to the couch and urges me to sit. "Don't mind me." Ky begins to strip, pulling off each article of his wet clothing. I can only see bits and pieces of his body as he waves the flashlight around, but it's enough to keep me riveted. Once he has nothing more than his boxer briefs on, he sits down and pulls me against him. "Body heat." He shivers slightly. His skin is so cold. I don't protest, I just wrap my arms around his neck and hug him, giving him all the body heat he needs.

"You drove back in the rain?" I ask curiously.

"Yup. I was inside when I heard the first crack of thunder. I knew you'd probably freak out, so I bolted."

"No beer?"

"No beer." He feigns disappointment. "See the things I do for you, Snow?"

"Oh, the sacrifices."

"No beer is definitely a sacrifice." We shift closer, Ky taking free liberty with his hands. He slides them under my shirt and caresses them along my abdomen, making his way to my back as I turn my body, pressing my chest to his. I can feel his warm breath on my neck and the cold drops of water falling from his hair onto my shoulders. I like being this close. I like being in his arms.

"You're so soft, Snow," Ky murmurs in the dark.

My heartbeat accelerates as I feel his nose brush against mine.

"I'm glad you're here," I admit, navigating through such uncharted territory. Ky is my stepbrother, but my attraction doesn't seem to give one fuck about that.

Our faces hover inches apart as we paw at each other, both exploring, learning, experiencing exactly what the other feels like.

I trace the lines of his neck with my fingertips, following the ridges of his shoulders and toned arms. I touch his hard chest before running my hands up and slipping them into his soft, golden hair.

"Shit, Kira." Ky wraps my hair around his wrist and tugs, forcing my head to tilt back. I wait in the dark, unable to see a thing. I can only feel. Feel him press himself against me, feel him breathe harder against my skin, feel his grip tighten around me.

I'm waiting for what still? I'm not sure. A moment of impact? A forbidden kiss?

Yes, a kiss. That's what I want. I want Ky to kiss me.

That's so crazy, borderline insane, but he's here, just as invested as I am, yet he's hesitating. I wouldn't say no. I wouldn't pull away or deny him. I just don't have the balls to initiate it myself.

"Kira?" Ky utters my name almost as if he's in a state of confusion.

"I'm right here." I place a hand on his cheek.

The tip of his nose touches mine, and we both stiffen. What's happening here? He claims he wants me. Throws out a pigheaded comment every chance he gets, so why is he wavering? Maybe he has the same reservations I do. Maybe he knows crossing a pivotal line will change everything. It doesn't have to. I'm not expecting a thing. We have a deal. One month, then I'm gone.

A man like Ky Parish doesn't come across as the relationship type anyway, and sometimes that's just what a girl needs. Something short, sweet, and fun. A distraction. A swipe right.

I'm going to spontaneously combust if he doesn't kiss me soon. I move my hand to the back of his neck and press gently, indicating I want this, want him — right here, right now. The first touch of his lips fires a cannon of excitement. A feeling that races between my core and my heart.

But a brief touch is all we're allowed as the lights flicker on abruptly, breaking the magnetic connection. It was more like a spell, and I think Ky was under it. Once he realizes exactly what's transpiring, a wall goes up. Something goes haywire. The look on his face as he stares at me is indescribable, and not in a favorable way. But he doesn't move, or release my hair, or push me away. We're just frozen in place. What's he thinking? What does he want? Why is he glaring at me with such . . . disdain? It makes me shrink like a dying violet.

"You can put your clothes in the dryer now." I retreat from his hold. He allows me to go, but he never takes his vigilant eyes off me. What is he looking at? What does he see? "Should we call the cops?" I stand unsurely.

"Hell no. No cops. I'll have my guys look into it." Ky follows suit, standing after he scoops up all his wet clothes. The thunder and lightning have seemed to stop, and even the rain is subsiding.

Maybe our encounter was just as random and haphazard as the storm, and we were just caught up in the quickening thrill of it?

I'm left unsure what to do. I'm totally freaked out, but my instincts are telling me to flee, flee from Ky and his personality shift. I feel beyond stupid. I feel alone and left drifting.

"I'm going to go to bed." I take a step back. The last thing I want is to be alone, but I can't be near Ky either.

"Will you be okay?" he asks in all his half-naked glory. I try not to look directly at his body, or at the writing tattooed across his clavicle – *"For those I love, I will sacrifice"* — or the sleeve of color inked down his arm, or the strategically placed, growling wolf face on the side of his thigh. He's so unlike anything or anyone I know.

His eyes are the hardest thing to avoid. The sharpness of his gaze is penetrating me like a searing ray of icy blue light.

"I'll be fine." I try to sound sure, but my voice betrays me. It's meek, and sad, and constrained. It's hurt. I'm hurt, and I know I shouldn't be. I don't mean a damn thing to Ky Parish, and he just proved that spectacularly.

"'Night, then. I'll stay up. Don't worry about anything," he all but dismisses me, almost eager for me to go.

8

Ky

KIRA IS GOING to be the goddamn death of me.

I've never jerked off to one woman so many times in my life. It's actually becoming torturous. Mainly because it's my own fucking fault.

I had her right there, right in front of me, a hate-fuck waiting to happen. And I choked. I froze. I fell to fucking pieces right in her arms. And now I'm more frustrated and pissed-off than ever.

I let the hard spray of the shower pelt down on my head as I recover from my umpteenth orgasm this week. Being in this house is motherfuckin' torment. Surrounded by the constant reminder of my divergent father and in the continual presence of his flawless stepdaughter.

I touch my face, feeling the raised bump of the scar across my eye. I am anything but perfect, but that's never bothered me before. I've always been confident about who I am, even after my father deserted me. But when I'm with Kira, everything is different. I feel different, and I fucking hate it. It's like I'm broken when I'm around her. It's like I broke in her arms that night in the dark. I still don't understand it, and I'm going to keep punishing her for it until I'm straight again. Until I'm me again.

Witches don't really exist, do they? I'm beginning to wonder. First, my dad with Kristen, Kira's mom, now me with Kira? Sinking into her like a stone in water. That's what it felt like when she touched me. Like I was drowning in the calmest, warmest water, and all I wanted was to drift deeper. To get lost in her, to hand myself over to her.

I don't hand myself over to anyone. Not a man, not a woman, not even a modern-day damsel in distress who looks as pure as the freshly fallen snow. Who I dream about, who I fantasize about, who, if I was any other sucker, would do anything for.

A hate-fuck is about all I'm capable of when it comes to Kira Kendrick. It's all I can offer, and all I was prepared to offer – payback for my fleeing father — until she got her hands on me.

Now I don't know what to do around her, except keep my damn distance.

"Ky." Kira bangs on the bathroom door. "Ky, I'm going to be late."

"Keep your panties on. I'll be out in a sec," I bark. I'm not nice, and I don't even attempt to be. I'm just trying to survive the next three weeks.

I let the water run for several more minutes just to piss Kira off. By the time I'm done with her, she'll hate me more than she can even believe possible. Then she and my father, and his perfect little wife, can live happily ever after and never have to think about me again. Which is exactly how I prefer it.

Once I'm out of the shower, I throw on a pair of jeans, a white T-shirt, and do a quick towel dry of my hair.

"Ky, c'mon, my professor won't let me in if I'm late!" Her voice carries up the stairs. This spurs me to move a little faster. Not because I don't want Kira to be late, but because if she is, and that's true, I'm stuck with her for the night. Can't happen. I've got plans.

I slide my rings on, grab my keys, and put a little more quickness into my step.

"I gotcha, Snow." I bound down the stairs. "You won't be late."

With a huff, Kira follows me out the door. She's beyond annoyed, and that's exactly how I like her. Fucking frustrated, just like me.

I climb on my bike, and Kira follows right along with me. This is the worst part, her touching me. All my hair follicles stand at attention. As much as my mind rejects her touch, my body has its own opinion.

I have considered using her car, but like I said before, I'm a glutton for punishment. A masochist, if you will. The torture is invigorating. It's an adrenaline rush. And I'm a fucking junkie.

Kira places her hands on my stomach, and my muscles clench involuntarily. I just react, no matter how or where she touches me. And I hate it. I. Fucking. Hate. It.

I hate that she possesses that kind of control. She'll never know it, though. I refuse to let her.

I start the bike with a roar of the engine, and we pull away from the obnoxious mansion I've come to despise.

The ride to Kira's school is short but still agony. I need to just go. Go blow off some steam and be with my guys.

I barely acknowledge Kira as she climbs off the back seat.

"Class ends at nine thirty," she reminds me for the tenth time today.

"Yup, I got it." I twist the silver ring around my index finger. Tuesdays and Wednesdays are her late classes, as I'm learning. You know what that means for me? Freedom. "I'll be right here when you get out," I assure her unenthusiastically.

"Still no word about the other night? Who it might have been?" She asks before taking off, she's on a constant pursuit for peace of mind. It's unfortunate I can't give her what I don't have.

I shake my head. "I'm going to see my boys tonight. We'll talk then."

By the expression on her face, Kira doesn't like the idea of me taking off.

"Don't look at me like that. I said I'll be back."

Her eyes tell me everything I need to know. The other night put a wedge between us, and now she's questioning whether or not she can trust me. I haven't given her a reason not to, except maybe for my bad attitude. That doesn't mean I'm going to bail; it just means I don't have to be thrilled about the situation.

"I'll see you later." She pouts her plump, pink lips. They are way too luscious and treacherously alluring. I know the exact image I'll be jerking off to tonight. I inwardly sigh. I'm fucking bewitched, I tell you. By the darkest magic known to man. Lust.

"You know you will," I promise.

Kira turns on her heel and heads for the steep stairs that will take her to the entrance of the building.

I watch her climb each and every one of them, her short shorts she's infamous for and the loose tank top shift seductively with every step.

Masochist, I tell you, because as I study her, all I want to do is chase her down and tell her how much I want to swim inside her. How much I want to drown in the water I was drifting in the other night. How much I want to fuck her until neither of us can see or breathe or even think. My heart palpitates like a jackhammer from just the mere thought. She's the nail being driven into my chest. She's the one who binds me to this cross. My anger and aversion grow larger as the hold she has on me grows stronger. I'm stuck in a hellish place. Between conscience and contempt, desire and disdain.

I want to abandon her, but I also want to stay.

I pull away from Kira and the school, bubbling with more annoyance than I know how to deal with. The only thing keeping me together is the knowledge that in just a little while, I'll be surrounded by my brothers, tossing back some much-needed booze, and blowing off a shitload of steam. I'll forget all about Kira Kendrick for a few blissful hours. Forget about how she touched me. How she said my name. Forget about how much I wanted to kiss her. How I could have kissed her. Forget about how frightened I was that if I did kiss her, I wouldn't be able to stop.

I twist the throttle and the bike rumbles down the highway. I weave in and out of traffic as the thunderous sound drowns out my aggravating thoughts.

When I pull up to The Lion's Den, the dirt parking lot is littered with bikes. It's a buffet of custom Sportsters, Fat Boys, and Low Riders with screaming chrome exhausts and don't-fuck-with-me fenders.

It's good to be home. I park my Softail right in the center of it all where a sign reads "Baumer Prez". Wiping a bit of dirt from the exhaust, I'm hit with a pang of remorse. I should fucking hate this bike as much as I hate him. He built it for me, but I just can't bring myself to let it go. I love it. I loved it from the moment he gave it to me. A totally custom Softail Breakout, chromed to the max,

with big, tricked-out wheels and a wicked tribal paint job. He said he chose the huge twin cam engine because it reminded him of me. Explosive, powerful, muscular, sleek. Those were the words he used. That's how he saw me. He built the bike in my image, and I was never prouder to be his son than the day he gave it to me.

I think there was one thing he didn't realize, though. That engine also gives you a swift kick in the gut when you open it up. It has massive torque, just like me. And he felt my brute force when he announced his sudden retirement. When he all but shoved the keys to the kingdom down my throat and walked away.

I shake off the escalating anger. I'm here to blow off steam, not explode like a steam pipe.

I step inside and am met with an abundance of familiar faces. It looks like the whole club is in here drinking. There are hoots and howls as I walk to the bar. Slaps on the back and handshakes all around. It's my first warm welcome in nearly two weeks.

"Slash." Popeye rests his elbow on the bar top. "The boy is back."

I take his hand and squeeze. He's the only one who can call me boy and get away with it. I've known him my whole life. He's a legacy member and like a second father to me.

"Just for the night." I sit, and Popeye grabs me a beer.

"You ever coming back?" he takes the opportunity to fuck around with me.

"Of course. Who do you think I am, my father?" I take an eager sip of the ice-cold brew.

"You do possess a slight resemblance to his ugly mug." Popeye laughs, and it's a thick, gurgling sound.

"Go fuck yourself, old man," I smirk.

Popeye laughs even harder, his gurgling voice morphing into a full-blown hack.

"Easy there. You're gonna give yourself a stroke."

"At least I'd go with a bunch of pretty ladies around me." He winks his one good eye, referring to Harley and Davidson — not their real names, by the way — who are manning the bar with him. Really, Meghan — Harley, and Davidson — Vanessa, are doing all the work. He just hobbles around back there, getting in everyone's way and drinking up all my scotch.

"How 'bout a little fire, Scarecrow?" A rush of heat passes across my face. I instinctively react, leaning back and grabbing the offender's wrist, yanking his body forward until his chest hits the bar top. There's a thud on impact, and then a huge, howling cackle.

"Gets ya every time." Breaker is in hysterics.

"Do you have a death wish?" I try to hold back my own amusement. Shithead is always pulling stupid stuff like that. "Messing with the Prez has its price." I kick his legs apart and knee at his nuts.

"Yo, yo, yo, watch the family jewels." Breaker uses his free hand to protect his balls. "It might be worth it, though. The look on your face." His body shakes with the fit of his laughter. It's infectious.

"I thought I lost an eyebrow for a second." I haul him upright, then give his head a good shove.

"Missed you, brother." Breaker puts an arm around me and nods to Davidson. "Hey, Pretty, a beer and a shot for the two of us." He winks and smiles, laying it on thick. Breaker lays it on thick to any woman with a decent-sized rack and a pulse. He redefines the term manwhore.

Damon La Rue, or Breaker as we affectionately call him because he can either be a heartbreaker or a ballbreaker, depending on the day, has been part of the Baumer Mafia as long as I have. He's one of my oldest friends. We grew up in this bar together watching our dads drink, fight, and womanize. Breaker's father, Griller, passed away a few years ago. Terrible bout with cancer. But like a true MC, he fought till the end. "To misplaced dads and angel wings," he toasts with the shot of Jack.

I ignore the misplaced dads comment and clink his glass to angel wings. I miss that ol' man. Griller, I mean.

"You two gonna make out at the bar all night, or are we gonna play some fuckin' cards?" a booming voice thunders through the room.

"Keep your fucking pants on, Bone." Breaker picks up his beer. "I was getting in some quality time with my Prez."

"Well, quality time is fucking over," he vibrates with anticipation.

Breaker shakes his head, and his unruly hair flops all over the place. "You gonna do something with this mop?" I give it a tug. "Or just wait for it to get caught in something?"

"Oh, I'm definitely waiting for it to get caught in something." He's lewd. "Tangled up in ten fingers while Davidson over there is screaming my name." He leans over and winks at her.

Davidson, or Vanessa, just rolls her eyes and serves another customer.

"Got a hard-on for that one, huh? She doesn't seem to want to give you the time of day."

"She'll come around." He blows a kiss at her. She ignores him like a pro. It isn't anything new that the bartenders get hit on. That's what they're there for. Booze and boobs. And they're called either Harley or Davidson so no one forgets their name when yelling for a drink. I made it easy for everyone.

Breaker and I finally meander over to a broad man with a thick, red beard and ponytail. He's decked out in leathers and looks ready to kill — which is Bone's normal appearance. Big, burly, and scary as all hell.

We follow Bone into the back room where several poker tables are scattered around. It's been known to get pretty intense in here on poker nights, but tonight, it's just us. Me and my boys. No bullshit, just cards and good booze.

I'm met with a warm welcome around the table. All the usual suspects are here. Breaker and Bone, of course, along with Hawk, Fender, Vet, and Tempest. Six of my favorite ugly mugs.

"Let's get this show started." Tempest shuffles the cards in a flashy display.

"Just a minute," I hold him off. "I need to have a word with Hawk first." Before this card game goes down, I need to know the status of his little investigation. It's been radio silence on his end. Hawk and I head to the back door to talk. It's a private entrance only utilized by the VIP members of the club. Once outside, I ask for the scoop. "Any word on Kira's father?"

"Not much." Hawk spies our surroundings. The rear of the building backs up to woods that the teenagers sometimes sneak away to drink in. Breaker and I had plenty of fun times back there. "I took a look at his financials and ran a background check. He's an outstanding citizen." There is extreme sarcasm in his voice. "He likes high-priced alcohol and high-priced ladies. Preferably at the same time. He also likes to gamble and has had several DUIs, which have all been mysteriously dismissed. He's got friends in high places. And some pretty low ones."

"Think he's got one of those friends messing with Kira?"

"If he does, there isn't a money trail. He's not in the country at the moment, though. Perfect alibi if he is fucking around with her."

"She said he's twisted."

"From what I found out, that's true. Sparkly clean on the outside, dirty and disgusting on the inside. I read some of the transcripts from his divorce from Kira's mom. Lots of abuse."

"Physical?"

"All fucking kinds."

"Kira, too?" I try to keep my tone even. I shouldn't fuckin' care about her past. I shouldn't fuckin' care about her at all. But that seems harder said than done.

"It didn't say, but I can dig deeper."

"Nah, that's okay. Just keep your eye on him. I want to be ready if he is planning something. She's convinced she saw someone that night."

"And you're not?" Hawk questions.

I shrug, fiddling with the thick silver ring on my index finger. "The cameras didn't catch anything."

"The power went out," Hawk argues.

"Even so. They should have caught something, no? That place is rigged better than the Bellagio. And if someone was lurking around, security should have picked up something. Movement, anything. That property is huge. And just to magically appear on the back patio? Too easy," I speculate.

Hawk rubs his forehead contemplatively. "In theory, yeah. That argument holds water, unless no one was there in the first place, and she just freaked herself out."

"That's what I want to find out."

"I'm doing all I can. Utilizing every resource."

"That's all I ask, brother." I clasp his hand in thanks. "Let's get back before Bone has an aneurysm."

"He's looking to lose all his money tonight." Hawk rubs his hands together, ready and willing to take it all.

"You look different," I mess around with him as we walk back inside.

Hawk shoots me a crooked smile. "Shut the fuck up, man." He knows exactly what I'm getting at. He's sporting his contacts. That means two things. He's out to get drunk and out to get laid.

"Ready for some shit?" Tempest resumes shuffling the cards.

"Let's do this." I settle into my chair and get comfortable for the ride. He shoots two cards out to each of us. I check my hand on the sly. King of hearts and a two of diamonds. Not a terrible start.

I watch the faces around me, reading each and every one of them. We've been playing together for years, so I know their tells. Most of the time. Hawk is the hardest to read. He's got a poker face as stone cold as my father's.

I push the thought of him directly out of my head. Not tonight Satan, not tonight.

Hawk and I both throw in the blind, or initial bet, and then we're off to the races. Bone calls, Breaker calls, and Vet and Tempest fold. Tempest throws out the flop. King of diamonds, three of hearts, and six of clubs. Things get interesting pretty quick. A round of bets go again. I raise, with a pair of kings. Bone raises, Breaker folds. Tempest flips the turn card, and it's a jack of spades. Bone's lip twitches, and I know right then he's got something in his hand. But I don't go down that easily. I throw in, wanting to see where this is going to go. Tempest turns over the river, and my pulse strikes my throat like a whip. This is what is so addictive about poker. It's a high-speed chase right at your fingertips. As fast as it is slow, I hold my breath, waiting to see what card is shown. A king of clubs stares back at us all.

Bone's face turns a lovely shade of red as he pushes all his chips forward.

"All in," he growls like a lion.

We all shake our heads. Bone loves poker, but he isn't the best at it. He's a go big or go home kind of guy, and when it comes to the game, he goes home a lot.

I call.

He snarls like a bull. "There's no way, Slash."

"We shall see, Bone." I urge him to show his cards, and he does. By slamming his hand down on the table, causing everything atop of it to shake like an earthquake just hit. "Two fucking pairs." He stands, shadowing the green felt in front of him. There lays the fourth king, the king of spades. Part of his hand. Along with a jack of hearts, as well.

"Impressive, Bone." I calmly turn my cards over one at a time. The two of diamonds first. Bone barks a laugh. He thinks he has me. Poor guy, when will he learn? I turn over my second card and reveal the king, and the table breaks out in rumbles. Three of a kind.

"Fuck no." Bone slams the table again. "Fucking no."

"You had a good hand, man, but mine was better." I collect the large pile of chips haughtily.

Bone lets out a roar. He's a sore loser. Always has been.

"Drill it down a notch, man." Breaker pulls at his arm. "It was only the first deal."

"I'm going to take all you motherfuckers down." He pulls out a wad of cash from his back pocket and tosses it at Tempest. "Cash in."

Tempest does as he asks, shaking his head slightly. We are all thinking the same thing. Bone is going to walk out of here broke, drunk, and pissed the fuck off.

'Tis life.

After the first high-flying hand, the next seems to move at hyper-speed. Before I know it, I have a hefty stack of chips in front of me and a nice buzz. This is just what the doctor ordered. Vet wins the next hand, and even Bone gets in on one or two. He still has the shortest stack in the bunch, though.

I check my watch, dreading the time. Quarter after eight. I remind myself to slow down so I can drive, but I really wish I could just stay here and drink my face off with the rest of these guys. None of them seem to be letting up anytime soon.

"Brewski, brewski, brewski, brewski." Breaker tosses fresh beer cans around the table. I catch mine but put it to the side while Vet, Tempest, and Bone all crack theirs open. My action doesn't go unnoticed.

"You done drinkin', Prez?" Tempest fishes. He's as rugged as Bone, lots of bright, gnarly tats all over his hands, plugs in his earlobes, and dark, slicked-back hair.

"Just takin' a break is all." I concentrate on my hand, wanting to avoid the subject at all costs.

An acute silence passes around the table, causing me to grind my teeth. I can hear their judgmental thoughts. They don't understand what I'm doing. Hell, half the time I don't even understand it. I just know Kira needed me, and my fucking conscience ordered me to go to her. I didn't have any choice in the matter. Of course, I wouldn't tell them that. The Prez not having a choice when it comes to a woman? Preposterous. That would be weak and pathetic, and I am neither of those fucking things.

"How's pick-ups been, Vet?" I spin the conversation right quick.

"Fine. Better than fine, actually. Envelopes have been heavier the last couple of weeks."

I nod. That's what I like to hear.

The table folds, and it's my turn to deal. I shuffle the cards with all their curious eyes on me. Tempest opened a fucking door, and all six of them scurried inside like the wet rats they are. They have questions. They want info, but I am reluctant to give them any.

I deal the cards, spinning out two to each of them. Tempest and Vet throw in the blinds, and we go around the table. Hawk and Vet call, as does Breaker. Bone folds. I barely see my cards. I fold, as does Tempest.

I turn the flop, and it's a beautiful sight. A pair of jacks and a queen. Hawk, Vet, and Breaker all sit up and pay a little more attention. Things just got interesting.

Hawk raises, and both Vet and Breaker call. There is some serious tension mounting. I flip the turn card, and it's an ace. Holy fucking shit.

Hawk raises, and again both Vet and Breaker call. I'm tempted to check my cards because I need to know who has a fucking jack. Hell, even a king. This hand is fucking juicy. I'm pissed my thoughts ran amok and I threw my cards away.

With a pounding heart, I go to turn the river card over when Bone interrupts me. "So, Prez, you gettin' any of that high-priced pussy, or what?"

All eyes land on him and then me. They are salivating for an answer.

"Seriously, Bone? In the middle of a deal?" I hiss.

"Just upping the ante is all."

"Is that what you're fucking doing?" I growl, clutching the cards so tightly in my hand they bend.

"Well, are you?" Breaker adds fuel to the fire.

I want to cut his tongue out with a dull knife.

I elect to remain silent and turn the card over, but no one is interested in the game anymore. They're all interested in where I've been dipping my stick lately.

"C'mon, Slash. You don't just up and disappear if you aren't eating the caviar and drinking the champagne," Vet throws his two fucking cents in.

"It's none of your goddamn business who I'm fucking."

I'm hit square in the face with a flashback of my father. He was just as secretive and shady about Kristen. Disappearing for days on end with no care or explanation. It pissed me off. It pissed me off so bad that he felt he couldn't trust me. Trust any of us. For half his life, this club had been his family. But he chose to keep her existence to himself. Because of the scrutiny, maybe? I'll never know. Kristen and Kira are so different than anything men like us come into contact with. They live on another level. A level many of us look down upon. Prissy, spoiled, selfish. That's how women like them are seen. Slumming with guys like us just for a good time. A one-night stand to tell their snotty friends about. "*I fucked the bad boy,*" I imagine them saying. And yes, all of us at this table are bad boys. As bad as bad can get, but along with the bad also comes some good. They all have something to offer, and maybe if women like Kira looked past the leather, tattoos, and loud bikes — past the scars on their faces — they would see what makes up the man inside.

Something suddenly dawns on me. Maybe Kristen did. Maybe that's what drew my father to her. And maybe Kira could do the same.

"He's totally not fucking her. Look at his face. He's got the worst case of blue balls," Breaker obnoxiously proclaims.

I realize then I'm scowling. Am I that fucking obvious? I might need to start working on my poker face.

"Fuck you all." I send the cards in my hand flying across the table like the Queen's deck in *Alice in Wonderland*. "Poker night is over." I stand up and drain the last of my beer. "Give my winnings to Harley and Davidson. They're gonna need it with this crew."

I walk out with my blood simmering and my boys in my rearview. So much for blowing off steam and a stress-free night.

I strap on my helmet and turn on my bike. There are a pile of different sensations gyrating through my body. I want to hit something. I want to ride fast and tell my father to fuck off. I want Kira's arms around me and her hands clutching my chest. I want to be alone and I want to be with her all at the same time. I want to stop feeling like a million broken pieces. I want worlds to merge but am terrified of the outcome.

I want to be the man I was three years ago. I want Kira to know that man, but I don't know how to go back, and I don't know how to move forward.

I'm stuck.

I ride into the night, letting the wind steal my fanatical thoughts,

racing straight for my greatest weakness and my most frustrating obstacle.

9

Kira

I RUN the bathwater until the tub is full.

I need to escape.

I need silence.

I need the whole world to disappear.

I discard my clothes and climb into the marble whirlpool tub large enough to fit six. It's situated right in front of a huge picture window, so I have a million-dollar view of the Pacific Ocean and a never-ending supply of its magnificent sunsets. The reflection off the water turns the stark-white bathroom pink and gold as the sun descends over the horizon. I breathe it in. I admire it, I appreciate it, then I sink down into the water and say goodbye to the world around me.

I find peace below the surface, holding my breath as the seconds tick by. My lungs slowly constrict, deprived of oxygen, but I don't come up for air. Not yet. I'm not ready. I close my eyes and concentrate, wanting to see nothing. Wanting to hear nothing, but even under the water, he's there. Invading my subconscious. Niggling his way into my tranquility. Into my escape.

He hates you, I remind myself. He leads you on, talks to you like you're a piece of shit, and disrespects the house your father and mother made your home. Yes, I call Gerard my father, because he is the first man besides my grandfather who treats my mother and me like true family. He loves us. Loves us like a husband and a father should, and Ky hates him for it.

He hates me because of my very existence, yet I can't stop myself from being drawn to him. From wanting him.

The night of the blackout haunts me. What would have happened if he kissed me? What would our relationship be like, then? I hiccup from the lack of air, but I still don't surface. Not yet, just a little longer. My lungs are burning now, but it's a sensation I crave.

I drift deeper into my thoughts, reliving being in Ky's arms. Reliving every touch we've shared. Reliving how enlivened my body became with each teasing caress.

I try not to let my thoughts wander there. Wander to him. To fantasize about him, but my attraction is uncontrollable. It's a speeding bullet, and my arousal is the bullseye. That annoying ache creeps up on me. I want to ignore it. Fight it. Beat it away with a bat. But I don't. I give in to it. I let it wrap itself around me, and I know then I'm a goner.

I come up for air sooner than I wanted. I'm pissed at myself, but I'm also so fucking needy. Needy for him. I slide my hand down my torso and find the apex of my thighs. The first touch makes me tremble even though I am submerged in warm water. I rub at the jarring throb hoping to subside the discomfort, but it only strengthens the sensations. My muscles tighten as I massage away the misery, my body responds in a mollifying way. Small, anguished moans escape from me as I climb each tormenting peak, coming closer and closer to the reprieve I'm dying for. I picture Ky; I feel him stroking me. His strong hands and commanding touch. It's him I want. Want on top of me, want inside me. I rub faster, breathe harder. My core constricting from the fantasy. *It's him I want, it's him I want*, I chant silently to myself.

"Fuck, fuck," I mewl out loud as I reach the pivotal edge. With the first caress of my orgasm — blissful and glorious — I allow myself to fall, but my pleasure is robbed as I'm startled to death by an ear-piercing sound. *"Shit."* I scurry out of the tub, dripping wet, frustrated as hell, and on a warpath. Wrapping myself in a towel, I rush downstairs to silence the alarm. Motherfucking thing.

Ky is covering his ears next to the keypad by the time I make it to the front door.

I punch in the four-digit code, and the blaring siren stops. I'm going to need an eardrum replacement if this shit keeps up.

"This fucking thing needs to be ripped out of the wall." Ky goes to do just that, and I stop him.

"Please don't. I'll call the company tomorrow. They'll send someone out . . . *again.*"

"You don't need a tech. You need a fucking priest to perform an exorcism."

"If I thought it would work, I'd do it," I smirk.

Ky crosses his arms and shakes his head, annoyed like usual. Miserable seems to be his perpetual mood.

Ky takes a deep breath, trying to calm himself down. He's so hostile at times. "Do you mind if I call one of my guys over to take a look? Maybe he can pinpoint what's wrong."

"You're asking my permission?" I try not to drop my jaw. Lately with Ky, it's an order. Like it or not.

Ky gazes down at me, as if he's noticing me for the very first time since the alarm glitched. Like I was invisible until just a second ago.

"It's not my house. Not my shit." He steals a glimpse at what I'm wearing. A towel and nothing else. I swear he likes what he sees. More than likes, but he's fighting his feelings to the death. Beating them down and kicking them out. If I was more of a woman, I would try to seduce him. Drop my towel right here in the foyer. Hand myself over to the domineering man I can't stop thinking about. Dreaming about. It's becoming a constant state of agony having him under the same roof. And what just happened in the bathtub didn't do anything but add fuel to my already raging fire.

Awkward. That's what we are. That's what we've become. There's no middle ground anymore. Not that there was much of one to begin with, but now it's like we are just drifting around each other. No connection at all except for the contempt crackling on his end. It makes me sad. Apart from my arresting physical attraction to Ky Parish, there is a part of me that really wants to get to know him. Who wants to know the man Gerard spoke so highly of. It's like he's two different people, and I can't decipher who the real one is.

"You should go get dressed." Ky clears his throat, crosses his arms, and walks away. "I'll make that phone call." His voice is so hard and cold I crumble a bit. Disheartened by the way he brushes me off. I wish I could hate him. I wish I could just put up a wall the way he does. Pretend he's nothing, like the way he sees me. But I can't. Something inside won't let me. I feel . . . *sorry for him*. And it's not out of pity; it's out of empathy. He's hurting so much, and there's nothing I can do. I'm helpless, and I despise that feeling. It's how my father used to make us feel. It's how he used to manipulate us.

I stare at Ky's back as he leans on the kitchen island. He's wearing a faded black T-shirt, blue jeans, and a backwards baseball cap with a logo of a round bomb sporting an angry face glaring directly at me. The stupidest idea pops into my head. I want to hug him. Just wrap my arms snuggly around him and let him have all my warmth. Maybe that's what he needs, a little compassion. Some affection. Someone he can relax around. I can be that person. If he'd let me. I take a step forward and inhale a deep, daring breath. Here goes nothing.

I take two more steps before Ky turns around.

"Why the fuck are you just standing there, Kira? Go get dressed," he snarls, and my plan is thwarted right on the spot.

Spoiled right to the fucking core.

I turn and head back upstairs, not wanting to agitate the beast any further.

This plan is going to take a bit more strategizing.

Straight back to the drawing board it is.

10

Ky

I PICK APART ANOTHER PISTACHIO, eating the nut and tossing the shell onto the floor. There's a pile at my feet.

Pistachios are my father's favorite snack, so it's no surprise I found a boatload of them in the kitchen pantry. I'm eating them purely out of spite. My plan is to eat them all and leave a mountain of shells for him to find.

I flip through Netflix searching for something else to watch. Three weeks holed up in this house, and I have seriously depleted my options. It's gotten so bad I was reduced to stalking Kira's playlist. A bunch of sappy love stories and teenage dramas are definitely not my thing.

I crack apart another nut and toss the shell onto the floor with the rest of them. The mess brings me a twisted satisfaction.

"You can at least use a garbage can." Kira places a small waste basket next to me, dressed in nothing but a white string bikini. I freeze in place, trying not to choke on the pistachio currently residing in my mouth.

I try to restart my motor functions as I ogle her half-naked body. Her perfect, sexy, seductive, spellbinding, vexing, half-naked fucking body that I want to slide my tongue all over and fuck until the desire is completely out of my system. Until it's fucking eradicated and I never have to think about Kira Kendrick ever again.

Out of pure vindictiveness, I lift up the toe of my shoe and crush a pistachio shell right into the floor. It crunches so loudly it echoes through the cavernous room. Fuck, that felt good.

Kira just stands there and watches me, barely bothered at all. Which, of course, only pisses me off more.

"Are you finished now?" She places a hand on her hip, seeming to pose like a supermodel. She's so fucking gorgeous she could be one. I hate myself for how fucking attracted I am to her, and if she takes one step closer, I might not be able to stop myself from grabbing her and pinning her to this couch.

A devilish thought of us defiling the white leather invades my thoughts. I'd come all over it, just because I could.

"No," I answer, crushing another shell into the stupidly expensive floor.

Kira rolls her eyes. "How 'bout now?"

"Maybe. What do you want?" I'm curt. I can't remember the last time I was truly nice to Kira. I'm such a dick.

"I want to go for a swim."

"Who's stopping you?" I crack open another pistachio and pop it into my mouth.

"No one's stopping me. I want to go for a swim with you," she clarifies.

Again, I pause all movement. "With me?"

"That's what I said," she confirms.

"Why?" I curl my lip.

"Why not? Maybe a little fun in the sun will do us both some good," she attempts to convince me.

"I don't have a bathing suit," I shut her down.

"You have underwear, don't you? I would offer you one of Gerard's bathing suits, but I don't want to send you off the deep end."

Smart girl.

I eye Kira speculatively. *What game is she playing?*

"All of a sudden you want to hang out with me?" I question.

Kira bites her bottom lip adorably before she answers. "It's not all of a sudden. We've both been under a lot of stress, and it's a beautiful day out. I thought we could take advantage of our pristine geographical location."

I crack a smile powerlessly. "Our pristine geographical location?"

"Is it not?" Kira motions to the back of the house, where a huge pool is situated and the Pacific Ocean waits just beyond the backyard perimeter.

She has a point. This place is as close as it gets to a Californian paradise.

"So, what do you say?" She juts her hip out, tempting me like a fucking siren.

I want to say hell yes. I want to live out every single wet dream in the pool, in the ocean, on the sand, under the sun. Take her every single way she'd let me, make her cry, make her scream, make her never want another man besides me again.

Rewind.

I'm getting way ahead of myself here. I calm my raging hormones before they reach the point of no return. There's no guarantee she'd let me put my hands on her if I agree. And wouldn't that totally suck?

But I can be persuasive when I want to be. I've even been called charming a time or two. Maybe I can turn on the Mr. Nice Guy act for just a little while if it's going to get me what I want — which is to get fucking laid.

I've been avoiding getting close to Kira at all costs. What happened during the blackout completely spooked me, but it's time to stop being a pussy and act like the red-blooded American man I am.

I have fucked a dozen-and-a-half women with no strings attached, and Kira doesn't have to be any different.

I let her get in my head that night, but I'm better prepared now. I know what to expect. I know how to control it. Purely physical. That's all I need and all I want. She can try to charm me all she wants. It ain't gonna happen.

I'm going to fuck Kira straight out of my system and then move right along with my life.

I stand up, towering over her petite frame. "Okay, Snow." I place my hands on her hips and drag her a little closer to me. "Let's go for a swim," I rasp in her ear.

Her breathing picks up as she places her hands on my forearms for support. This is going to be too easy. I look into her dark eyes, and they are bright with something . . . excitement, uncertainty, arousal, perhaps? I notice her nipples poking through the thin material of her bathing suit top. I am going to suck the shit out of those two little points.

"Pool or ocean?" she asks a tad bit shakily. I definitely affect her.

"Whichever. Wet is wet." I let go of her and pull my T-shirt over my head, tossing it onto the couch.

The expression on Kira's face is priceless. It's clear she enjoys looking at me as much as I enjoy looking at her.

"I was thinking the beach, but now I'm reconsidering." She's staring straight at the tattoos on my chest.

"Why?" I ask.

"The pool is closer."

I beam. "Faster for me to get you wet?"

Yup, that statement was littered with innuendos.

The exhilaration that flares in Kira's eyes hits me straight in the gut. Her gaze is so penetrable, I swear to God I can feel it everywhere. Slithering all throughout me like a savage serpent.

"Ky." She places a hand on my chest, right where the writing dips below my collar bone.

"Kira." I grab her arms, locking her close to me. "Don't say anything." I lean in to kiss her, unable to escape the avalanche of attraction burying me alive. But the second before her lips touch mine, a ringing sound breaks the spell. It tears our moment apart, and we trip over reality.

"That's mine." Kira looks at where the sound is coming from. The charging station set up on the kitchen countertop next to the refrigerator. "I should check that." She steps away, and I reluctantly let her go. My heart is pounding, and my head is light, and my dick is on fire. I need a minute.

I never take my eyes off Kira as she scurries across the palatial room and grabs for her phone. She is ball-breakingly beautiful in that barely there bikini. This phone call better be fast. I'm tuned up now, impatient, and ready for more.

I saunter over to where she's standing, unbuckling my pants as I go. No sense wasting time.

I eavesdrop on Kira as she answers the phone. "Mom? Hello?" Her voice elevates excitedly. In the three weeks I've been here, I don't recall Kira ever talking to her mother. "Oh? Gerard? Hi, how are you?" Kira turns to look at me, and my blood runs cold. *My* father is calling *her*.

Kira continues with her conversation while I shoot laser beams at her and the phone. "No, everything is good. How is Paris? Is everything okay with my mom?"

I watch her intently as her facial expressions change. I'm not close enough to hear exactly what he's saying to her, but I am close enough to hear his deep timbre. "Yeah, the alarm has been giving me some problems. I called the company again. I'll figure it out," she assures him.

Yeah, the problem is that alarm system is an expensive piece of shit. I had Hawk come over and take a look at it while Kira was at school. He did all kinds of tests and diagnostics and came to the same conclusion as the company. Nothing is friggin' wrong.

"I know, I miss you. Both of you." She looks right into my eyes as she tells him that, and my blood races from negative one degree to a thousand degrees in a nanosecond. "I love you, too." There's so much reverie in her voice my head nearly explodes.

I love you, too . . .

Those four words rock me to the very core. Rage, resentment, and jealousy claw up my throat like a deranged demon hunting for blood.

Kira hangs up, and I can barely stomach being in the same room as her. That one phone call reminded me of everything I lost and everything she gained. Everything she and her mother took from me. The one person I loved most, needed most, depended on most. *My* father. *My* real father. Not hers.

Illogical anger alters my existence. It rings in my ears and pulls at my fingernails.

"Ky?" Kira hums my name, and it is the softest, sweetest sound, but it does nothing to vanquish my beastly temper.

"What?" I hiss maliciously.

"Are you okay?"

Am I okay? *Am I fucking okay?*

"No, *Kira*," I spit out her name. "I am not fucking okay." I storm off. I need air. I need space. I need to go fucking beat the shit out of something.

"Where are you going?" She trails after me.

"Away." I continue through the house.

"Away, where? What about our swim?"

I stop dead in my tracks. I cannot fucking deal with this right now. *With her.* Slowly turning on my heel, I step toward Kira, towering ominously over her small frame. "You want to go swimming, Kira? Do us all a fucking favor and go drown yourself." My words drip with disdain, and Kira's eyes instantly well with tears. The tiniest little pang of guilt hits me in my heart, but it's not enough to apologize, or atone, or even want to take it back. At this very moment, I truly mean it.

I stalk off, leaving Kira visibly heartbroken in the kitchen. It's so wrong, but I'm glad she's in pain. At least now, I'm not the only one.

Misery sure as shit loves company.

I HIDE out in the spare bedroom I've taken up residence in. It's huge, obnoxiously white, and sterilely decorated, like the rest of the house. The only thing tolerable about it is the dark green bedding and the sick terrace off the back that overlooks the pool and vast, turquoise blue ocean. I stalk by the doorway and spy Kira standing at the edge of the massive pool. She's just staring down at the water, arms wrapped around her waist, hair blowing in the breeze. That small pang of guilt is now a heated sword, stabbing me over and over straight through the heart. I can be a mean motherfucker sometimes, but what I said to her was downright cruel. Of course, I regret it now. And of course, I hate apologies, but my words definitely warrant one.

Kira finally dives into the pool, and her form disappears under the surface. I expectantly wait for her to come up for air. And wait, and wait, and wait.

But she never does. I rush to the clear glass enclosure of the terrace and find the faintest hint of her body on the bottom of the pool.

What the fuck is happening right now? My pulse begins to pulsate in an alarming sort of way. Something is wrong. Something is so, so wrong. I take off for the pool, sprinting through the house in my bare feet and jeans. It feels like I'm running for a lifetime. My legs just not carrying me fast enough.

Internal panic sets in. She's trying to commit suicide, and it's all because of me. She was already fragile, scared, in need, and what did I do? I used all those things against her and more. I deflected my own anger on her. I blamed her for all my problems, for what happened to me. For the actions of my father. And is it really her fault? No, how could it be? Kira Kendrick is just too easy to fall in love with. I know what my father sees. A pure soul. A kind spirit. A strong will. How do you reject someone like that? Even the coldest of hearts could thaw at the hands of Kira. Mine started to. As much as I fought it. As much as I didn't want it, she got under my skin without even trying. One touch, and I was toast, and now I'm seconds away from possibly losing her.

My mouth has gotten me in a lot of trouble in the past, but this may be the absolute worst of it.

I dive into the pool, pants and all, and swim as fast as I can to the bottom. She's just floating there, like a lifeless water lily stem.

As soon as I grab her arm, she flails, startled that I'm there. I tug at her, but she fights me.

Hell, no, sweetheart, there's no way I am leaving you at the bottom of this pool. I'm here to protect you, not put an end to you.

I yank harder, overpowering her, pushing off the floor of the pool to propel us to the surface. As soon as we come up for air, Kira coughs and chokes.

"What the fuck do you think you're doing, Ky?" She kicks me in the ribs and swims to the ledge.

"Saving your fucking life." I swim after her.

"What?" She coughs again, sucking in oxygen.

"I didn't actually mean drown yourself, Kira."

She looks at me like I have ten dragon heads.

"I wasn't trying to kill myself." She hoists herself out of the water. "I'm a free diver, you fucking idiot," she yells at me before she storms off.

"A what?" I pull myself out of the water and follow her.

"A free diver. I dive under the water and hold my breath for long periods of time." She dumbs it down for me with no uncertainty. "I started doing it in middle school to escape my father. It's what helped me cope with his crazy." Kira stomps into the house, leaving a trail of wet footprints. She heads straight for the laundry room where a stack of plushy white towels are lined up on a shelf. "And what the fuck do you care anyway? You clearly don't want to be here. You clearly want nothing to do with this family. So why don't you just fucking leave, Ky? Why are you wasting your time?"

"Because you're scared and in trouble."

"Oh, now you suddenly care that I'm in trouble?" She pushes past me and stomps off into the kitchen area.

"I'm here, aren't I? I've been here for the last fucking three weeks."

"At what fucking cost? You have done nothing but disrespect me and this house. If I drowned, I would have done you a favor."

"Don't say that, Kira." I stalk toward her, and she steps back until she hits the wall, but her mouth keeps running.

"You hate us. You hate me, and my mother, and your father, and I have no idea why."

"Kira, stop," I warn, but she continues without any regard.

"What did we do to you? Gerard has done nothing but love us and take care of us. And you spit on him like he's dirt. Besides my grandfather, he's the first man to ever treat my mom and me right."

I try to push back the fury, but the more she talks about my father, the more pissed off I get.

"He's a good man, and I love him. He's an amazing husband and father." Her sweet voice raises. "What did he do to make you hate him so much?"

"He chose you over me!" I finally explode, punching the picture hanging next to her head. The glass shatters, and Kira screams.

He's an amazing father. Yes, I fucking know that. He raised me.

"Get out, Ky," Kira orders, sliding away from me, her back never leaving the wall.

I pull myself together and focus my fuzzy vision on her. "No." I follow her, and she moves faster, darting back into the laundry room and locking the door.

"Ky, get the fuck out," she screams through the thick barrier between us.

"I'm not leaving, Kira," I stand firm, beating down the door.

"Please just leave." I hear her tears, and they rip me apart. I did this. I did all this.

"Kira, just open the door." I pull at the handle.

"No," she sobs, and the sound just makes me want to tear into that room even more.

"Kira, please," I begin to break down.

"Just go away and leave me alone."

"That's not what you really want."

"Yes, it is. I want you gone. I want you out of my house and out of my life. I'll deal with my problems on my own." Her voice is brittle yet somehow still strong. That describes Kira to a T — soft as a petal and sharp as a pin.

"I'm not going anywhere." I slide down to sit on the floor. That's when I notice the blood. It's seeping from my knuckles onto the pure white marble. Look at that. I wasn't even trying to make a mess this time. I press my finger into one of the larger dots and draw a heart between my legs. Then I add squiggles down the center to make it broken, just like me.

After a few quiet minutes, I try again, "Kira, please come out."

"No," she sniffs. At least she isn't sobbing anymore.

"C'mon," I try to coax her.

"Nope." She's stubborn as an ox. It actually makes me smile.

"Remember when I said I was good at making a bad situation

worse? See? It's true." I bang the back of my head lightly on the door. I'm slowly going mad without her.

Nearly an hour passes before I decide to change tactics. Begging and pleading is clearly not working.

I stand up, my hand still bloody and now slightly swollen.

"Kira, please come out?" I ask with the tamest, most tender tone I can muster. "I want to take you somewhere."

"Where the fuck could you possibly want to take me?" She's harsh.

I exhale a deep, pleading breath. "On a date."

A nerve-racking minute later, the lock clicks. Kira cracks open the door and gawks at me like I have gone completely insane. Maybe I have, but my gamble paid off. We're making eye contact now.

"You're bleeding." Kira notices my knuckles.

"It's just a scratch," I brush it off.

She looks down at my feet. "There is blood art on the floor." Along with the broken heart, I added a skull and crossbones and a star to my masterpiece.

"I'll wipe it up. I needed something to do while I groveled."

"You did not grovel," Kira begs to differ.

"For me, that was groveling."

She rolls her pretty, slightly puffy eyes.

"Go put something comfortable on. We're gonna go for a ride." I wipe away a tiny teardrop caught on the corner of her bottom lash.

"I don't know, Ky."

"C'mon, Kira. One ride. I'll be on my best behavior. Scouts honor." I grin.

"You are no Boy Scout."

"That's no secret, Snow," I hum provocatively in her ear.

She glares at me without an ounce of faith or trust. I guess I deserve that look, but I'll fix what's broken.

I always do.

11

Kira

KY WANTS to take me on a date five minutes after he basically told me to go kill myself.

I must have finally lost my mind, 'cause I agreed, have changed, and am now walking down the stairs to meet the man who is more confusing than an evil Sudoku puzzle.

Ky is waiting in the kitchen, also dressed in a fresh set of clothes. His blond hair is styled wildly; his fingers are adorned with thick silver rings, and a wallet chain is hanging from his jeans. But it's the surprised look on his face when he sees me that I take notice of most of all.

"Nice outfit, Snow." He smiles, and it actually seems genuine.

"Glad you like it. It's the same thing my mom wore on her and Gerard's first date." I'll never forget that day. Finding my mom dressed in a black sheer shirt, leather leggings, and a pair of my moto boots. I nearly fell over. It was a new look for the business woman, but it fit her perfectly. Gerard brought out a whole new side of her from the very beginning. "I thought I'd replicate it."

"I can get down with that." He nods approvingly. "I like you in leather."

I could have bet money the mention of Gerard would have sent Ky off the deep end again. Maybe he really is on his best behavior?

I guess time will tell.

After arming and disarming the alarm a nauseating amount of times for a sanity check, I climb onto the back of Ky's bike and hope to God this decision doesn't blow up in my face. One Ky Parish explosion is enough for one day. Maybe even for one lifetime.

As soon as I wrap my arms around his waist, he rests his hand on mine. It's such a sweet, surprising gesture my stomach actually flutters.

Then we take off for parts unknown.

We head south down the coast. I'm still not privy to where we're going, so I take each moment as it comes and just enjoy the ride.

If there is one thing Ky attracts, it's attention.

I couldn't keep track of all the stares we collect on the road. Adults, teenagers, even kids take notice of us. I've never been one for the spotlight, but this kind of attention is sort of enlivening. It makes a little tiny piece of me feel badass.

I mean, who wouldn't feel that? Look at the man driving. He epitomizes the meaning.

Just like his father.

When my butt finally starts to hurt from sitting on the firm-ass pillion pad, Ky pulls off the highway and continues onto the main drag of Manhattan Beach.

What in the hell are we doing here?

We head down Highland Avenue, past posh shops, crowded restaurants, and busy sidewalks, drawing attention with every rev of the engine.

When we stop at a light, Ky checks on me. "Hangin' in there, Snow?"

"Sittin' pretty," I assure him.

"You sure as hell are." He rests one of his hands possessively on my calf. "Everyone is staring at you."

"Um, I think everyone is staring at you and your loud-ass bike."

"Nah, no one cares about a loud-ass bike, only the chick riding on it."

I shake my head. "We can agree to disagree."

"Have it your way." Ky's mood is light, which is refreshing and oddly terrifying. Although I can't say I hate the attitude adjustment.

After a few more blocks, Ky pulls into a parking lot right near the beach where a burnt-orange food truck is dishing out dinner to a line of people not far from the pier. The writing on the side reads The Shrimp Shack, and a cartoon shrimp with black sunglasses proudly projects the thumbs-up to us.

I'm baffled, but I'm going with it. Ky parks, and we hang our helmets on the handlebars before we get in line.

"This was your master plan? A food truck in Manhattan Beach?" I don't mean to sound underwhelmed.

"Not just any food truck."

"Does it sell golden shrimp?"

"Somedays." Ky grins down at me like he knows something I don't.

The line moves fairly quickly, and when the guy taking orders sees us — *ahem*, let me rephrase that — sees Ky, his face lights up.

"Slash." He runs out of the truck to clasp hands with him. He's super skinny with a backwards baseball cap, a sleeve of tattoos, white apron, and ring in his nose. He kinda-sorta looks like a guy Ky runs with. Maybe? Possibly? I don't know. "What do I owe this visit for?"

"Just doin' a pick up and wanted to grab some dinner with this little beauty here." Ky nods at me.

"Beauty, she is." He puts his hand out to shake. "I'm Cutter. Welcome."

"Nice to meet you." I smile.

Cutter whistles. "You got yourself a knockout, Slash."

I want to inform Cutter that Slash doesn't have a damn thing, but mamma always taught me if you don't have anything nice to say . . . so

I just bite my tongue. "What'll you have?" Cutter hops back into the truck. All our socializing has made the line longer.

"Mind if I order for us? I know what's good," Slash asks politely. I try the nickname out. It doesn't really work when I use it.

"Be my guest. Dazzle me," I reply dryly.

"Challenge accepted. Two Top Secret Shrimp plates and two sodas."

"Comin' up," Cutter responds buoyantly. It's clear he enjoys his job, or at least enjoys when Ky comes to visit.

We wait for our food off to the side of the truck. Now that it's just us, the silence is a little awkward. I keep asking myself if this is really a date, or is Ky just playing some twisted game? She didn't drown herself in the pool, so maybe I can get rid of her by abandoning her on Manhattan Beach? That seems a little farfetched, and so far, he's been nothing but nice. My paranoia is resurging with a vengeance all while making leaps and bounds.

"Slash," Cutter calls from the front door of the truck. Only his head is poking out.

Ky puts a hand up to me. "Hang out for a second, Snow." So I do. But I also watch. I watch Cutter hand Ky a thick white envelope. It's shady as all hell. Ky seems pleased as he shoves it into his back pocket and covers it with his shirt. They clasp hands again, and Cutter passes Ky two soda cans.

"Hey, Snow, catch." Ky tosses me one and then the other. I catch both with no problem. Then Cutter hands Ky two plates of food.

"It was nice meetin' ya, Snow. Come back for water ice before you leave," Cutter calls before he disappears back into the truck.

My name isn't Snow. I want to yell back, but what's the point? That's who I am tonight. *Ky's Snow.*

"Ready?" Ky walks off toward the beach, and I follow. "Pop a squat." He chins to a parking chock that just meets the sand.

We are getting fancy tonight.

I make myself as comfortable as possible as Ky hands me my dinner.

"Golden shrimp," he voices proudly.

"We'll see." I push around the hearty shrimp smothered in a golden yellow sauce. It smells delicious, I'll give it that.

"Cheers." Ky holds a shrimp up on his plastic fork.

"Cheers." I tap my shrimp to his, then we both take a bite. "Holy shit." I cover my mouth, 'cause one, I'm shocked by the incredible taste, and two, I don't want to display my half-chewed up food.

"Told ya." Ky is cocky. *What else is new?*

"What is in this sauce?"

"Not a fucking clue." Ky holds another piece of shrimp up and inspects it. "I just know it gets the same reaction every time someone new tries it."

"Are you selling drugs out of that truck?" I don't beat around the bush. I saw the money exchange. I'm not an idiot.

Ky chokes a bit. He wasn't expecting that question. I sprung it on him on purpose.

"No." He starts to laugh.

"What's so funny?"

"You would peg me for a drug dealer."

"Are you not?"

Ky stays silent.

"I have my answer."

"I'm not tonight. Some shady stuff does happen around me, but this" — he nods back to the truck — "this is all kosher. Cash money."

"You get a cut of what he earns?"

"He's my employee. I own the truck."

"You do?" I can't hide my surprise.

"Don't take me for an entrepreneur?" Ky bites into another piece of shrimp.

"No," I snicker. "Not the mobile food kind."

"I have three others, and I want to buy a fourth. Put them in the right spot, they're little gold mines."

"Such the education I'm getting."

"Sometimes I'm good for something." Ky stabs at his coleslaw and stares out into the ocean. The sun isn't quite setting, but it isn't directly above us anymore either.

I let that statement linger before I respond. "You're good for a lot of things when you want to be."

"Not lately," he disagrees, disenchanted.

"Why do you hate me so much?"

Ky regards me with so much remorse. "I don't hate you, Kira. I'm just . . ." He searches for the right word.

"Angry?" I try to help him out.

He nods. "Angry and resentful and confused and hurt and so many other fucked-up things. They're all just raging inside me twenty-four hours a day."

"Sounds exhausting."

"It is."

"I know a little something about emotional turmoil," I confess.

"Your dad?" Ky guesses right. "Funny thing is, the thought of anyone hurting you drives me mad," Ky admits.

"Except you." Yes, I throw a dig. He deserves it.

"I am sorry, Kira. I'm sorry for what I said, and how I acted, and if I scared you."

"I'm still deciding if I want to forgive you."

"That's fair."

"What did you mean when you said Gerard picked me over you?" I think this is the burning hot question that has kept a stake wedged between us since we met.

Ky puts down his half-eaten dinner and runs his hands over his face. "When my dad met your mom, he became a different person. Almost instantly. It wasn't noticeable to most, but I'm his son. He raised me. I know him. He started pulling away, and sneaking around, and being secretive. And when I confronted him about it, he shut me down. We told each other everything. He was my rock. He got me through some of the toughest times in my life, and then, just like that" — he snaps — "he turned his back on me, and his club, and people we considered family."

"That doesn't sound like the Gerard I know." I shake my head.

"I don't know the Gerard you know. I couldn't pinpoint that man if I wanted to. For all I know, he hates my guts."

I shake my head vehemently now. "He doesn't hate you. He's never said a bad thing about you. Every time he talked about you, it was with such pride. He spoke so highly about you that I felt like I already knew you. That I already trusted you. It's why I came to you. Because of him."

Ky frowns.

"I hate him, Kira." Ky rests his elbows on his knees and presses his palms to his forehead like he's praying.

In this moment, I feel incredibly sorry for Ky. He's suffering.

I don't know what I would do if my mom walked away from me. If she just up and divorced herself from my life. I'm pretty sure I'd be devastated, too.

I place my hand lightly on his arm. "I'm sorry you're hurting."

Ky lifts his head, startled by my touch.

"I'm sorry I hurt you." His blue eyes are so anguished and raw.

"I'll forgive you if you promise to never do it again." I try to shed a little light on the dark conversation.

"Never again, Kira." He brings his forehead to mine, closes his eyes, and inhales me.

I believe he's sorry. I believe he's remorseful. And even on some deep level, I believe it when he says he'll never hurt me again.

But where does that leave us? Who are we now? So much damage has been done.

Forgive and forget and just move on? Forgive, but don't forget, and proceed with caution? Forgive, and distance myself completely? The thought of that last option stings too much.

"I'd really like to get to know the man Gerard talks about. The one who's funny and strong and brave."

Ky scoffs. "I don't know where that man is anymore."

"Maybe we can find him together?" I offer.

Ky stares at me. Long and hard.

Maybe it's an unreasonable proposition?

"Maybe we can," he surrenders.

I smile sweetly at him.

He touches my cheek tenderly.

This Ky I could grow to like.

"How 'bout we get some water ice and go watch the sunset on the pier?" he suggests.

"I think that sounds like first date material."

"This is a first date," he reminds me.

After grabbing some lemon water ice for me and some raspberry for him, we stroll down to the pier, and just as we take our first step onto the dock, Ky takes my hand.

We walk with our fingers entwined to the roundhouse at the end, tossing our empty cups into the trash once we're done.

The pink hue the sunset is casting is making everything feel magical. More enchanting, more marvelous, more alive.

Ky props me up onto the railing so we are face to face. He gets comfortable between my legs and wraps his arms around my waist. We're close and intimate and maybe a little spellbound because of our mystical surroundings.

"I really am sorry, Kira," Ky apologizes once again.

"You said that."

"I want you to believe me. I want you to be able to trust me."

"Trust takes time, and I do believe you. You just can't use me as a punching bag for your frustration. If it's too hard being with me—"

"It's not too hard," Ky cuts me off. "Being with you isn't hard. Forgiving him is what's hard. Being reminded is what's hard. Being with you is easy. It's what I want."

"To be with me how?"

"Every way." Ky slides his hands down to my hips. "I want you on the back of my bike, and in my bed, and on my lap for breakfast."

"That sounds quite specific."

"I'm a visionary."

There's no turning back when he leans in to kiss me. It's a heart-pounding, showstopping connection that consumes me completely. It's deep and passionate and sexual, and its intensity communicates so many things. Pent-up frustration, affliction, and physical urgency.

Luckily, we're hidden behind the roundhouse so no one can see the mess of hands and lips and tongues we are becoming.

I struggle for breath as much as I struggle for more. The heat rising inside me like a thermonuclear reactor.

"I think it's time to take you home," Ky speaks between hot, hungry kisses, his grip on my body insanely restrictive.

"I think that's a good idea. Maybe we can still go for that swim," I offer, winded, lightheaded, and woozy with lust.

Ky places his hands on my face and touches me almost reverently. "I would give almost anything for that."

"All it will cost you is a ride home."

"Snow." He presses his lips to mine. "It's going to cost me so much more than that."

12

Ky

I CHASE Kira down the beach.

She changed back into that sexy white bikini, and her body is on full display just for me.

She runs into the calm water, giggling playfully and carefree. Her energy is infectious, and for the first time in a long time, I feel a true sense of happiness. Of freedom and ease.

"Gotcha." I lift her up into my arms, and she screams with a thrill. "Didn't think I could catch ya?"

"I was hoping you could."

"I always can when I really want you."

I let her slide down my chest until her feet are touching the ocean floor.

"Are you telling me you want me?" She stays pressed against my body. Her skin is warm to the touch and softer than silk.

"Since the moment I laid eyes on you," I confess softly, purposely tickling her ear with my lips.

She shivers, and I know it isn't from the cool temperature of the water. I run my fingertips gently down her arms, chasing after that same reaction. I execute it perfectly because she shivers more, and her nipples harden under the thin white material.

"Do you like it when I touch you?"

"Yes," she brazenly answers. Her dark eyes fastened to mine.

"I like touching you." I skim my fingertips back up her arms and then down over her chest. When my pinky grazes her nipple, she inhales sharply. "I want to touch you all night." I lean in to kiss her.

"What's stopping you?" she questions right before our lips meet.

"I hope nothing. I don't want anything to come between us tonight."

"I won't let anything, if you don't," she promises.

I nod, calling her ante. I'm not going to let a damn thing come between us tonight.

We pick up right where we left off on the pier. Tongues tangling and hands roaming and breaths heavy. Except now, there's nothing limiting us. We can go as far as we want, and my plan is to take it all the way.

I break our bond, wanting to look at her as I touch her. The moon is round and full and bright, acting as our very own spotlight. Everything is lit up in a silvery glow, the surface of the water, the beach, the house, and both our bodies.

Slipping my fingers under her bikini top, I slide it up, exposing her perfect, round breasts. I pant harder at the sight of them and revel in the feel of them. Massaging both of them at the same time, I reclaim her mouth, kissing her harder and more aggressively, but still with some consideration.

"Mmm," a little moan escapes her, and I get goosebumps. I want to hear more. I want to feel more.

This time Kira breaks our kiss. Her eyes are starry, and her lips are plump. She explores my body with her fingertips, tickling my skin with her feathery contact. Up my chest, over the wording across my clavicle, down to the sparrows on both my pecs to my side where a hand is flipping over two cards — a pair of aces. She continues to move lower, testing the waters by the hem of my underwear. I'm not going to stop her. The bulge of my erection is no surprise. I've been hard since the second she put on that bikini. Tormented with anticipation.

When she dips her finger under the waistband and skims the head of my hard-on, my entire body locks up. Completely seizes from one tiny touch.

"More," I demand, pressing my pelvis into her palm.

Kira slips her hand inside my briefs and grips my erection firmly. I crumble under the contact.

With my head floating in a haze of bliss, I trap Kira's face in my hands and kiss her like a desperate man. Sucking her lips and stroking my tongue with crucial need.

"God." Now it's my turn to moan as I palm her ass and press her against me.

If she was any other woman, this would be escalating a thousand times faster. I would be more aggressive, rougher, less patient, but with Kira, everything feels different. *I* feel different. It freaked me the fuck out the first time we got close, but not tonight. Tonight, I want it all. I want everything she's willing to give.

I hoist her into my arms, just so we can be closer. So she can be wrapped around me.

I strain under the pressure of her pussy against my throbbing cock, but I don't rush a thing. I'm indulging in each step closer we take. To what I hope is our inevitable destination. Me inside her. Me coming inside her.

We kiss more boldly, more forcefully as the minutes pass by, the uptick of desire ratcheting our arousal higher and higher.

As much as I want to take this slow, to give Kira all the time she needs, the friction of our bodies is testing my resolve.

I slow it down, barely able to retain oxygen in my lungs. Kira peers into my eyes, her nose resting against mine. When she touches my cheek tenderly, with so much raw emotion, something inside of me cracks, just ruptures right open.

"I don't think I will be able to handle it if you say no to me tonight."

Kira swipes her thumb slowly across my bottom lip, entangling us in the definitive moment.

"I was under the impression nothing was coming between us tonight." Her voice is so sweet and so soft it's an unyielding velvet rope bonding us together.

"No, nothing," I agree, pressing a kiss on her collarbone as I push my underwear down. The wet material clings to my thighs as I lift Kira just enough to tease her entrance with the thick head of my cock. Sliding her bathing suit bottoms to the side, the last obstacle keeping us apart, she sinks down onto my erection, and my skull nearly splits from the warm, tight heat.

"Fuck, Snow." I latch my hands onto her tight ass as we begin to teeter in a maddening motion, and once the floodgates open, there is no closing them. There's no turning back or reconsidering our decision. The brainwashing passion takes over, and we both give in to it like puppets.

Kira rides my cock with explosive rapture, and I find as much pleasure watching her as I do feeling her.

"Ky," she squeaks my name as she paws at my face and kisses my mouth. I nip at her bottom lip and growl as we fuck slowly but fitfully, a storm of necessity building between us.

Kira's moans and sighs begin to climb octaves. Her pussy's clamping tighter, and her nails are digging into my skin. I know she's getting close. Her beautiful, thin frame bowing in the moonlight reveals all the ecstasy flowing through her limbs.

I thrust deeper and harder, wanting nothing more than to watch her ethereal being come to life.

"Ky . . . Ky," my name spills from her lips as she claws at my neck. Then she opens her eyes and kisses me as she comes. The connection she establishes in that one fiery moment rocks me to the very core. She becomes a part of me as she shatters to pieces. As she stares directly into my eyes and holds me hostage in the peak of her orgasm.

There's no holding back after that. Not for me. My jaw tightens as severely as my balls, and then it's a full-on release. A climax to the *nth* degree.

"Fuck," I bark out as Kira clings to me, thrusting my hips as hard as my body will possibly allow. I still inside her as a blast of euphoria paralyzes me, sending us sinking down into the water as my knees give out.

I crush her to me as I battle to recover. Battle to keep our heads above the surface and oxygen flowing through our lungs.

I'm lightheaded as we drift through the silvery sea. Kira's soft, sensual kisses elongating the high.

No woman has ever kissed me the way she does. They're so penetrative it's as if they're sprinkled with crack cocaine and a little bit of fairy dust.

They bubble under my skin and reach the places I ignore exist.

"I'm getting a little cold." Kira glides her nose along my jawline.

"So let's get warm." I stand with her still in my arms, barely weighing anything. I walk us both back onto the shore.

Placing her on her feet, I scoop up the towels she tossed on the sand. The air is balmy, so it aids in ridding the chill the salty water left behind. And once we are both dry enough, we head back to the house.

Inside, we shower together, giving me the first real, clear look at her body. I explore her skin as I lather her up, noticing all the little nuances I ignored before. Like the little squiggles of waves tattooed on the most obscure parts of her body. One on the front of her shoulder, another on the back of her neck. One more on the inside of her wrist, yet another on her hip. Finding them all is like discovering one tantalizing prize after the next. The one on her rib cage I find the most intriguing. It's the same small wave as all the rest, except it has some cursive writing attached, which reads "Into the sea." I trace the letters with my fingertip, and Kira quivers. Something inside me lights up from her reaction. She responds so strikingly to my touch.

"I want to go to bed," I purr in her ear.

"I'm ready, too." Kira lifts up onto her toes and steals a wet, delectable kiss.

It spurs me to pull her closer and grope her ass, squandering all sense and reason.

After a quick dry off, we dim the lights in Kira's room. It's a massive, white space with pops of pink, gray, and gold and a multi-million-dollar view of the Pacific Ocean. It's an heiress' room for sure.

We climb into her highly decorated bed, pushing what feels like a million throw pillows onto the floor. Pulling the comforter down, I urge her to lie on her back and then get comfortable right beside her.

Propping my head in my hand, I resume exploring her naked body. I've never had a woman take my breath away like Kira does. Succumbing so sincerely. So untaintedly.

She transforms me in a way I never knew possible. Molding me into a man I don't even recognize.

Skimming my fingertips down the center of her chest and torso and then back up, I watch her physical reaction take form. Her nipples harden, her skin prickles, and her breathing picks up. As much as I want to attack her right where she lays, I also want to hunt. Hunt all the places that make her weak. Discover all her secrets and then exploit them for my advantage. I also want to make her feel like she's never felt before. I want her obsessed with only me. With what only I can do and how I can make her feel. I want her body to be all mine.

"Spread your legs, Snow," I hiss commandingly.

Kira opens her eyes, looks straight into mine, and drops to her knees.

Something about the whole thing is so . . . *life-altering*. That sounds dramatic, but it's true. I don't know what it is with Kira. I'm not usually *aware* when I'm with a woman, but with her, I'm attentive to every single touch. I want each one to affect her the same, if not more, than the last.

Moving my hand down to the apex of her thighs, I use all four fingers to massage her clit. Circling around the soft flesh until it's swollen and wet.

"Ky." Kira huffs my name insufferably, our eye contact never breaking. She has no idea I'm just beginning. I move the radius of my fingers out, rubbing her entire pussy, spreading her wetness all over her folds. "God." Her back bows from the onslaught of pleasure, and it's a beautiful sight.

Sliding my middle digit inside her entrance, I finger her, slow and controlled, memorizing each of her actions and reactions.

I continue the provoking pattern of in and out and around until her cheeks are a deep shade of pink and her breathing is erratic.

"Huh, huh, huh, huh." She kisses me crazily between gasps of breath, pulling at my neck and jerking her hips as the sensations become too much.

"You want me inside you again?" I provoke her.

"You know I do." She licks her lips and then mine. How someone as sweet and innocent-looking as her makes the slightest gesture so sexually charged I will never know. But I eat it up, every last bit with a cherry on top.

Repositioning us, I beckon Kira onto my lap. I have to watch. I have to see everything. All of her.

I pump my erection with bloodthirsty anticipation as she straddles me, then sinks down slowly onto my cock.

"Christ." The friction is instant. It's earth-quaking sensation and pulsating need.

Wrapping her hair around my wrist, I pull, forcing her head back as she rides me. I don't want this to move quick. I want to draw out the time and elongate the pleasure.

"Slow, Kira," I instruct as she fights to chase her orgasm.

"Faster, Ky," she argues, but I ignore her plea.

I bite her neck and lick her skin as she bobs up and down, each rock inducing her to tremble.

"You're gonna come with me, Kira. When I'm ready, you're ready." I hold on tightly to her long, golden-blonde hair.

"I'm ready now," she whines, and I get the most selfish satisfaction that it's my cock making her feel this way. Making her achy, and needy, and weak.

A handful more of quivering undulations, and we are both at the brink of madness.

"Ky, please," Kira begs, deflating all the fight left in me. I want to come, and I want to come hard with the purest fucking woman I have ever encountered riding me with unadulterated reckless abandon.

Releasing her hair, I bury my face into her chest, sucking and biting each breast as I set Kira free.

She instantly moves faster, sprinting after the orgasm that has been just out of reach. I watch her facial expressions contort as she comes closer and closer to the breaking point, dragging me right along with her.

"Ky, Ky, Ky," she pants my name with every thrust as if it will keep her on the ground. I lift my hips, meeting hers until the rhythm is just too perfect. Until the flow is inescapable and we both succumb.

Kira climaxes only seconds before me, her pussy clamping around my cock and vibrating like high-power voltage.

"Oh, shit." I grab onto her ass, captive beneath her, allowing her to milk my orgasm for every single thing it's worth.

Our labored breathing and strangulating sounds fill my ears and the room as we peak together, entangled in a rare and spectacular spasm.

Rare and spectacular for me anyway.

Kira softens on top of me, her forehead resting against mine, her breaths choppy and limbs weakened. We stay connected this way until I carefully lie back down, keeping Kira securely fastened in my arms. Tonight, she isn't going anywhere. Tonight, she's mine.

"How long do you think we'd get grounded for if our parents found out about us?" Kira asks adorably, and I bark out a laugh.

"We're adults. They have no grounds to punish us. Besides, no one tells me who I can fuck, especially my father."

FRIDAY HAS JUST BECOME my favorite day of the week. Kira has off on Fridays, minus the stupid study group I plan on making her ditch so I can keep her naked and in bed all day.

"I'm starving." She stretches like a cat as she wakes up.

"I have something you can eat." I pop my eyebrows at her.

"You're so crude," she giggles, pushing me playfully.

"Just honest." I grin. "Besides, he's a little jealous."

"Why is that?" she entertains me.

"Because, he didn't get to experience what that sexy little mouth can do." I trace the end of my fingertip around her plump lips.

"The day is still early." She steals a kiss, then hops out of bed.

"Hey." I grab for her gloriously naked body. Damn, it gets me every time. "I'm only down for naked breakfast," I protest as she covers herself with a loose tank top.

"How about clothes for breakfast and skinny dipping for brunch?" she offers an alternative as she picks through one of her drawers for a pair of underwear.

"More of you naked and wet? I could do that." I try to play it cool. But let's face it, inside I'm a savage salivating for more of Kira. More of her naked, more of her wet, and more of her mine.

Breakfast consists of eggs, toast, orange juice, and coffee. And Kira sits exactly where I told her she would — on my lap.

It was a good warmup for skinny dipping. We spent the morning just as promised, naked and wet, Kira showing off her crazy freediving skills.

Holding her breath way longer than any human should.

"That shit freaks me out," I admit when she finally comes up for air.

"It shouldn't." She grabs hold of my shoulders and kisses me playfully.

Kira and I swim over to the tanning ledge, lie in the shallow water, and chill.

"Why do you do it? I mean, why do you like it?"

Kira stares off beyond the pool into the glistening ocean only yards away from us.

"It's my escape."

"From what?"

"Life, I guess. I started doing it around thirteen. When things would get really bad with my dad. He was so mean to my mom. Mean. That's what I called it back then before I understood the term abuse. He would yell, and break things, and then he would hit her. It was always the same pattern. We both knew when and how it was coming. She always protected me, though." Kira doesn't look directly at me once through the whole story, but I can still see the tears forming in her dark eyes, threatening to spill. "One day, I was desperate to escape, so I filled the tub and submerged myself under the water. Everything went quiet. That's all I was after was quiet." She sits up straighter, and the tears fall.

"Kira. You don't have to go on."

"Sorry." She splashes her face with pool water.

"Don't be. I don't want to send you on any trips down memory lane that are going to make you cry."

"I don't usually get so emotional." She smiles like she's being silly, but seeing her so upset does something inexplicably crazy to me. It makes me feel homicidal. Maybe it's a good thing Kira's real dad is out of the country. If he wasn't, I'd be making a phone call. Then a house call.

"He never hurt you?"

"Not physically, no. But he knew how to manipulate me. He knew what would upset me and push my buttons when he was in the mood. One time, he made me stay and watch while he hit her. He said if I left the room, he would kill her, and I believed him."

"Jesus, Kira, enough." I put my arm around her and secure her close to my chest. "You don't have to tell me anymore. I get the picture. I get the tattoos now, too."

"Into the sea. It's my escape."

"You nearly gave me heart failure when you 'escaped' into the pool yesterday."

"I just needed to clear my mind. I had no idea you were watching me."

"I'm always watching you, Snow." I press my lips to her head. "Even when I didn't want to."

Kira tilts her face up, and I capture her chin. Then I deliver a kiss I didn't know I was capable of. A kiss that's strong and passionate, but also full of sincere emotion.

"How 'bout I help you clear your head right now." I skim my palm across her bare abdomen before heading farther south.

Kira grabs my wrist. "As tempting as that sounds, I have to get ready for study group."

"Blow that shit off." I press onward, reaching her clit just in the nick of time.

"Mmm," she moans as soon as I touch her, and I know I have her.

"Ky, I can't. Finals start next week. I have to show up."

At least, I thought I had her.

"Finals?" I freeze.

"Yeah, one more week and then you'll finally be rid of me." She pecks me on the cheek. Then she pulls herself out of the pool and runs inside buck naked.

I watch her dumbfoundedly.

In the past twenty-four hours, getting rid of her never crossed my mind.

13

Kira

Sebastian reads aloud, addressing the questions that may arise as we give our final group presentation. For Managerial Economics, our final consists of one-half written exam and one-half oral presentation.

I try to concentrate, I really do, but all that seems to occupy my mind is Ky.

I'm counting down the minutes I will be out of this place and back with him. I really can't afford to be this distracted, but I just can't help it. The last three weeks have been a volatile teen drama with a surprise twist ending. I'm still debating if it's happy or not.

Sebastian takes a hard left, as he usually does, going off on a heated tangent on ethical business tactics. I listen with one ear open, darkly wondering how unethical it is to sleep with your stepbrother. Your hot, rough, rugged, panty-ripping — I take my own hard left, fantasizing about Ky again, when Sebastian shatters my dirty daydream.

"Kira, do you have anything to add here?"

I don't have any idea what he was going on about, so I just shake my head and pass on joining the conversation.

"Are you all right, Kira?" Evie nudges me once Sebastian calms down. She's an international student from the UK with the cutest English accent. "You seem a little off today."

"I'm fine," I assure her. "It's just been a long week."

"Oh, I hear that. I am so ready for a break." She chomps on a piece of her customary KitKat bar. I don't think we've had one study session where she didn't have the chocolatey safety net.

"One more week." I smile.

"Cheers to that."

We continue to review the study guide, each of us taking a section to outline, but I barely see the words. All I can think about is Ky and relive the way he made me feel last night. And this morning, and in the pool during naked brunch.

A little bit of regret niggles at me, though. I opened up too much today. Showed too much of myself. I try not to get overly sensitive about my past. Usually the emotions are compartmentalized in a tiny box, buried deep beneath my subconscious. It's how I've been able to move on, but there are things about myself I don't discuss with anyone besides my mom or my therapist. But today, with Ky, I almost shared one of my darkest secrets, the largest skeleton in my closet. During a moment of complete transparency, I wanted to tell him everything. I wanted him to understand. Understand what my mother went through. What we both went through. Understand how much happiness Gerard has brought into our lives. I shared just enough before he stopped me dead in my tracks, and maybe that's best for everyone. I don't exactly know where this is headed. My educated guess? Nowhere. I foresee a fun time, a good fuck, and then a farewell. I'm sticking to the original plan. Heading to Paris after my last exam. I'm not going to make this any more complicated than it has to be. I'm not going to hold him to anything. I like Ky, when he's not acting like a total adolescent dick, but catching feelings seems like a gamble. A broken pair of deuces. Gerard would tell me to fold.

The end of study group feels like a relief. Like a weight has finally been lifted off my chest.

I pack up my stuff, ready to bolt for the door.

"Hey, Kira, wait up," Sebastian calls after me.

I slow my pace through the hallway. Begrudgingly.

"Good group today." He pushes his eyeglasses up his nose.

"It always is. You run it like a Nazi." I smile.

"I just want everyone to succeed."

"I know. I've never been more confident to take a test before."

"Good." He grins. "Have you given any more thought to my question?"

I pause just as we get outside. Standing at the top of the building's stairs, I turn to face him. He isn't bad looking or a jerk. He's just not my type.

"Sebastian, I'm flattered that you want to take me out. I just don't think it's a good idea." He's asked me out in some way, shape, or form since the beginning of the semester. For coffee, to study, a game of tennis, a movie, and just this last time to dinner. I have let him down nicely for each and every attempt.

"Why? Because I'm not some rich, movie-star type from Hollywood?" he accuses.

I'm caught off guard. "No, not at all."

Then my attention is pulled away from him by the deafening sound of a revved engine. A Harley Davidson engine, with a mean-looking motherfucker sitting atop a leather seat. "I gotta go. My ride's here." Saved by the biker.

I run down the steps to where Ky is waiting.

"That guy bothering you, Snow?" he asks as he hands me my helmet.

"No." I glance up at Sebastian who is sourly watching me with Ky. "Just a guy who doesn't like to hear the word no."

Ky peers up at Sebastian through his dark sunglasses, hostility radiating off him like the midday desert sun.

I hop on the back of the bike and slide my arms around Ky. The connection seems to break him out of his unfavorable fog.

"How was your study group?" he asks as he rests one of his hands on mine. I'm caught off guard for a second time this afternoon, because Ky has never cared how a class, or a study group, or my day has gone.

"It was good. But I'm glad it's over now." I snuggle a little closer to him, and I catch a faint smirk on his lips right before he turns his head.

"Up for a ride before we go home?" He makes the engine purr before we pull away.

"Hell yeah."

And away we go.

WE DON'T GET BACK to the house until well after ten. Along with a ride, Ky also took me out to dinner, which was a nice surprise. No food truck this time either. A pretty nice place with tables and chairs and everything. The conversation didn't suck either. I told him about my year backpacking through Europe, and he told me about his time in the military and his very eccentric, hippy mother who had him smoking pot when he was eight and advocating for 'guitars not guns' at rallies all over the state. When he stopped showing up for school, Gerard stepped in and filed for full custody, which is how his time at the Baum Squad Mafia began.

"Time for bed?" Ky locks his hands around my waist and walks me toward the stairs.

"Time for a bath and then bed."

"I'm totally down for that."

"You might not like this bath."

"'Scuse me?"

"You'll see." I drag him up the stairs by his shirt.

In my bathroom, I turn on the water and pull out a stopwatch from one of the vanity drawers.

"Here." I hold it up.

"I don't like the direction this is taking." Ky grabs his crotch.

"It's not to time you. It's to time me."

"Doing what?" He answers his own question as he looks down at the running water. "Hell, no, Snow."

"Oh, come on. I'm trying to beat my best record."

"Which is?"

"Eight minutes, forty-two seconds."

"Fuck, no. I will be pulling you up after thirty seconds. That shit freaks me out."

"Ky, I've been doing this for years." I place the stopwatch in his hand. "Trust me."

The look on his handsome face is full of doubt.

"I do trust you. I hate this." He closes his fingers around the watch.

"When I'm done, it'll be bath time," I promise seductively as I do a little strip tease.

Ky makes no secret of ogling my body or stealing touches wherever he can. "Start the clock as soon as I go under."

I step into the tub, sit down, and breathe calmly. I inhale deeply and then exhale everything in my lungs, Ky's eyes on me the whole time. I then inhale another immense, deep breath, as deep as I can, and think of anything except the fact that I am holding my breath. I release that one and prepare to submerge myself. I take three more breaths, one partial inhale, one maximum exhale, and then one-hundred percent inhale. Nodding at Ky, I hold it and submerge myself under the water.

Once under, I enter into a state of relaxation.

That's the secret. Letting go of everything. Relaxing your mind and your body so none of your tense muscles steal precious oxygen.

This is what draws me to freediving. The full body calm. The separation from stress. The severance from nerves.

This is part of the therapy that got me through. Ironic, isn't it? Lack of oxygen can kill you, but for me, it saved my life.

As time passes, I recognize all the usual bodily responses. The general urge to breathe, the first contraction, but I've been doing this a long time, so I channel my training and press on. All I want is a second more. One second more to be better.

As the compression on my diaphragm starts to build, the deeper into my headspace I go. I'm familiar with my limitations. I know at exactly what point I can withstand. It's making it past that point that's the challenge. Surrendering to the discomfort and pushing on.

When the first air bubble escapes, I know my time under the water is winding down. I have mere seconds left before I blackout or choose to come up for air.

The need to deflate my lungs or CO_2 wins out. I break through the surface of the water and gasp for air. I pant, sucking in oxygen, allowing my muscles to feed.

"How long was that?" I wipe my eyes and ask Ky.

He looks down at the watch a little pale. "Holy shit, I forgot to press the button."

"Are you fucking serious?"

He shows me the screen. All zeros.

"Ky!" I splash.

"I told you that shit freaks me out. I kept picturing myself giving you mouth to mouth."

"I bet you did." I roll my eyes and pull the plug in the tub.

"Hey, what are you doing? We were supposed to have bath time."

"I'm draining some of the cold water." I turn the faucet back on. "I can't imagine you'll enjoy a polar bear plunge."

Ky dips his hand in the draining water and then pulls it out right away. "Jesus, woman, how do you survive in that?"

I shrug. "Cold water is better for slowing the heart rate and metabolism."

"I'll definitely stick to warm water where your blood keeps pumping." Ky pulls his shirt over his head and gets rid of his pants. I don't know if I'll ever get tired of looking at his naked body. All ripped and chiseled and covered in ink. I try not to giggle when he steps into the cool water. It's getting warmer but still needs a few gallons to cross over. It's not his reaction to the temperature that makes me laugh — even though that's entertaining, too — it's the tat across his pelvis. Of course, I noticed the writing last night, but I chose not to make a comment until now.

"Interesting choice of words." I tickle the tattoo.

Ky makes a devilish little sound. "I was eighteen, stupid, and drunk as all hell."

"I can picture that."

"Want to see if it's true?" He pumps his erection. I peer down at his hand and the words "choking hazard." "I definitely want to know how those lips feel on other parts of my body."

The devil is taking over, I can see it in his crystal-blue eyes. He's becoming possessed with lust, and the only person who can vanquish the demon is me.

"After bath time, I'll put my lips wherever you want."

"After bath time, you don't have a choice." He floats next to me, pulling my body right up against his. Then he kisses me, and it's as surprising as all the other kisses he's bestowed on me. I'm always expecting rough, thoughtless, sloppy. I don't know why. Maybe it's because that's the way he's treated me for the last few weeks. But every time he puts his mouth on me, it's possessive, provoking, and dare I even say it, sincere.

Ky Parish is definitely a puzzle I enjoy playing with.

Ky urges me on top of him, and we continue to just kiss. To just touch and explore and enjoy.

He cups my face and stares up at me with starry eyes. "I have never encountered a woman as beautiful as you."

His declaration has rendered me speechless. A compliment from Ky? A heartfelt compliment I never saw coming. There's a little twinge in my stomach I choose to ignore. *Don't fall for him.*

I tenderly trace the scar marring his face, and he closes his eyes.

"Did this happen in the military?"

"No," he answers evenly. "When I was thirteen." He flutters his eyelids open to look at me, placing his hand over mine as he continues to speak. "One of the older kids who grew up around the club. He used to push me around because I was scrawny. Because he was angry and because he thought he could. I had enough one day, so I challenged him to a fight behind The Lion's Den. There's woods back there, so it was the perfect place. Or so I thought. We got into it pretty good. A couple of other club kids were there egging us on. My dad had been teaching me how to box, so I thought I had a good chance to kick his ass."

"And did you?"

"I got a few good shots in. But he played dirty. Had a knife. He didn't like the fact that I was holding my own, makin' him look bad. So, he came after me. I dodged a few swipes by only the grace of God. But he got me good once." Ky drags my fingertip along the puffy line. "My dad and a couple of the other guys heard the commotion and came to break it up just in time, but Slash was born that day."

I frown, sympathizing with his younger self. Picturing a young, scared Ky. The same scared picture I have of myself at that age.

"Don't feel sorry for me, Snow. I got lucky. I kept my eyesight and only walked away with a superficial wound."

"I don't feel sorry for you." I kiss his scar. "I was just thinking that you're beautiful, too."

We get caught up in a moment, ensnared in a sensual silence.

Ky takes my face firmly with both hands and stares at me as if he can see right through me. "What are you doin' to me, Snow?"

It's a rhetorical question I hope, because I have no good answer.

Am I doing something? Am I affecting him? The hard-nosed Ky Parish is actually penetrable?

He kisses me then, a deep, passionate embrace that resonates all the way to my core. *Whoa.*

"I think I'm ready for bath time to be over," he licks his lips eagerly, and I wholeheartedly agree.

I can barely open my eyes or stop my body from responding to him. I'm aching for him in every way.

We abandon the tub, not even bothering to drain the water. There is only Ky and me and the need suffocating us like vining ivy.

Ky sits me on the edge of my bed, and I know exactly what he wants. He doesn't need words to communicate; all he needs is actions.

I open my mouth as he guides the head of his erection to my lips. It passes over my tongue, and I suck gently once it's halfway inside.

Ky watches me the whole time, biting his lower lip in pure pleasure. I take him deeper, keeping with the slow, controlled motion.

"Shit, Snow." He lifts my damp hair by the root and tugs as his cock slides easily in and out of my mouth.

"Enough." He pulls away, leaving me licking my lips. "Lie down," he orders, bossy as always, but I give in, knowing there will be a happy ending whichever direction this goes.

Circling the bed, he climbs on the mattress with his knees near my head. "I want to feel it when you come." He straddles my face and guides his shaft back between my lips. Then he leans over and puts his mouth on me, and my whole body spasms. He sucks monstrously on my clit before circling his tongue and sucking again. I fade beneath him, melting under the oppressive heat of the arousal he's bringing forth. Demanding to emerge. I squirm and strain, trapped under the weight of his body, concentrating on all the sensations he's conjuring around the girth of his erection.

I suck with everything I have, muffled moans vibrating up and down my throat.

I widen my thighs from the demand of his tongue, his mouth acting as my maestro. Marshaling the laws of my desire until I can't take it another second longer, until my body gives in, shuddering from the massive quake his ministrations brings on. I claw at his back as he licks up the dew from my orgasm, moaning like it's a delectable treat.

My form is limp and my head is light when he finally shifts on top of me. Circling his body around so his pelvis is snug against mine.

He isn't quick to move, or maybe that's just my perception. Everything seems to be progressing at a crawl.

"Kira, look at me." Ky spreads my legs and lets his gaze linger on me.

I lift my blurry eyes to his. The blue sharp, fierce, and entrapping. I'm the animal; he's the hunter.

Ky hovers himself over me right before going in for the kill. A split second of delay before he thrusts into me. Fully, powerfully, taking me completely. I cry out from the force, my head spinning from the same potent ecstasy again.

Ky fucks me hard but slow, slamming into me each time with the same measured strikes.

I spread my legs and bow on the bed while he overtakes every inch of my body. Using all his strength and all his power to dominate my pleasure, leaving me a helpless woman beneath him.

That twinge of anguish scorches me again, warning of another earth-shattering climax.

"Ky," I whine, paralyzed by the unstoppable pangs of lust and warfare on my body.

He groans in distress, his cock thickening inside me, his hips grinding in a maddening motion.

Something inside me cracks, just crumbles right to pieces, and I fall, spiraling into a black abyss. No sound flows out of my mouth, just a silent gasp that seems to engulf me. That holds me hostage until Ky comes so deep and violent inside me, that for a flash I split right in two.

Ky sinks down onto my trembling body, touching me in ways so foreign I question if it's even real.

He traps my head, brushing his lips against my temple, then my eyes, down to my lips. We kiss as if intoxicated, doped up on desire, inebriated on stripped inhibitions.

I crack my eyes open to steal a peek at his face. He's in his own state, celebrating in the feel of my lips and the call of my curves.

I try not to read too much into the moment. We were both swept away. We have insane physical chemistry, and I wouldn't want to ruin that by getting icky emotions involved. By seeing something that isn't truly there.

Even if it is too late. Even if I am getting attached. Ky could be easy to fall in love with, and I'd be all too willing to fall.

I see so much of Gerard in him. So many of the same characteristics my mother adores.

Ky isn't Gerard, though. He has his own life, his own agenda, and I don't think either of those include a permanent me.

14

Ky

I WAKE WITH A FRIGHT.

Flying up from my pillow, I glance around the room frantically. For no good reason, my heart is pounding, and my senses are on high alert.

Turning on the bedside lamp, I check on Kira. She's sleeping peacefully beside me.

Sliding out of bed, I creep around the room, inspecting every dark corner.

A slight gust of air tickles my bare back, and I turn to see the slider cracked open.

I think back to earlier tonight. Did we go out on the terrace? Did Kira wake up and get some air? A million scenarios run through my head as my skin prickles from the eerie awareness.

I walk out into the dark night, standing watch over the backyard.

There are no sounds besides the ripple of the ocean and only the sea breeze blowing against my naked skin.

We're alone, as far as I can tell.

I gaze back at Kira as she sleeps, recalling her blatant fear the first time we met. She was convinced someone is watching her, still is. I'd think it, too, if I woke up every night with the creepy crawlies.

There's one thing I'm certain of. If there is someone out there watching her, who wants to hurt her, they're going to have to get through me and a barrier of Baum Squad MCs.

IT'S MONDAY MORNING, and Kira is cramming for her last exam, reading over notes as she shovels cereal into her mouth.

"If you don't got it by now, Snow," I hint the obvious. She studies just about as much as we fuck.

"I've been distracted this past week." She cocks an accusatory eyebrow at me. "I just want to make sure I didn't miss anything.

"You're gonna ace it, just like all your other ones." I have full faith in her.

"Thank you for the vote of confidence."

"You're welcome, and I promise when we get home, I'll have a surprise waiting for you." I nibble her neck.

"An erection does not count as a surprise," she jokes dryly.

"You are no fun." I bite her, and she squeals.

"Stop that. You can't send me to Paris with love bites. I will never be able to explain them with a straight face."

A lump forms in my throat at the mention of Paris. We haven't exactly talked about what's going to happen after this exam. I've felt extreme pressure as the minutes ticked away this past week but never dared voice my thoughts. And now, the hour of truth is speeding toward us like a rocket, and I have no idea what to do about it. My pride is a beast, and I don't want to come off weak. I don't want to be the one who caves first. Who confesses their true desire. That I don't want this to end. But Kira hasn't dropped a single hint about staying. No matter how many emotionally charged moments we've had or flaming-hot physical encounters. Doubt and insecurity spring. What could I possibly offer a girl like her anyway, besides my dick? Maybe she realizes it, too. She is nothing if not pragmatic.

"We gotta go." She turns her head and steals a kiss before hopping off the kitchen counter stool.

"Go. Right," I mutter.

Kira barely takes notice in my change in attitude, and maybe that's a good thing. Start the separation now so it's easier in the end.

I drop Kira off at school for the last time, and I'm tortured with pins and needles. Watching her bounce up the stairs in her short shorts and a pretty tank top eats away at me.

She's mine. I mean, I want her to be fucking mine.

I take off, aimlessly driving back and forth up and down the coast. I have three hours to kill, but Kira's absence on the back of my bike makes the ride seem empty. Seem lonely. I've gotten too used to her there.

A depressing mood sinks like a stone in my stomach. I know this feeling. It's a dark place plagued with sadness and gloom and dejection. It's what I felt when my father left. It's the place I had to drag myself out of in order to go on. A place I never ever want to go back to again, and I think Kira is the one other person on this Earth who can send me there.

Racked with indecision, I notice the time. I'm going to be late getting back to Kira, so I open the throttle and step on the gas, hurrying back to my greatest weakness and my most frustrating obstacle.

When I pull up to the school late, I find Kira talking to that button-up wearing douchebag.

He's standing way too close and smiling way too much like a scumbag for my liking. Kira also told me he doesn't like to take no for an answer. Well, let me fix that right quick.

I pull my bike up directly in front of them. I clutch the brake and remove my helmet in a deft move, then swing my leg over the seat. I go straight for the preppy four eyes coming on to my girl.

"You're standing too close." I shove him.

"Hey, what the fuck, man?" He steps forward, and I make a fist.

"Ky." Kira jumps between us, pressing her hands and chest to mine.

"You defending this nerdy prick?" I lay disloyalty on her. It helps justify my actions in my mind.

"Ky, what the fuck are you doing?" She pushes me as I press forward. I am going to rearrange this motherfucker's face. He bobs and weaves, unsure whether to stay and fight, or flee. He looks like a crackhead cricket, if you ask me.

"Ky, Jesus Christ, cut it out. You're gonna get me kicked out of school. Is that what you want?"

I stop. "What I want is creeps like him staying the fuck away from my girl."

Something in Kira's eyes goes dark. An intensity I have never seen before springs like swords from her dark irises.

"Sebastian, get the fuck out of here. Now." The guy hesitates for a second but ultimately decides to listen to her. *She just saved your fucking ass, buddy.*

"Take me home," she orders.

"Fine," I spit. "We can talk there."

"We're not talking." She clips her helmet on.

"Oh? Are we fucking?" I'm obstinate.

"Definitely not that either."

"We'll see." I take off.

Once back at the house, Kira all but jumps off the bike while it's still moving and slams the front door in my face.

I'm still ragey, but Kira has a surprisingly calming effect.

"So, we're not gonna talk, and we're not gonna fuck, so what are we going to do?" I ask as she storms through the house.

"We're gonna say goodbye."

I stop dead in my tracks. "'Scuse me?"

"Did you not hear me? Want me to spell it out? G-O-O-D-B-Y-E."

"What the fuck are you talking about?" My voice cracks a little as panic takes over.

"I'm going to say this once, and I'm going to be crystal clear. I'm no one's fucking property. No one is going to control me, or tell me how to live my life, or dictate who I can be friends with." She points and yells. "I spent my entire childhood watching my father make my mom's life a living hell, and I won't go through that." Angry tears start to well in her eyes. "I won't make the same mistakes," she screams, and huge crystal droplets run down her pink cheeks. "Now get out."

"I'm not leaving," I argue.

"Fine, stand there." She stomps off toward the stairs.

"Where are you going?" I demand, quickly unraveling.

"To pack. I have a plane to catch in the morning." That statement does it. I shatter into twenty different pieces. "Kira, don't go!" I howl, nearly ripping my hair out. The thought of her leaving, leaving *me*, I can't bear it. "Don't leave." The disparity in my voice shows all my cards. All my feelings. Shows my weakness for her.

She stops dead in her tracks and turns to face me. We are only feet apart, but it feels like an ocean is between us. "Please don't go." I step forward, my heart on my sleeve. "Stay with me."

She shakes her head in resistance. "I need you, Kira. I don't know when it happened or how it happened, but I need you. And the thought of you getting on that plane tomorrow is slowly destroying me. It has been all week," I finally confess.

"Why didn't you say anything?" She sounds small, and saddened, and full of hurt.

I shrug. "I don't like admitting I need anything or anyone."

"Is that why you went after Sebastian? You felt threatened?"

"Partially. And partially because he really was standing way too close. I'm the only one who should ever be that close to you."

"He was apologizing."

"I don't care what he was doing. He was too close."

Kira rolls her eyes. They're still wet with tears. "I'm not an object, Ky. You can't treat me like a possession. That will never work."

"I just want to protect you. Isn't that what you came to me for? To protect you?"

Kira doesn't appreciate that line of defense, but I'll use everything in my arsenal to get her to stay.

I take a step closer. She doesn't back away, and I interpret that as a good sign. "I will never hurt you like your father. I would never try and control you or stop you from living your life." Those tactics would never work with Kira; it's abundantly clear. Besides, I don't want a robot. I want what Kira has to give. A pure soul, compassionate eyes, an emotion-fueled touch.

"You proved otherwise ten minutes ago."

"I just protect what's mine."

"I'm not yours. You've never said that until right now."

"You're right, because I was a coward. I wanted to claim you as mine the second you walked into my bar."

She has a hard time believing that. It's written all over her gorgeous face. We didn't exactly get off to the best start.

"Ky, I want to believe you."

"So stay, and I'll show you I'm telling the truth. I'll show you that you can trust me. One more chance, Kira." I take a final step closer and grab her hand. Lifting it up, I tangle our fingers together. "Please, Kira," I actually beseech her. "Don't go. Stay here, with me."

Her eyes begin to water again as she fidgets right in front of me. "Don't break my heart, Ky. There are a lot of issues you need to work out with your father. He's going to come back. You'll have to hash it out if you truly want to be with me."

She's fucking right. We are going to have to hash things out. But just like Kira is the only other person who can send me to that dark place, she's also the only one who makes me want to reconcile my relationship with my father. For Kira, I would do it. For her, I would do anything.

"Are you saying your heart is already involved in this?" I kiss her knuckles.

"Too much," she admits.

"Mine, too," I whisper. "How did that happen?"

"I'll never know." She cries frustrated tears, and I pull her close, hugging her with all my might. "How is it you can be so nice one minute and such a dick the next?"

"It's a gift," I laugh.

"You should definitely return it." Kira wipes her wet eyes on my shirt.

"I'll think about it." I press warm kisses all over her face. Silently thanking God she's still in my arms. "The one thing I'm definitely not returning is you, Snow. You're mine. From this moment on."

"No more accosting my classmates," she stipulates.

"Only if they deserve it," I make no promises. I'll accost anyone who gets in our way.

"You're impossible."

"Sometimes." I hoist her up and throw her over my shoulder.

"Ky!" she yelps. "Where are you taking me?"

"To bed, where else? I'm going to show you all the ways you belong to me."

"Sounds intense."

"It will be, baby." I march up the stairs to her bedroom. I toss her on the bed with a little bounce and stand over her, casting a shadow of authority. If Kira Kendrick wants a proclamation, I'll give her one. She's mine. I've declared it. And now the whole world is going to hear her scream it.

"Take your clothes off." I cross my arms dominantly above her.

Kira doesn't rush at my authoritative command, but she does obey.

She may not want a man controlling her life, but her pleasure is a completely different story. That I own. That I'll wield. That I'll control.

Kira naked never gets old.

"Hands over your head, Snow."

In that I'm-so-sexy-I-don't-even-need-to-try way, Kira lifts her arms. Her whole body elongates, and so does my resolve. Being stretched to the point of snapping. I am a fucking fool for this woman. A sucker, a dope, a sap. A victim of weakness. Because that's Kira's power. She makes me weak. She breaks me down. She makes me kneel. And through all that, she somehow makes me better. Makes me stronger. Makes me able.

I like who I am when I'm with her. She changed me, and she doesn't even realize it. I didn't realize it either until the moment she threatened to leave.

I kneel and place my hands on her thighs. "Who does this body belong to?"

"You?"

"Me? You don't sound sure, Snow."

"I'm not."

"Why?" I push her legs apart, exposing the sweetest, most vulnerable part of her body.

"Because you make me question everything?"

"Question the way I truly feel? What my true intentions are?"

"Yes," she huffs as I blow on her clit.

"I'm going to put all those doubts to rest tonight." I kiss the pink piece of flesh. "No more doubts. No more secrets. No more fears. I'll give myself to you right now, if you do the same. If you tell me you're mine. Pledge it to me." I suck on her clit, hard enough to send a message, soft enough to make her respond.

"Ky," she mewls.

"Do you want to be mine, Kira?" I lick and suck, gliding my tongue along her slit in light, airy strokes.

"Do you want to be mine?" Kira buckles, crunching up to look at me, her cheeks pink with need.

"I'm already yours, Kira. All yours." I look her dead in the eyes. I have never given myself to another human being the way I have given myself to Kira. I'm drawn to her in ways I can't explain. On a level so profound I can't even comprehend it. The only thing I truly understand is that I need Kira in my life.

Period, end of story.

"Promise?" She latches onto my neck, desperate for my word. And I'll give it to her. When it comes to Kira, I'll give her anything.

"I promise." And I mean it with every breath and every fiber. Every cell that swims through my veins.

We seal our pact with an intense, emotion-filled kiss that sets the sheets on fire and ignites the passion boiling right beneath the surface.

"Scream my name when you come. Scream that you're all fucking mine." I eat her out with no reserve or restraint or repression. Pulling out her pleasure as fast and as hard as my lips and hands will allow.

"Ky, Ky, Ky," she pants, oppressed by the weight of her ecstasy. I finger her fast then slow, her pussy spasming from the oscillating sensations. A seesaw of highs and lows that drive her straight to the edge. Her body tenses, her breathing shallows, and her nails claw at the back of my neck. "Fuck, I'm yours," she declares seconds before she shatters in a beautiful display of bliss. "I'm all fucking yours," Kira nearly cries as she comes, and it's a stunning stretch of surrender I wasn't prepared for. Even though I wanted it, pushed for it, essentially begged for it, the reality of it reduces me to almost nothing. Kira has taken my heart hostage and is now holding it for ransom. A ransom I'm positive I'm never going to pay.

"Ky." She murmurs my name so purely I rush up her body to kiss her. To lose myself in her. To hand myself over to her.

"You fucking destroy me, Snow." I press my lips, hot and hungry, all over her face, and neck, and naked chest. I have finally come to realize I need more than just her body. I also need her love. "I—need—you." It's as close as I can come to professing my true feelings and not stumble all over myself.

"You have me," she promises between emotive kisses. Kisses that hypnotize me. That break me down and nearly annihilate me.

"Roll over." I urge her onto her stomach and pull her up to her knees. Making quick work of my fly, I release the fucking projectile my dick has suddenly become and sink into the one place that will cover the explosion.

"Ah, Ky," Kira's voice pitches as I thrust, the force too much.

"Fuck, sorry." I cover her body with mine, anchoring one hand over hers, and tilting her chin up. "I told you I needed you." I kiss her deliriously, hard up, and hungry to fuck. Kira clutches the comforter as I continue to pound away at her. "I'm yours, I'm yours, I'm fucking yours." I hold her tightly against me, our choppy breaths mingling with each brutal thrust.

I've never been so rough with Kira before. Possessive, dominant, demanding, maybe, but not rough. Tonight is different, though. Everything is different. I need her more, crave her more, just demand so much fucking more.

And she gives me everything. Her body, her trust, her entire self.

Hard, fast, deep. Hard, fast, deep. Hard, fast, deep the rhythm goes until the tip of my cock becomes so sensitive it could burst like a carnival balloon.

"Kira." I shudder as my thighs go numb and all my energy drains rapidly in a rapturous way. "Fuck, baby." My body and mind drift through a euphoric space, high off the woman I'm buried deep inside of.

I press a long, lingering kiss against her temple. "You take it like such a good girl."

"You give it like such a bad boy."

I growl and bite her neck. "I play to my strengths, Snow."

"I want to be one of your strengths, Ky."

"You already are, baby. You already are."

15

Kira

I WAKE up to soft vibrations next to my head. I crack my eyes open, my limbs a tad sore from last night's sheet shenanigans, and check my phone laying on the pillow.

I read the text from Ky: **Stay in bed, Snow. I want you naked when I get back.**

I smile like a stupid idiot making note of the time. I'm supposed to be leaving for the airport right now instead of just waking up. However, I'm choosing to stay in bed. Choosing to stay in the States with Ky, my stepfather's son, whom I'm falling madly in love with. My therapist would officially diagnose me insane. For the first time though, insanity has never been so appealing.

I TEXT BACK: **Naked brunch?**

. . .

KY: **Fuck yes**

I LIE in bed waiting for far too long. I'm antsy, and I need coffee. Ky said he wanted me naked, so I have a fix in case he comes home while I'm downstairs. Throwing my hair up in a bun and putting on a sheer white nightie with ruffles on the hem, I head downstairs.

It is a glorious fucking day, so I open up the whole house. The glass walls separate along the entire back of the first floor, making an indoor space an outdoor space. I inhale the sea air as the sound of the waves crash against the shore and the seagulls soar in the wind.

I hear a *vroom-vroom* of an engine. And not a bike engine either. No, I know the sound of that exact engine. The way it purrs and idles.

I sneak to the foyer to peek out the window, and I find a surprise. Ky getting out of an electric blue Viper with white racing stripes. Holy fuck, he didn't.

I watch him enter the house, punching in the key code, juggling two coffee cups and a brown bag. I step back until I'm nearly in the kitchen. He catches me out of bed. I can't see his eyes because they're covered by his dark Oakleys, but I can read his body language. He's surprised to find me, but not upset. He stalks toward me, and I stay completely still until he's right next to me.

"Snow, you were supposed to stay in bed." He presses a firm kiss on my head. "You didn't listen."

"I'm still naked. I half listened," I defend my position.

"That material is getting ripped the fuck off your body as soon as I put this down." The corners of his lips curl up sinisterly.

"I can just take it off right now and save you the trouble."

"Ripping it will be more fun." He leans over and catches my mouth with his, delivering a paralyzing kiss.

"Mmm," I moan, and my response has him sporting a shit-eating grin.

"Damn right, baby. All it takes is just one kiss."

"One kiss for who?" I challenge. Not wanting to come off as weak for him as I truly am. So fucking weak and feeble and tamed.

He snickers slightly. "Maybe both of us. C'mon."

Ky sets his haul on the kitchen island, then hands me a cup. "Lavender latte."

I take it utterly surprised. "Seriously?"

"Seriously." He tosses his glasses onto the marble top and rolls his eyes.

"But you hate Bradlee's."

"I know." He shrugs. "But that's what you do for love, right? You stand in a shitty coffee shop you despise for an hour getting stared at just so you can order the girliest fucking latte on the menu. Which, by the way, is totally disgusting. I tasted it. I stand by my original assumption."

I hold the coffee cup to my chest, with my heart about to burst. Who is this man? Could it be the person Gerard always talked about? The one I was so desperate to meet?

"Love?" is my only response.

Ky shakes his head lightly, like I caught onto his card trick. "What else am I supposed to call it?"

"I guess what it is."

Ky balls the sheer material clinging to my body in his fist and drags me slowly to him. I place my latte down right before he kisses me. Kisses me like he's never kissed before. So slow and torrid and deep and consuming that I lose myself in the feel of him. Ky could so easily be my destruction. His gentle side makes me weak, and his dominant side makes me wet. It's a detrimental yin-yang I love being entangled in.

"Maybe I'll make you keep this on?" He tugs on the nightie. "You look sexy as shit in it."

"I thought you might appreciate it."

"I do, baby." Ky slides his hand with the material in it down my torso and touches me right between the legs. "I'm going to fuck you in it and then I'll rip it off your body." He sneaks his finger between my folds and strokes my clit, and just like every time before, I turn into putty from his touch.

"You better hurry up, then, 'cause I've been waiting for you all morning."

"I need some foreplay first."

"Oh, yeah?" I go for the button of his jeans. One blow job, coming up.

"Not that." He stops me.

"No?" I pout. *What, then?*

He picks up the latte. "I want to watch you drink this."

"You kinky bastard," I laugh.

"I have my moments."

I sip the latte as seductively as possible just to appease him. He watches my face the whole time.

"Did that turn you on?" I tease. Ky grabs my waist and presses his erection right into my hip. "I guess so."

"It's what you do to me."

"I've got skills." I take another sip of my latte.

"And one hot, sexy body." He lifts me off the ground and places me on the countertop. It's cool underneath my bare bottom.

"Is that all you want me for?" I toy with him. "My body?"

"Pretty much." He scoots himself between my legs. "I'm a caveman. What can I say?"

"Who likes fast cars," I fish.

Ky opens his mouth to respond, then catches himself. "Cars?"

"Yeah, you borrowed Gerard's Viper to get breakfast."

"It's fucking sweet. I needed four wheels, so I checked out the garage. My bike doesn't exactly have cup holders."

"My mom gave it to him as a wedding present."

"She's got good taste."

"She does know her cars."

"Yeah, there was a hot Vette in the garage, too. I almost took that."

"Good thing you didn't. She's overly protective of that car. Even I need permission to drive it."

"Why's that?" He gropes my body.

"It was my grandfather's. Last thing she has left of him. That was kind of their thing. Working on cars."

"I get it." Ky nods. "Family is everything. Even when it's gone."

That statement says so much about Ky, and his slashes of resentment that run so deep.

"Speaking of family," I tiptoe lightly around the subject. "I have to call my mom and tell her I'm not coming."

Ky's eyebrow raises ever so slowly as he contemplates this. I still feel like the subject of our parents is touch and go, but he said he would try for me. Begin to let go of the past and look forward to the future.

"I think that's a great idea. Let's FaceTime them." There's something devious in his suggestion.

"Are you sure?"

"Absolutely. Let's do this."

I'm a little stunned. And a little skeptical. I was expecting a fight. At the very least hemming and hawing that he doesn't want to speak to his father.

"First, let me put some clothes on." I slide off the counter.

"Bummer." Ky curls his lip.

"You can have me naked the rest of the day. The rest of the summer, if you want."

"Now that's what I'm talkin' about," Ky approves.

I run upstairs to grab a tank top and shorts and am back down in the kitchen in no time.

"Let me have a few minutes to talk to her alone first." I backtrack toward the laundry room. "Two minutes."

"Alone?" Ky isn't keen on the idea, but he lets me go, and I barricade myself into the laundry room, getting a bout of déjà vu when I shut the door. That day started out horrendous and ended up like a fairytale. I just never imagined my handsome prince would be my stepbrother. Wonder what the Brothers Grimm would make of that?

I dial my mother with my heart beating like a baseline in my chest.

"Hi, sweetheart," she answers the call cheerfully. It's dinnertime overseas, so her hair is done and so is her makeup. She looks radiant. Paris agrees with her. "Are you at the airport?"

"Not exactly." I bite my lip.

"Oh? Is there a problem? Can you not find your passport?" She goes all parental.

"No, I wouldn't call it a problem."

I see her glance up at someone, no doubt Gerard.

"Then what would you call it?"

"I would call it a change of plans." I make a clownish expression.

"I'm not sure I'm following."

"I'm not coming." I just go ahead and rip the Band-Aid right off.

"What? Why?" My mother's face falls.

"Because, I met someone." I hold my breath, anticipating her reaction.

"You what?" She bats her long, thick eyelashes incredulously. "When? How?" These questions are all legitimate. When she and Gerard left for Paris a month-and-a-half ago, there wasn't even a whiff of a man in my life, so I understand the shock.

"It's all really new, and I know this feels like it's coming out of left field, but I really like him, Mom . . . I may even love him." I admit softly.

I do love him.

"Love?" My mother looks like she was just hit with a baseball bat. I hate springing this on her, but it did just kinda happen. "Kira," her tone becomes serious. "You know if you're happy, I'm happy, right?" I nod. "But have you been completely honest with him? Does he know about your past?" She hints. My past. *Our* past is a delicate subject.

"He knows some," I admit.

"All?" she presses.

"He will. I'll tell him everything. I trust him. But we're still getting to know each other. It's sort of complicated. I didn't want to drop all my skeletons on him at once."

My mother considers this rationale. "Okay, sweetheart. Just as long as you trust him. I don't want you to give your heart away to a man who doesn't know how to handle it."

"He's pretty strong. I think if anyone can handle my past, and my heart, it'd be him."

My mother nods, accepting my decision. That's the one thing she's always had, my back. "Do you want to meet him?" I open the laundry room door and head back into the kitchen where Ky is impatiently waiting.

"Meet him?" My mother perks up. "Of course."

"Is Gerard around?" I slide onto one of the kitchen island stools. I steal a glimpse at Ky, trying to pick up any animosity from the mention of his father's name. There seems to be none.

"Yes, he's right here." She tilts the phone sideways so both their faces are smooshed on the screen.

"Hey, Little Darlin', I hear you're ditchin' us this trip."

"It's for a good reason."

"It better be, or he'll have to deal with me," Gerard threatens, and not in a joking manner either. When it comes to the guys in my life, he's a protective papa bear.

I feel Ky shift behind me. "She's in good hands. Don't worry about a thing, ol' man." Ky leans over so his face can share the screen with mine. Gerard nearly passes out. "Ky?"

"Hey, Pops."

"What in the fuck?" His eyes dart from me to Ky and then back again.

"It's a long story." Ky places a hand on my shoulder.

"It's a Greek tragedy, is what it is." Gerard does not sound one ounce of pleased. Shit. "Gerard," my mother steps in right in the nick of time. He's starting to turn red. "Ky and Kira are both adults. And I'm sure they didn't intend for this to happen?" My mother shoots me a sidelong glance, like, *right?* She's thrown, too. "You can't help who you love. As bizarre as it may be sometimes. Look at us." She vindicates.

"We aren't related," he replies with clenched teeth.

"Neither are we," Ky points out. "Marriage doesn't really count." He's smug. Ky is loving this, seeing his father squirm on a hook. It's written all over his face and is audible in his tone.

"Kira, are you really serious about this? It's not some crazy joke?" Gerard grills me.

"No." I glance happily at Ky. "What can I say? Attraction to bad boys must run in the family."

Gerard shakes his head. "Oy."

"*Madame, Monsieur,*" a man with a thick accent addresses my parents. "*Bon appetit.*"

"Oh, sweetheart, our dinner is here."

"Show me."

My mom flips the camera and exhibits the glorious piece of steak and asparagus bunch sitting on her plate.

"That looks amazing."

"It smells amazing. We were supposed to have so many wonderful meals while you were here."

"I know." I frown slightly.

"There's still time. We'll book you another plane ticket," Gerard chimes in.

"Sorry, not happening, Pops, she's staying with me." Ky plants a protective kiss on my head, and my mother nearly melts. At least she approves.

"Little Darlin', what I said still applies. If he doesn't treat you right, he'll have to deal with me," Gerard continues with the threats.

"I think I can take care of myself."

In this situation anyway.

"We'll let you two eat. And have some wonderful dinner conversation." I can't keep a straight face. I wish I was a fly on the wall to hear what they have to say. Gerard especially.

"Okay, sweetie. I love you. I'll call you later, and we'll talk some more." My mom nods hopefully. Pressingly is more like it. I have a feeling we are going to have a very long, involved chat

"'Kay," I agree. "Mom, make sure you take a bunch of pictures of the Eiffel Tower. Oh, and the L'Arc de Triomphe. Oh, and that little cafe we love getting lemon chiffon tea at." I beg dreamily. Maybe I'm going to miss visiting Paris more than I realized.

"I promise, sweetheart. All of it."

"Thanks. Love you."

"Love you, too, baby."

"Ah, before you hang up." Gerard motions to my mom to give him the phone. "Ky, you may be my kin and all, but I'll kill ya if you hurt her."

Ky huffs. "Well, gee, thanks, Pops. It's great to talk to you too after all this time."

Gerard scoffs a bit. And luckily it's more amused than agitated. It's fascinating watching them finally interact.

"You look good, son." Gerard winks at me. Maybe he isn't as pissed as he originally let on.

"You look older," Ky makes no qualms about talking trash.

"Glad to see things haven't changed much." Gerard bears his pearly whites.

"Oh, things have changed a whole hell of a lot." Ky chews on the inside of his cheek. "It's good to see you, though." They're making nice. Which makes me very happy. And relieved. No more bloodshed to worry about in the house. "Go have dinner. We'll talk when you get back." Ky nestles up against me.

Gerard nods, concentrating heavily on his son. His blue eyes full of a manifold of emotions.

"'Night, son." Gerard's tone is stern, yet affectionate.

"Oh, hey, Pops, one more thing. She's a sweet ass ride." Ky winks at his father.

Gerard turns red as a tomato. "Ky, you better be talking about the fucking car."

Click. Ky hangs up on him.

"You're so mean." I exclaim.

"I know." He chuckles manically. "Did you see his face? I wish we took a screenshot. I'd blow it up and hang it behind the bar."

"My mom heard that dirty little joke."

"*Pfft.* She's married to my father. She's heard a hell of a lot worse."

"Not about her daughter. Hopefully." I smack his stomach.

"Aw, don't be mad," he pacifies me. "It's all in good fun. And it's the truth. You're one fucking hell of a ride." Ky tilts my head back and kisses me. He's so lucky I love him, or I'd punch him out for that comment. "Now that that's done. I'm totally ready for you to ride me." He wiggles his eyebrows.

"I bet you are." We both laugh.

"Breakfast be damned."

"I can live with that." I lift my arms and wrap them around his neck, picking up exactly where we left off. Getting hot and heavy right in the middle of the kitchen.

Ky manhandles me, taking every and all liberties with my body.

Not one inch is off limits. He gropes my breasts then my ass, licks my lips then my neck, bites my collar then my thigh.

"You going to go down on me right here?" I rest back on the edge of the counter as his mouth works its way north from my knee.

"Why not? We're the only ones here. I can take you wherever, whenever, however I want." He brings his face to mine. "You belong to me. You said it last night."

"Screamed it was more like it," I mutter under my breath.

"Damn right, baby." Ky lifts me off the stool and plops me onto the island counter. "And I plan to make you scream it again. Now spread your legs. And let me eat."

"Kiss me first." I appeal, utterly lovestruck.

"Snow, I plan on doing that, too." Ky leans in, and I'm washed away by the first firm press of his mouth. Jesus, I'm powerless against him. His tongue teases its way under my loose-fitting shorts before he shifts the material over enough to lick me with no obstacles in his way.

"Oh, oh, oh," I twitch with each hard slash of tongue, my pussy throbbing from the ambush of ecstasy.

"Fuck, that sounds so hot." Ky spies up at me as he eats me for breakfast right on the countertop. I watch his mouth close over my clit, and the concentrated sensation forces me to drop my head back and mewl. "You look so fucking hot," he spreads my thighs farther apart, splaying his fingers across my kindling flesh. I dig my hands into my hair and pull as Ky continues to feast, my muscles pulling tighter and tighter with every maddening ministration of his tongue.

"You're gonna make me come," I grab onto the back of his head with one hand and hold on tight, panting and squirming and pleading.

He moans against my pussy in a gluttonous way. "On me. You, come, all over me." Then he stands, ripping open the fly of his jeans. Shoving them down, he grabs me chaotically and guides the head of his shaft straight to my soaking wet entrance. We both gasp as he penetrates me, his cock thick and hard and eager.

"Damn, Snow," he grunts, circling his hips in a furious motion. The pressure and the angle are so good, so precise, the orgasm that's hovering comes in for a crash landing.

"Ah! Ah! Ah!" I jerk upwards with each powerful plunge of his cock into my flooding heat, coming in a frantic array of passionate sounds and fervent gestures. I'm shaking all over, clawing, scraping, and scratching at Ky, gripping onto him for dear life as his cock sharpens and swells, stabbing into me like a meaty knife. He grunts animalistically when he comes, his thrusts turning lazy and fitful while his body spasms. The masculine features of his face twisted with a titanic amount of pleasure.

"Mmm," he clutches my cheeks and kisses me sloppily, dazed from desire. Drained, he catches his breath by resting his head on my heaving chest. "See. I promised I would kiss you."

"Kiss is not a strong enough word to describe it." I run my fingers through his hair, sated, satisfied and feeling utterly sublime.

"Why do you still have clothes on?" He complains.

"Because you to were too distracted to take them off."

"We need to rectify that. Now." Just as he goes to slide off my shorts, the doorbell rings, and we both jump.

"Holy shit. Gerard just sprinted across the pond to kill you."

"Shut it. That senior citizen couldn't run across The Lion's Den parking lot. Stay put." He pops a kiss on my lips. "I'll get rid of whomever it is."

My very large, very hot, very intimidating boyfriend walks across the expanse of the room. He's a dark constitution amongst all the light. Just like Gerard. And just like his father, he fits. Right here in this house, in my life.

I watch Ky, overly invested. He speaks to whomever it is for a good, long minute before he says, "Kira, we have company."

A man I don't recognize follows Ky through the house. He's dressed similar to Ky, black T-shirt and jeans, and is carrying a yellow file folder. The man's T-shirt has a logo on it, though, the same angry bomb that was on Ky's hat with words that read "Baumer Mafia." His hair is dark, and so are the thick-rimmed glasses on his face.

"Kira, this is Hawk," Ky introduces us. "He's the one who came over and looked at the alarm."

"Oh, right." I put my hand out. "Nice to formally meet you." I dangle my feet on the counter top.

Hawk just nods. Not very social I take it. Or maybe he just isn't a fan of me. He's giving off some serious hate vibes. I pull my arm back, dissed.

"Slash, can we go someplace private and talk?" He's all business.

"Is it about the club?"

"No, not exactly."

"Then Kira can hear."

Hawk rubs the back of his neck. "I still think we should talk in private. It's about that situation you asked me to look into."

"The situation with Kira and who's stalking her? That situation?"

"Yes, exactly that," Hawk responds, miffed.

"Then Kira should definitely hear," Ky makes up his mind. My pulse flies one-hundred-and-eighty miles an hour at the mention of the word stalking.

"Suit yourself. You're the Prez." Hawk throws the yellow folder at Ky. "Read it."

More curious than a cat, Ky picks it up and inspects its contents.

His face scrunches as he reads, "Diagnosis: post-traumatic stress syndrome, depression, early onset of psychosis, with instances of hallucinations and delusions. Attempted suicide."

The hairs on the back of my neck stand up. "Where the fuck did you get that?" I hurl myself across the counter at Ky, trying to grab the folder out of his hand.

He steps away faster than I can move. "Kira, what is this?"

"It's . . ." I began to hyperventilate. "It's . . . *my* past."

Ky looks at me like he's never seen me before. "Attempted suicide? And what exactly is psychosis?"

"It's a mental disorder," Hawk feels compelled to explain.

"It's not a disorder," I snap. "It's a symptom."

"Of a mental disorder," he patronizes me.

"No, I don't have an illness. And I haven't had an episode in years."

"Ya sure? Cause you're sure selling it hard to my Prez over there that someone is after you." Hawk makes it clear he thinks my claims are bullshit.

"Someone is."

"Really? Has there been any more spooky incidents? Any more

freaky feelings that someone is following you? Has the alarm even tripped on its own lately?"

I swallow hard, running through the last week. No, none of those things have happened recently.

"Maybe Ky scared whoever it was away?" I try to rationalize.

"Maybe there was no one to begin with," Hawk tries to throw me under the bus.

"There was. I know it," I push. I'm not crazy. Someone was following me.

"Not far as I can tell," Hawk disagrees. I want to punch him in his smug face. "Far be it from me to deny help to anyone, but when something seems off, I dig in deep."

"And you decided to dig into me?" I hiss. I feel violated. That file is *my* personal record. *My* cross to bear. It should have been *my* decision when and where I told Ky about it. Not have it dumped all over the table like a barrel full of rotten fish.

"She's been playing you the whole time, bro."

"I have not. "I strongly deny his accusation. "Why are you trying to poison him against me?"

"Because he's my Prez, and one of my best friends, and it's my job to protect him." Hawk gets in my face.

I want to break his glasses right off his nose. "You're an asshole."

"Enough." Ky inhales a deep breath. He's quiet for way too long. "Kira, I'm going to ask you once." Something strange sparks in his eyes. "Have you been playing me this whole time?"

The question nearly breaks me. *"No."*

"Were you ever going to tell me about this?" He waves the folder in the air.

"Of course I was. I just needed to find the right time. I needed to trust you." I fumble over my words, panic threatening to choke me.

Ky's gaze turns as dark as a thunderstorm. "You needed to trust me?" he repeats coldly, chillingly so. "And when exactly was that going to happen? 'Cause from what you've been spewing out of your mouth, you trust me already."

"That's not how I meant it," I backpedal.

"Then how the fuck did you mean it?" He turns on me.

"Ky, please don't get like that."

"Get like what? Pissed off? Feel played?"

"I didn't play you, I swear," I insist. "Why would I? What would be in it for me?"

"Entertainment." He tosses out a ludicrous response. "Something to buy your time until you went to Paris."

I shake my head insanely. I can't even believe what he's accusing me of. And so easily. It's like he's a stranger.

"Bored, rich girl plays with the dumb biker? Stupid, simple Neanderthal."

"Stop." My eyes water uncontrollably. "That's not true."

That person I thought I loved is gone. Just poof, like a puff of smoke. The man who was mistrusting, mean, and jaded taking his place, reemerging with a vengeance.

"I don't know what the fuck is true anymore," Ky gripes.

"We are." I try to grab his arm, but he jerks it away.

"Are we?" His eyes are hollow, void of any admiration.

"Yes, of course. I never lied to you. I never deceived you." Images of last night play through my mind. We broke so many barriers. Overcame so many obstacles. And now everything, our entire relationship, is on the line because one of his jerk-face friends is here accusing me of shit. Shit he knows nothing about.

"It doesn't feel that way." Ky peers down at the folder in his hand. I start to suffocate. He doesn't believe me. Maybe, he doesn't really want to believe me.

"I can't be with someone who deceives me, Kira. It makes me look weak and makes me vulnerable. And I can't afford to be either of those."

I'm grasping at straws, trying to rapidly figure out a way to convince him I'm not lying, or deceiving him. That I love him.

"Ky," my voice breaks.

"I gotta go." He steps back, and I'm left in shock. What is happening? How is it all falling apart so fast?

Ky walks to the front door with Hawk right behind him. "So that's it?" I yell with fury. "You're just going to walk away, just like that?"

"It's what needs to be done." Ky doesn't turn around. Chickenshit. He can't even bring himself to look at me.

Angry tears drip down my cheeks. "Gerard knew what was going to happen the whole time, didn't he? He knew exactly what you were capable of. You're a traitor."

"You fucking leave my father out of this," Ky turns and explodes.

"You were right about one thing." I wipe my wet face.

"And what's that?" He sneers.

"You are a coward."

Ky stares me down like his eyes are two rocket launchers ready to fire.

"You have no idea who I am, Kira. You can't accuse me of shit."

"Oh, I know exactly who you are . . . " I contest. "Fucking no one."

Hawk pulls at Ky as he tries to rush toward me. "She ain't worth it, bro. Leave her in her fucking palace, and let's be out."

Ky hesitates, our eyes fixated on each other, the connection red hot.

My heart is breaking into a million little pieces right now, and he doesn't even fucking care. No explanation is allowed to be had. Just *BAM!* You're trash, no matter what we pledged to each other last night.

He told me he loved me not a half-hour ago, made love to me not ten minutes ago, the smell of sex still potent in the air, and now he's just walking right out the door. Not a flying fuck about me to found.

My limbs feel weak, but I won't break, not in front of him. Not in front of anyone.

Ky and Hawk walk directly out the front door without a second glance, and once I hear their motorcycles pull away, I fall to the ground, sobbing inconsolably.

The pain is like a blazing sword cutting straight through my chest. I fight to catch my breath, but the hiccups are stealing all my precious oxygen.

I cry harder as I find myself at a loss. Alone, abandoned. My world is spinning, and I don't know how to stop it.

I look out the back of the house, and the glistening pool catches my undivided attention. I crawl across the smooth travertine to the patio.

With what little life I have left, I fight to stand. I see my reflection in the surface of the water. It isn't the first time I looked like this. A fucking mess. But there's one thing that always helps me heal. I step off the edge and submerge myself into the blue. I need the quiet. I need the solitude. I need the reprieve. I need the whole world to just fucking disappear.

I need to fucking disappear.

I close my eyes and find sanctuary at the bottom of the pool.

Alone, abandoned, and yet again at another loss.

16

Ky

I'M A FUCKING TRAIN WRECK.

Kira's hollow eyes keep haunting me.

I broke her fucking heart and mine in the process.

I haven't stopped drinking since I walked into The Lion's Den last night.

I want to be numb. I want to forget. I want the ghost of the only woman I ever loved exorcised from my life.

No one is left in the bar except Popeye, Hawk, Breaker, Vet, and Harley. They've been babysitting me. I haven't spoken a word about Kira. Just sat here and tossed back shot after shot with a bottle of Wild Turkey keeping me in excellent company.

I'm a fucking dick.

I'm a deserter.

No man left behind, my ass. I'd be court-martialed if I was on the battlefield.

Walking out of Kira's house yesterday felt like a warzone. I didn't even entertain the idea of letting her explain. I formed my own conclusion, and ran with it. I'm good at that. A pro, really. I believe what I want whether it's the truth or not. It's my biggest downfall. My most unjust flaw, all for nothing in the name of perception. To uphold my stature and shield me from vulnerability. If you don't allow anything to hurt you, nothing ever will.

But that's bullshit. None of us are immune to emotion. Not even me.

I tried to turn it all off. Put up a wall, and strut around like I don't need a goddamn person to survive. What bullshit that turned out to be, because here I am wallowing in my own self-inflicted misery. Karma taking a fucking sledgehammer to my head and that shitty wall.

My heart has shriveled up in my chest, and it seems no amount of booze is going to kill off the pain.

"Maybe we should call it a night, seeing as the sun's up?" Popeye tries to persuade me to give up my bottle.

"I decide when I call it a fucking night, ol' timer. Back off, or I'll put that knife through your fuckin' hand."

The knife I'm referring to is the one my father stuck in the bar top ten years ago, no one is supposed to touch it. It's a reminder of what happens when you cross the Club, and most importantly, its president.

"Easy there, Slash. I'm just looking out for my boy."

"I'm not your fuckin' boy. I belong to a fuckin' man traipsing all around the world with his expensive pussy. He doesn't give a rat's ass about any of us anymore." I tighten my fists till my knuckles are white. "You should have seen him eating at some fancy French restaurant dressed in a suit that probably costs more than my bike." *Cop out, deserter, cocksucker.* We really are related and have way too much in common when it comes to bouncing on the people we supposedly care about.

"You saw him?" Popeye inquires.

"FaceTimed him. Yesterday." The thought of that conversation kills me. For the first time in three years, I was able to speak to my father, and for half a second, life was good. It was almost perfect. And then *BAM!* T-K-O.

I never saw it coming, but oh, man, did I feel it. I still feel it. And I have a feeling I'm going to feel it for a long-ass time.

Love is torture. A death sentence, and I've been convicted.

"How about I take you home, Slash?" Harley seductively slides her hand across the bar and rests it on mine. Her thumb ticks back and forth over my clammy skin as she gazes at me with come-fuck-me eyes.

Even in my drunken state, the touch feels wrong. It's hard and heavy compared to the light, loving, dusting of my Snow's. With blurry vision I inspect our adjoined hands. The contact makes my stomach twist into sickening knots. It feels criminal. Misguided, like a betrayal.

"I'll take you home and make you forget all your problems," she promises, leaning over the bar, her tits pouring out of her shirt and practically into my mouth. The busty brunette is hard to pass up, she's a vixen blessed with wicked ways. I know because her lips have been wrapped around my cock more times than I can recall, and if I was another man from another time, I would take her up on her offer, lickity split. But I'm not another man. I'm Kira's man. Kira's possession. I belong to her, mind, body, and soul, whether I want to or not. She has possessed me in ways I can't explain, and as easy as it would be to leave with Harley right now and forget all my problems in her warm pussy, my loyalty would never allow it.

No matter how I desperately need the distraction.

Sadly for me, the come-on isn't even a turn-on, I'm limper than a dead fish in the seafood section of the supermarket. Nope, only one fucking woman can command this body, and I have done a spectacular job of amputating that relationship.

"I think you should take Harley up on her offer," Popeye encourages. He and everyone else knows what she's willingly serving up to me on a silver platter. A hell of a good fuck. No strings attached.

But I can't even entertain the idea. I reject the notion. Kira has ruined me. Fucking destroyed me.

The recollection of her sweet surrender has me aching. *"Fuck, I'm yours...I'm all fucking yours."* I steal a large swig of bourbon straight from the bottle, eager to numb my mind and kill off the memories invading it like the enemy. They haven't given me a moment's peace since I left her. They're my demons dragging me into hell, and the only way to atone is to crawl back on my hands and knees and offer Kira something so rare it's only witnessed during a full, blood red moon.

My remorse. My regret. My repentance. My admittance that I was wrong.

"Thanks for the offer, but there's someplace else I have to be." I push the bottle in her direction and stand. Swaying slightly on my feet, Hawk is in my face before I take two steps toward the front door. "Hold it."

"Get the fuck out of my way, Hawkeye." I command. That's right, not order, not instruct. Fucking command.

"You aren't going anywhere. You've been drinking all night."

"I'll take a fucking cab." I push him.

"Slash," he slams his hand on my chest and cocks his head. "How the fuck do you know you can trust her, man?"

"Because I fucking do." And that's enough.

"Don't let some high-price pussy cloud your judgment." He lowers his voice and achieves pissing me off in a new-record time.

"She isn't just some high-priced pussy," I wrap my hand around his wrist and squeeze. "She's the most important person in my life, and I fucked up because of you." Hawk's expression morphs into surprise. He wasn't expecting my blame, and was surely thinking what everyone else in this room was thinking. That I was just getting laid. Using Kira to get my rocks off, and maybe that was the original plan. But things changed. Everything changed. I changed. "Now get the fuck out of my way before I knock you into next week."

We are tangled up in a face off when there's a bang at the front door.

"Answer it." I nod at Vet. Who the fuck would be rollin' up in here this early in the morning?

I can't see whom Vet's talking to, but he shuts the front door holding a Tiffany-blue box. "He says it's for you." Vet places the box down on the bar top in front of me.

"Who said?" I ask, confused.

"The kid outside. Said he has a delivery for Slash."

"And that was it?" A girlie, blue box.

Vet nods awkwardly. He isn't the best with people. Relates better to animals than humans, hence the nickname.

"Is it tickin'?" Popeye pokes the box with his walking stick.

"Not as far as I can tell." I pick it up and shake it. It's light as a feather.

"What's the card say?" Breaker asks over my shoulder. Everyone has now crowded around me and my new mysterious box.

I take the white envelope and slide the card out. It's white with black writing. It reads:

SLASHES ARE SO PRETTY *in the Snow.*

SOMETHING about the message gives me the chills. I rip open the box to find something puzzling inside. Locks of blonde hair tied with white ribbon. There must be a dozen pieces of them.

"What in the fuck?" Breaker expresses.

Just as I lift one piece up, my phone rings. My heart jolts, and I rush to answer it.

"Ky," Kira cries my name in a bloodcurdling way.

My entire body turns cold as ice as the puzzle pieces snap together rapidly.

"Kira? Where the fuck are you?"

She's so hysterical I can barely make out a word she's saying, but *home* and *hair* come through loud and clear.

"Kira, calm dawn, I'm coming. Lock yourself in the bathroom and don't let anyone but me in. Understand?"

There's nothing but sniveling on the other end of the line. "Kira, say you understand," I press.

"Yes," she shrieks.

"Gimme me a gun," I order Popeye. We keep a few Glocks behind the bar. "Give them one, too." I nod back to Hawk, Breaker, and Vet.

"Prez?" Vet voices.

"We're going to Kira's. Shoot to fucking kill."

Popeye pops out 9mms onto the bar like it's a fuckin' gun range.

"Roll out." I stick one in the waistband of my jeans as I head for the door.

"Popeye, don't let a fuckin' soul into this place until I get back."

"Done," he complies.

Outside, the morning sun is bright and warm. It heats my icy veins as the gang of us tear down the highway toward Kira's house. All I keep hearing is her panicked voice and the way she called my name. Nothing has ever sobered me up faster in my life.

I was a fucking moron to leave.

I left her defenseless.

I left her unprotected.

I left her, plain and simple, and it was the stupidest decision I have ever made.

We pull up to Kira's in record time.

Jumping off the bike, I punch in the code to the front door and barrel inside.

"Spread out. Shake it down," I order the others.

Hawk, Vet, and Breaker all go their separate ways as I pull the gun from my pants and creep upstairs.

The house is as silent as a morgue. Making my way down the hallway, I come to Kira's door. Pushing it open slightly, I inspect the room.

Nothing's out of place. No one is here.

"Clear," I hear Hawk yell from the first floor.

Sigh of relief.

"Kira," I rush inside her room and bang on the door. "Kira, it's me. Let me in."

Nothing. I wait. "Kira. Open this fucking door, or I'm going to break it down." I bang harder. A mix of fear and panic asphyxiating me.

The lock finally clicks, and I hurry inside. I find Kira in a ball in the corner, shaking and crying and . . . her fuckin' hair.

"Kira." I fall to my knees and gather her into my arms. She's limp and lifeless and terrified. "It's okay. You're safe now." I hug her tightly, thanking Jesus she isn't hurt. Well, physically anyway.

She sobs in my arms, and all I can do is hold her until she lets it all out. She clings to me like I'm life. Like I'm air. Like I'm the sea she uses to escape.

When she finally settles, she looks up at me with red, puffy, fragmented eyes.

It destroys me.

I did this. My pride allowed this to happen.

"I'm so sorry, Snow." I kiss her head.

"Someone was here. They cut my hair."

Jesus, she's been reduced to a scared child. I'm falling to pieces inside.

"I know. I'm getting you out of here." I haul us both up to our feet. I walk Kira out of the bathroom and head for her closet. I grab a book bag off the floor and hand it to her. "Pack it, and let's go."

"Where are we going?" She holds the pink backpack warily in her hands.

"Outta here. You'll stay with me until we can figure out whoever this psycho is." I finally take a good look at her. A real look at her. This motherfucker really did a hack job on her hair. It's nearly all gone, the ends choppy and all uneven. "Change. C'mon, hurry up." I grab her toothbrush and comb out of the bathroom and throw them in the bag.

Kira puts on a pair of three-quarter-length jeans, and leaves on the flowy white tank top she's wearing. She throws a few more items into the bag, and then we're out.

When Kira notices her reflection in the mirror hanging in the hallway, she stops dead in her tracks. She inspects herself, touching her hair like it's a foreign object.

She looks over at me and the tears start to well again.

"It's okay; we'll fix it." I take her face in my hands. "You're still beautiful, and still my Snow."

Kira doesn't humor me with a response. I'm sure there are a cyclone of emotions spinning inside her right now, many I'm responsible for.

I lead Kira downstairs where Hawk, Vet, and Breaker are waiting.

She tugs her hand out of mine when she sees Hawk. They are going to have to learn to play nice later, 'cause we are getting the hell out of here.

"Ignore him," I tell her. "The only person you need to be concerned with is me. No one else matters," I speak softly, wanting to keep her calm.

Kira gazes at the three men staring back at her. They're all similar to me. Rough, rugged, edgy, and fearless.

But the way they look doesn't seem to bother her. It's the way she looks that does. When she puts her hand on her head and hides behind me, I die. I drop dead of heartbreak right on the spot. Kira has never shown insecurity. Never shown weakness. Not once, even during our worst times. Our nastiest fights. She has always stood tall and proud and confident. But this? This is tearing her down.

"Hey." I put my arm around her.

"I need to fix this fast." Her voice is so tiny.

"Then I'll take you wherever you want to go."

"I don't know where to go. I can't walk in to my regular salon like this. It will get back to my mom immediately."

"Fuck," I hiss.

"Um, Prez?" Vet clears his throat. "If you need some place to take her, Petie's ol' lady owns a salon in West Hollywood. I'm sure she'd fix her up."

I look down at Kira. "Whatya think?"

"What other choice do I have?" She's at a total loss.

"All right, call Petie. Tell him to let his ol' lady know we're on our way and text me the address.

"Dahlia. His ol' lady's name is Dahlia. She's real nice," Vet addresses Kira.

"Thanks." Kira clings to me.

"All right, let's go." Just as I take my first step toward the door, the alarm trips.

"Sonofabitch." Kira skyrockets through the ceiling.

"Fucking Christ." I punch the code in, then slam my fist into the keypad, cracking the touch screen. "I've had just about enough of this goddamn thing."

"That's one way to fix it," Hawk grunts.

"Well, someone needed to do something." I drag Kira out the door with Vet, Hawk, and Breaker behind us.

Handing Kira my helmet, I give my guys instructions. "Head back to The Lion's Den. Check on Popeye. I'll be back later to sort this shit out." I throw Kira's backpack to Vet. "Drop it at my place."

They all give me the thumbs-up, and we drive off to our different destinations.

Kira rests her head on my back the whole ride. It's like I can feel her despair seeping out through her cheek.

All I keep thinking about is how I want to hold her, hug her tight, and promise that I'll never leave her again. Promise that she'll always be safe. That she'll always have me.

Promise that I'll never break another promise again.

That's what I really want to tell her. What I really want to confess. I failed her. I failed us, and we were only just beginning.

I have a lot to work on. Pledging your loyalty and actually sticking by your word are two very different things.

I like to think I'm loyal. I try my hardest to be, but I seem to fail miserably when it comes to the people closest to me.

I rest my hand on Kira's as we pull into the strip mall parking lot where Dahlia's is located.

The neon sign reads "Rockin' Redners."

Kira slides off the bike and takes in the outside of the establishment. It isn't terrible, in my opinion. A little flashy, but definitely not a dump.

"Better than I thought it was going to be." I reach for her hand.

Kira shrugs. "I wish I had a hat."

"You can leave the helmet on."

She shakes her head. "Let's just get this over with." Her tone is shaky but sounds like it's getting stronger. Maybe the shock is starting to wear off.

We walk into the salon hand in hand to find it's completely empty. A tall, curvaceous woman with long, jet-black hair and blue streaks immediately greets us.

"Hi." She smiles brightly, taking an inconspicuous notice of Kira's hair. "I'm Dahlia. Welcome."

"I'm Ky. This is Kira. Thanks for taking us on such short notice."

Now that I see Dahlia's face, I recognize her. She doesn't come around the bar much, but Petie has taken her on some club rides.

"Well, when Petie tells me his Prez needs my help, I help." She grins warmly at Kira. "Let's get you in a chair." She reaches her hand out.

I hold my breath and pray that Kira takes it.

17

Kira

I STILL SORT OF FEEL LIKE I'm in a fog.

I stare down at the proffered hand in front of me, wanting to take it, but for some reason am hesitant.

"Go on, Snow," Ky encourages me.

I don't have much of a choice, so I place my hand and some faith in Dahlia's palm and let her lead me through the salon.

As she washes my short, chopped hair, I want to crawl into a hole and die.

This is humiliating.

I'm still trying to process the shock. Process the image I saw in the mirror when I realized what had happened. That someone had been in my house. In my room. That they violated my privacy and took away a part of me. All while I slept in my own bed. I begin to shake as I replay the memory, falling back into that black place when I felt alone and scared.

"You cold, sweetheart? I can make the water warmer."

"I'm fine," I force out, at the same time fighting back tears.

Dahlia peers down at me with warm, dark eyes. She seems very sincere. She knows something went down and is trying her best to temper a bad situation.

"Okay, all done." She helps me sit up with a towel around my head. Not sure what I need it for. Most of my hair is gone.

Once I'm in her chair, she towel-dries my wet head. "Where is everyone?" There are eight other stylist stations in the place, yet there's not another soul besides us. Me, her, and Ky.

"Sent them on a break. Figured a little alone time was in order." She winks at me through the ornate mirror.

"Good call," Ky adds as he sits in the waiting area flipping mindlessly through a magazine.

"Okay, let's see." Dahlia combs my hair, piecing it apart to inspect the damage. As I watch her move my short stands this way and that, a chunk of emotion erupts from nowhere.

"I'm sorry." I cover my face and hide the tears.

"Oh, sweetie, don't cry. We'll fix it." She places two consoling hands on my shoulders.

"I don't care about my hair." It's not a total lie. I hate the way it looks and that all my beautiful length is gone. It's more the fact that it happened at all. That my heart is broken, and the man who abandoned me yesterday was so quick to come to my rescue today. I'm confused. I'm a mess. I'm tired, and I feel so ugly. Ugly inside and out.

"Kira?" I hear Ky's voice next to me. When I take my hands away from my face, I find him on one knee beside me.

"I'm fine." I suck it up. I have so many mixed emotions when I look at him. So much I want to say. So much I want to scream.

I take a few deep breaths and calm myself. Wiping my face, I send him away. "I'm okay. Go sit down." I then look at Dahlia. "Let's do this."

Dahlia puts on her bravest expression for me.

"Let's do this. You have a gorgeous face. I know exactly the cut that will look fabulous on you."

I may have only met Dahlia fifteen minutes ago, but I decide I like her. She's genuine, and I can really use some of that in my life right now.

I close my eyes as Dahlia snips away, shaping and evening what's left of my hair.

When she turns the blow dryer on and I feel the warm air against my bare neck, I open my eyes. What I see is a little shocking, but I've learned to judge a haircut once it's completely finished.

I watch Dahlia brush and blow dry my hair simultaneously. She smooths it out until it's pin straight and the blonde is shiny and dry.

"All finished." She steps aside, confident in her work. I gaze at myself in the mirror. The bob haircut is actually beautiful, even if it's a style I never considered before. The front is a tad longer than the back, but it all still moves in a light and airy way.

I look over at Ky meekly. "What do you think?"

"Actually." He stands and strides over to us. "I love it. It's sexy." He touches the end of one strand.

"I agree," Dahlia adds. "It's beautiful and edgy and enhances the features of your face."

"Thank you." It's nice to hear a compliment.

"Anytime." She really is so sweet. A young, hot brunette who rocks leather is definitely not what I was expecting when Ky's friend called her an "ol' lady."

"What do I owe you?" Ky goes to grab his wallet.

"Not a thing," Dahlia stops him.

"C'mon," he pushes.

"Nope. Just take care of this one." She taps her curled finger under my chin.

"That goes without saying."

I steam a little from his response. I hold back my irritation, saving it for later. He may be trying to make things right, but he's not just going to waltz right back into my life like yesterday never happened.

Fuck. No.

Ky places a twenty on Dahlia's station. "No arguments."

She stops while she's ahead.

"Kira, maybe our paths will cross again soon." She sounds hopeful.

"I'd like that." I slip out of the chair feeling, surprisingly, world's better. I can now blend back into society without weird looks or insecurity.

Ky slides his arms around me protectively, and we walk back out into the sunshine.

"You good, Snow?" Ky drags his hand up to the back of my neck and leans in for a kiss, but I jerk away.

Ky isn't keen on that response. "Okay, I get it." His voice is even, but his expression is cross. "We'll get back to where we were. Even better than we were before."

I'm glad he's so confident, because I have serious doubts.

"Where to now?" I climb on to the bike and strap on the helmet. "We'll head back to the Lion's Den. Regroup."

"Do you think we should go to the cops?" I suggest. Now that my mind is right, I'm thinking a little more clearly.

"No cops. Waste of time. If you want something done right, you need to do it yourself."

Vigilantism. Fantastic.

"What would have happened if there was still someone in the house when you got there?" I don't know why I ask the question. Morbid curiosity, maybe.

Ky glances back at me as he turns on the bike. "I would have shot them in the fucking face. Hold on."

Ask an honest question, get an honest answer.

He releases the throttle, and I grab onto him just in time to keep me from being kicked off the back from the acceleration.

Jesus. I think I put him in a mood. Tough shit. Misery loves company. And right now, I'm fucking miserable.

The ride down the highway is uncomfortable. You can feel the tension surging through both our bodies like lightning conductors.

My emotions are a mixed bag of tricks, and I never know which one I'm going to pull out next. One side of me bursting with love for Ky. He came for me. He didn't abandon me when I needed him most. He's showing he wants to fix things. The other side is filled with anger. I resent him for walking out on me the second he found out something he didn't like. That he accused me of things that weren't true and didn't even entertain the idea of letting me explain. He made his own conclusions and left, opening me up to all kinds of vulnerabilities. My biggest concern is that he'll do it again. That this is a habitual habit of his. That's it's a personality trait. I'm not perfect. No one is, and if he's going to cut me out every time his trust is tested, there's no hope for us. Trust is the foundation of a relationship, and if Ky has none, there can be no us.

An annoying rumble of an engine pulls me from my jarring thoughts. The black car next to us veers over into our lane, nearly hitting us.

"Holy shit." I cling tighter to Ky, my pulse rate spiking.

"Asshole," Ky spits as he accelerates a bit. He can't go much faster because of the line of cars in front of us.

The highway is congested this afternoon, so switching lanes is difficult at the moment. The black car hangs back, giving us the room we need. Ky uses the little stretch of road allowed to break free from the cluster of traffic.

I hear the same roar of the engine again and turn to see the black car following us.

"Do you have any idea who that is?" I yell to Ky.

"Not a damn clue." Just as Ky answers, the black muscle car is on our ass, accelerating at frightening speed.

"Ky, drive faster," I screech as I see the tip of the headlight dangerously close to the back tire. One tiny bump, and it's lights out Ky and Kira.

"Hang on." Ky swerves out of the lane, but the car follows. A cat chasing a mouse down the highway at death-defying speeds.

The car catches up to us again, and again comes terrifyingly close to the back tire.

"Ky, watch out," I scream in horror. There's nothing around us, no doors or roof to protect us. No airbags or safety features. We are sitting ducks, and the highway is the Grim Reaper waiting to claim us as his own.

The engine in the black car wails, and I feel my life coming to an end. He's going to hit us. *He's going to hit us. He's going to hit us.*

"Ky," I wail into the whipping wind. I hold on tight, tears streaming down my cheeks as Ky takes matters into his own hands and shoots between two cars that are parallel to each other in front of us. Driving right down the dotted lines, he squeezes us into the barely there space. The sedans honk and curse, but neither of us care. We just need to get away from the psycho muscle car trying to kill us. Ky stays sandwiched between moving vehicles using them as a cover to escape. I don't look back anymore; I just bury my face in Ky's shirt, praying for our lives.

I only choose to look up when I feel the bike veer off the highway.

"Is he gone?" I stutter.

"For now." Ky's tone is chilling. It's a mix of calm and crucify.

Once we arrive at The Lion's Den, I all but fall off the bike onto the ground. I hyperventilate on all fours, never so grateful to feel dirt beneath my fingers.

"Just breathe, Snow." Ky rubs my back, trying to calm me. "You're safe now."

"Safe? I feel like I'm in a fucking horror movie." Tears careen down my cheeks and saturate my skin.

Ky scoops me up, and I lock my arms around his neck and weep. I just need to get it all out. All the emotions massacring my insides.

I don't know how long I cry or who sees me falling to pieces in the parking lot, but I can't imagine this is good for Ky's image. He doesn't seem to be bothered, though. He just holds me securely, whispering sweet, consoling words until I go limp in his arms. Until I can't shed another tear.

I lift my puffy, soaked face up to his. It feels as if all the life has been sucked out of my body.

"Better now?" he asks.

"Not at all, but thank you." I sniff.

"Anything for you, Snow." He begins to lean in to kiss me, but stops. We linger there, our lips inches apart. As pissed off as I am at him, I need him equally as much. I squeeze my arm, closing the last bit of distance between us, and kiss him with more ferocity than I knew I was even capable of. Ky tightens his hold, deepening the kiss, massaging his tongue furiously against mine. He steals my breath. And steals my fear. And offers all the stability I'm desperate for.

Ky sucks lightly on my bottom lip at the tail end of the kiss. We're both wound up and winded, but have found some calm in each other's arms.

"Let's go inside."

I nod silently as Ky gets us onto our feet. We're covered in dust and most definitely look like we narrowly survived a high-speed car chase.

Ky takes my hand and leads me up onto the front deck of the bar. I have flashbacks of the last time I was here. I was so out of my element and nearly accosted.

"I'm not going to get surrounded again, am I?" I ask only half-joking.

"No one is going to come near you unless I give the okay."

We walk through the threshold, and as soon as we cross the divide, every single eye lands on us. There aren't a ton of people in the place, but there's enough to make it uncomfortable.

"What the fuck happened to you two?" that asshole Hawk exclaims.

"We had a lovely run-in with a Challenger that tried to run us off the road."

"What?" Half the men in the room stand at attention.

"Did you get the fucking license plate?" Hawk is up Ky's ass in a nanosecond.

"No, I was too busy trying to avoid being roadkill."

"What about you? Did you get a look? See any numbers or letters?" he addresses me.

"No," I snap. I can't stand him. Looking at a license plate number was the last thing on my mind as I stared down the throat of death.

Ky definitely picks up on my animosity. "I think we need a drink." He locks his arm around me possessively and walks me to the bar. Plopping me on a stool, he orders from the busty brunette lingering beside the beer taps. "Two shots, two chasers."

She definitely wasn't manning the bar last time I was here. Jesus, if that shirt was any lower, her nipples would be showing. I try not to gawk, and she barely acknowledges my existence.

"Did you get a look at the driver, at least? Anything distinctive on the car?" Hawk continues to interrogate Ky.

"The fuckin' windows were tinted. There were no markings that I could see. The fucker came outta nowhere." Ky picks up the shot glass the bartender places in front of him and pounds the dark liquid immediately. "Another." He slides the little empty glass back.

I follow suit, drinking the nasty brown liquid. *Yuck.* I grab for the chaser of soda and immediately suck it down.

"Slash." Hawk leans in closer to Ky. "I have to ask." His voice lowers. "Has Kira been out of your sight at all? Even for a minute?"

Rage erupts inside me. Does he honestly think I can't hear him? "You think I had something to do with this? That I orchestrated it? Who exactly do you think I am? A criminal mastermind?" I leap to my feet, and Ky catches me in an arm-hold.

"I'm just investigating it from all angles. You have mental instabilities."

"I am not crazy!" I explode. "I am the victim." I try to fight my way out of Ky's grasp. If Hawk wants to see crazy, I'll show him crazy.

"Chill out, Snow." Ky actually finds this humorous. "I know you want to scratch his eyes out, but they barely work anyway. It's not even worth it. Now, if you want to kick him in the balls, I'm all for that."

"Slash." Hawk covers his crotch with both hands. Everyone around us, except Hawk, laughs.

"Have a drink, Snow." Ky pulls me onto his lap and pushes the shot glass my way. I shoot it without a second thought. It's still disgusting. "Good girl." He kisses my neck.

I try to calm down, I really do. But Hawk airing all my dirty laundry is making me homicidal. "I'm going to say this one last time. What you read in that file was a manifestation of things that happened in my past. Post-traumatic stress from my abusive father. I am not proud of it, but I have worked fucking hard to escape the shadow of that emotional trauma. And I am not going to let you use what happened to me back then as a scapegoat for what's happening now."

"I'm not going to let him do that either. Hawk is just doing his job," Ky tries to play mediator.

"And what job would that be? Grade-A asshole?"

"He has been known to wear that patch," one of the other guys who was at my house this morning chimes in. I don't know anyone's names except I've-got-a-hard-on-to-ruin-your-life Hawk.

"He definitely needs to get laid more," another adds.

"Will you two shut the fuck up?" Hawk snaps.

"Sucks when someone gangs up on you," I sneer.

"All right, enough. This isn't getting us anywhere," Ky puts the kibosh on the all the bickering. "Hawk, look into any stolen Challengers in the area. Maybe that will be a lead."

Hawk nods. "I'm ten steps ahead of you."

"Good." Ky stands, sliding me gently off his lap. He drinks the last shot, then slams the glass upside-down on the creaky worn wood. "I'm taking Kira home to rest. If anything pops up, call me."

"I have one more question for Kira," Hawk delays our departure.

"What now?" I cross my arms.

"Your mom, she's a pretty high-profile figure, right?"

"You could say that. Where are you going with this?" I eye him suspiciously.

"Has she had any issues with anyone? A crazy fan? A jealous business partner?"

"No, everyone loves my mother. The only person she's ever had an issue with is my piece-of-shit father."

"We're already looking into him." Hawk scratches his stubbly chin. "That lead seems cold, though."

"I still think it's time to go to the police." I offer my opinion on the matter.

"Hawk pretty much is the police," Ky informs me. "If anyone can snuff out who it is, he can. He has access to all their resources."

"Please forgive me if my faith is tested when it comes to his abilities." I'm obstinate.

"You two will learn to get along, eventually." Ky is confident.

Glad someone is.

Ky bumps fists with the three men around us. Then one of them holds his fist up to me. I touch my knuckles to his. "I'm Vet, by the way. And that's Breaker." His tone is mild, same as it was this morning when he suggested Dahlia's salon.

"Nice to formally meet you." I try for polite.

"You need anything, we're here. We protect the Prez and his ol' lady."

I grimace at the name. He called Dahlia that, too, and she was nowhere near old.

"That's enough talk of ol' ladies," Ky interjects. "Kira and I have some stuff to hash out."

Do we ever. "No thanks to Hawk," I mutter irritably under my breath.

"Easy, killer." Ky takes my hand and presses a kiss to it. I suddenly feel like I'm under a microscope. Everyone in the place is scrutinizing us. All the men, and especially all the women. There aren't many, but definitely enough.

Once we're outside, I share my thoughts with Ky. "They don't like me."

"Who doesn't?"

"All those people in there. They don't like me with you."

"Are you with me?" He probes.

Fair question.

"I'm still undecided."

"Gonna make me beg for it, huh?"

"Maybe."

"Then maybe it'll happen."

"I have a feeling you've never begged for a thing in your life."

"On the female front, no." He laughs. "But you may be an exception." He places his finger under my chin.

"We'll see." I'm skeptical. I've spent enough time with Ky to know he's proud. Way too proud. So proud, it blurs his vision, causing him to make rash decisions. Decisions that can be detrimental.

"You have my heart, Snow, whether you want to believe it or not."

He has mine, too, and that's a huge part of the problem.

18

Ky

KIRA HAS BEEN RUNNING hot and cold all day.

I know she's scared. I know she's upset. And I know she's confused. I also know a majority of all that is my fault.

What Kira doesn't realize is that I have been in dire situations before. I've been knocked down, shot at, left behind, and I've always come back swinging. This time is no different. I will fight to fix things. Fix everything, because Kira is all I want. I want her safe, I want her happy, and I want her with me.

"My bedroom is upstairs." I walk her through my condo. It's a two-story end unit with a nice view of the expansive courtyard with gazebo and small duck pond. "Go lie down, and I'll be up in a minute."

"Can you bring me a drink, please?" She climbs the stairs slowly, physically exhausted.

"Water or beer?" I offer. It's about all I have.

Kira snickers. "Water is fine."

I watch her disappear to the second floor. Grabbing a bottle of water out of the fridge, I crack it open and take a sip. I want to pour it over my head and wash away everything that went wrong in the last twenty-four hours. But a baptism isn't going to change the past. It can only help me do right in the future.

In my room, I find Kira curled up in the fetal position. I sit down next to her and hand her the water. She gulps it down wearily. I brush her hair away from her face once she places her head back on my pillow. I like her lying there. I like her in my room, in my bed, part of my world.

"Do you want me to lay with you?" Kira looks up at me with unsure eyes. She's keeping me at an arm's length, and it's fucking killing me. "I just want to hold you, so you feel safe." It's the complete truth. Right now, I just want to be the man she can lean on.

"Fine." She rolls over. I guess that cool response is better than hell no. I'll take what I can get for now. I spoon myself against her, trapping her body in my arms. Imprisoning it. We lie there without saying one word. There's so much we need to talk about, but the time just doesn't seem right.

Kira's breathing becomes heavier and heavier, and soon she's fast asleep. I love her just being next to me. Feeling the warmth of her body and hearing the tranquility of her slumber. I dot soft kisses across her skin, pressing a tad harder when my lips reach the wave tattoo on the back of her neck. She moans so soft and sweetly I nearly dissolve. I cannot live without this woman. She has so quickly become everything. When we're together, I die ten-thousand deaths from just one sigh. That's her power, to bring a man like me to his knees. A man who thought he didn't need a fucking soul to survive, but was proven wrong in a blindsiding instant, because when Kira walked into my bar, my entire existence changed. I remember my father telling me something similar about Kristen, and I didn't believe him. I didn't even want to hear what he was trying to tell me. In my eyes, he was a hypocrite. He preached how important family is, then he turned his back on us. Walked away from everything he was accustomed to for a woman he barely knew. I may not be walking away from my family, but I am beginning to understand the connection he has to Kristen. The undeniable force, the extreme need, the dire fear of losing her.

I'm not sure I will ever understand the motivations behind his actions, why he felt the need to disassociate himself, but I am beginning to understand love, and the commitment that goes along with that binding sentiment. I committed myself to Kira, I promised to take care of her, and I'm going to stay true to my word.

Now all I need to do is convince Kira of that.

No problem, right?

Fuck.

I PUSH the eggs around the frying pan.

It's six p.m., and Kira is still asleep. At least that's what I thought, until I turn around and find her standing behind me.

"How long have you been spying on me?"

"Just a minute." She rubs her sleepy eyes.

"Feeling any better?" I slide my fried eggs onto the plate next to the stove.

"A little." She tucks her hair behind her ears awkwardly, still getting used to the short length.

"Want some eggs?"

"Sure." She sits down at the little eat-in countertop at the end of the kitchen. My home isn't as fancy as hers, but it does the job for a single guy like me.

"Scrambled?" I already know what she likes.

"Yes."

"Coming up."

"I can't believe I slept so long."

"It was a pretty rough day." I crack two eggs into a bowl.

"It was a pretty rough two days." Kira throws that out there. I whisk the eggs harder than I mean, but the mention of yesterday puts me on edge.

"Yeah. We've got some shit to talk about." I pour the eggs into the hot pan, and they sizzle, just like a bug under the baking sun and a microscope. Me being the bug in this metaphor.

"That was an asshole thing you did to me yesterday." She doesn't pull any punches.

"I know it was. I regret it, and I'm sorry." I push the eggs around the pan as they cook.

Kira doesn't respond, so I find my balls and look over at her. Her expression tells me some half-ass apology isn't going to cut it.

"You're saying the words, Ky, but I am having a really hard time believing them."

"Jesus, Kira, are you going to crucify me forever? I fucked up. I know it. I'm sorry," I pop off.

I am a pro at this apology thing.

"Christ, I can't do this." Kira gets up off the stool, frustrated already.

"Can't do what?" I question her as I pull the pan off the heat.

"Have a civilized conversation with you. You jump down my throat the first opportunity you get."

"I'm not jumping down your throat. I'm just not good at admitting when I'm wrong."

"So I've noticed." She's curt.

"Well, what do you want from me, Kira? I apologized. I came running to you when you needed me. I was here for you all day, and I'll be here for you tomorrow and the next day and the day after that."

"Until you find out something about me you don't like. Or life throws a curveball you weren't expecting, and you walk out on me again."

"I'm not going to do that," I argue, but even I hear the lie in my own response. I don't like surprises. I never have. And I don't respond well to ones that alter my life.

"What Hawk dumped in your lap was my most painful secret. It was my story to tell. And I was going to tell you. I *wanted* to tell you everything. But I had to do it in my own time. When *I* was ready."

"Kira, I get that, I do. I was just put on the spot and didn't react very well." I follow her into my living room where she's pacing.

"What concerns me is that I'm seeing a pattern."

"Pattern? You're a fucking shrink now?" I'm exasperated. Kira stops dead in her tracks. "This is exactly what I'm talking about, Ky.

You're so defensive. You think everyone is attacking you. I'm just trying to explain to you why I'm upset."

"I get why you're upset. I'm an asshole." I spell it out, point blank.

"I think you're just lost." She veers off in a different direction.

"Not when I'm with you. When I'm with you, I know exactly where I am. I know exactly who I am."

"Then how was it so easy for you to just walk out on me? I can't be scared of the person I'm with."

"Kira, I would never hurt you." I take a stern step forward.

"Maybe not physically. But emotionally? You're more than capable of that." I don't know what it is, but something in her tone is so alarming. So resolute, it actually scares me.

"I will never hurt you," I assert.

"You already have. You asked me to trust you, and I did. I handed you my heart, as fragile as it was, and all you did with it was smash it to pieces. You accused me of horrible things, when all I was guilty of was caring about you. I'm not perfect—"

"Neither am I," I interject.

"There's just this huge pit of doubt inside me I can't ignore."

"So, what the fuck are you saying?" My frustration returns with a vengeance.

Kira shakes her head unsure. "If I can't trust you, and you can't trust me, it's over before it even began."

"Kira, no." I don't accept that. The thought of it being over is unbearable. It rattles me so hard it feels as if all the inanimate objects around me are exploding. Everything in my condo just spontaneously combusting, creating mass chaos.

"Life is full of surprises, Ky. And hard decisions and obstacles. I need to know the man I'm with will stand by me through those things, not fight against me. Not abandon me or isolate me. I refuse to go through what my mother went through. I refuse to be unhappy. I lived that way for too long." Her big brown eyes begin to water, and I begin to realize just how scarred my Snow really is. There are so many invisible slashes, it may take me years to discover them all.

"I can be that man," I promise.

"You weren't yesterday."

"Christ almighty, Kira." I snatch her hand and yank her across the room. I take a seat on the couch right in front of her and grab hold of her hips. "I can be everything you need me to be. I made a fucking mistake. I hurt you. I know it. I own it. I don't know how many times I need to apologize until you believe me, but I will keep saying I'm sorry until I lose my voice and your ears bleed." I take a deep breath, putting it all out there. Everything. Every part of myself. The broken pieces, the defective parts, my crushed constitution. "I know there are a million reasons for you to go, but all you need is one to stay."

"And what would reason would that be?"

"You need me."

"What—?"

"And I need you," I continue before Kira has a chance to object. "I need you, Kira. I need to be the man I am when I'm with you. Leaving you yesterday made me realize that. It made it soul-crushingly clear. I have lived in a prison of sadness for years, and you freed me from that." I squeeze her hips, silently pleading for her to hear me. To truly listen to my words. "I like who I am when I'm with you." I look up at her a desperate, broken man, dying for her to stay with me. To still be mine. "Don't give up on me yet. Please."

Kira peers down at me with dark, molten eyes that are so emotive and sincere, they destroy me. "Ky Parish, you almost sound like you were begging." She trails her fingertip softly over the mutilation across my eye.

"A man would be a fucking fool not to beg for you." I touch her hand. "Not to fight for you."

"Are you really going to be that man?"

"I'm already that man." I pull her down to the floor so she's kneeling between my thighs. "I'm the one who's going to heal all your scars, guard your body, protect your heart, be a better man than I was the day before, and love you with everything I have. Everything I am."

Kira visibly softens. "That's definitely the kind of man I need."

"Say the word, and you have him."

"I have something better than a word." She leans forward and presses her lips to mine. I take full advantage of the opening, crushing her body and mouth to me. It's the most reassuring and consoling kiss

I have ever experienced. Trapping her face in my hands, I smother her with affection and earnest embraces. Embraces that communicate *I'm sorry, I love you, I want you, I need you, I'd fucking kill for you.*

Soft caresses soon becomes fanatical petting, and emotional kisses become an intensified clash of tongues.

The rift between us is mending, recalling what was almost lost. I pull at Kira's shirt as an overwhelming need ensues. A primal growl vibrates in my throat as my desire is torn in two. One part of me wants to fuck Kira like an animal, while another wants to shower her with passion and love.

I all but maul her while she's on her knees, biting, kissing, sucking every part of her exposed skin.

"I fucking need you," I snarl against her neck, a savage hankering to be set free. "I need to show you. I need to be inside you."

"I want you inside me." Kira's breathy pants set fire to my arousal.

I rip at her shirt, stretching it out as I yank it over her head. There's no bra to stop me from attacking her breasts, sucking on them deep and hard, fitting as much in my mouth at one time as I possibly can.

"Jesus, Ky." Kira buries her fingers into my hair as I nip at her nipples, making them pucker and pebble under the force of my mouth. I move to the button of her jeans as I continue to lavish her chest in a lust-filled frenzy.

Once the button is popped and her zipper is down, my hand dives inside to find the sweetest spot of ecstasy on the planet. I slide a finger into her pussy, and Kira releases a blistering sound.

"Oh, God." She disintegrates as I work her fast and slow, massaging my palm firmly against her clit. I refuse to relent until she's soaked and dying for more. Dying for me.

Hearts pounding, breathing labored, desire running rampant, I lift Kira off the floor and place her on the couch. I make quick work of removing her pants, then attack her pussy. I don't want to give her time to think, I want her just to feel. Feel me and all the things I'm capable of.

I lick the sugary spot between her legs emphatically, flicking my tongue against her clit and licking up the candied juice flooding from her entrance. Her afflicted sounds are so fucking arousing my cock is boxing like a prize fighter behind my zipper. I want her bad. I want her fast and dirty and slow and sweet.

"Oh, fuck, oh, Ky." Her words are choppy and her body tense. I know what that means. I'm bringing her close. Way too close. I dial back my tongue and suck on her clit one last time. "Oh, no, why?" she whines, winded and weak.

"Because I want you to look me in the eyes when you come. I want you to see me, and I want to see you. I want us to see everything. Together."

"See everything?" Kira repeats, clearly confused.

"This is the part where you trust me, Snow." I peel off my Baumer T-shirt, then lose my jeans. It's an even playing field now. Bare body to bare body. I stalk onto the couch, collecting Kira in my arms.

I position us the way I want, hooking my arms under Kira's knees. She's propped on the back of the couch, her shoulders braced against the wall.

I drink her in, all nakedness and perfection. My cock is humming to be inside her, to just slide right into the sweetness a torturous inch away. I don't know how I got so lucky, or why I'm so fucking stupid, but I was a moron to ever deny this woman, and an even bigger asshole to have ever walked away.

"Ky, what are you doing?" Kira heaves wantonly. She's feeling the exact same thing I am — greed, lust, hunger, desire. A conglomeration of craving clawing right below the surface.

"Admiring what's mine." I tease her pussy with the engorged head of my pounding erection.

"You like what you see?" It's such a shy, honest question.

"I love what I see." I lean forward. "I love you."

Kira traps my face in her hands and kisses me torridly. I lose my head in the connection, the ache in my balls winning out.

With a slight shift of my hips I sink inside of her, my swollen shaft stretching her wide, taking her by surprise.

She fights for oxygen as I steal it away, thrusting solid and steady and excruciatingly slow.

"Watch, Snow. Watch how perfect we fit together." I lean back so we can both see. See the way my cock slides in and out of her body and glistens with her arousal.

She's so wet, and so tight, and so fucking warm, my mind is swimming in self-indulgence. At one time, I was afraid to drown, but now I welcome the submergence. Because now I know, once I go under, I won't be alone. Kira is there, and we'll drift through the darkness together.

"Oh, fuck." Kira quivers as I continue to fuck her gradually, taking all the time in the world, even if it's slowly destroying us. "I need more," she pleads, and I gain way too much satisfaction in her appeal.

"Are you begging, Kira Kendrick?"

"Shit, yes." Kira begins to crumble right before my very eyes.

"Touch yourself." She's so open and exposed I can't control the request. I want our climaxes to be volcanic, and watching Kira pleasure herself will send me right over the jagged edge.

"You're a bastard." She brings her fingers to my mouth, and I soak them with delight.

"Sometimes." I agree. "But I promise, baby, it will all be worth it."

Kira caresses her clit, and my head nearly explodes. It's so fucking hot it could light the goddamn room on fire.

"Don't take your fucking eyes off me." I move my hips faster, in a steady, circular motion.

Kira whimpers in pleasurable pain as she massages the reactive little piece of pink flesh and her pussy painfully contracts.

"So close, Snow." Every muscle in my body strains as my gaze jumps between Kira's face and her hand.

"Too close." She closes her eyes and gives in to the temptation.

"Look at me." I touch my forehead to hers. The small shift in my position forces me deeper, intensifying our connection. Kira's mouth forms an erotic O as she stares into my eyes and lets go, coming in a star-studded array of high-pitched pants and tortured moans.

The flash of heat and pornographic display sends me on my own rapturous ride, and I find myself caught in Kira's climax, thrusting away, achieving the volcanic eruption I was after from the very start.

Everything is tight — our bodies, my thoughts, and Kira's pussy.

Time slows down and my pulse rate speeds up as the simultaneous climax causes a physical landslide. We're both sticky with sweat and saturated with fluids by the time it all passes.

I breathe heavier than I have in a long time; my energy is spent, my thoughts are foggy, and I can barely remain upright. We slide down the heated leather, disconnected from each other, but still exceptionally close. I lie with Kira trembling in my arms, the aftermath still viable. I kiss her head, her face, her lips, clutching her new, short strands tightly in my fist.

"Never ever doubt me again."

"Never ever give me a reason to."

I think that's a fair trade-off.

Kira and I lie together, limbs entwined, reconnecting. Would I sound like a total bitch if I said I enjoy snuggling with her as much as I enjoy fucking her?

"Will you tell me about the file?" I ask, playing with a lock of her pale blonde hair.

"If you really want to know."

"You know that I do."

Kira snuggles a little closer to me, burying her face in my neck for a beat before she speaks. "I didn't tell you the whole story about my freediving venture. Things were really bad between my parents. The worst they had ever been. They were fighting again. It was loud and vicious, and my mom was crying and screaming." Kira sniffles, and I realize she's holding back tears. I tighten my hold around her and give her the time she needs to continue. "I just wanted it all to stop. I wanted it to be quiet in my head. I wanted my mom to stop getting hurt. I even wished that my dad would die. I don't know what made me do it, but I filled the bathtub in my parents' room. It was this huge Jacuzzi thing that I loved taking baths in. I filled it all the way to the top, then I got in, clothes and all. I was like in this trance. I didn't mean to stay under so long, but it was so peaceful. There was no sound, no hurt, no yelling. I just embraced it. I went to sleep, and I almost never woke up."

"That sounds chilling."

"They say drowning is the most peaceful way to die."

"That's fucking morbid, and I'll take your word for it." I press a kiss on her forehead. "How did you . . . not end up dying?" I don't know how else to phrase it.

"My mom found me. She pulled me out and gave me CPR. I think that day was a turning point for all of us. It put everything into perspective. She started to plot her escape in the ambulance on the way to the hospital. I went through a lot of emotional shit after that. I was really lost and broken and fucked up. And it's not something I'm proud of. Shit." Kira hides her face against me, concealing her tears. "But I fought really hard to make it through to the other side."

God, I'm such a fucking dick. Kira has gone through hell in a handbasket, and I'm over here all resentful because my father met a woman and wanted a better life. I have tortured both her and him over it. I've only thought about myself and never considered anyone else's stake in it. Kira was right when she said I was lost. I am, but I really want to find my way back. Maybe I am, little by little, with her by my side.

"I get it. We don't need to talk about it anymore. I know enough. And I fucking hate seeing you cry."

"I'm not a fan of it myself." She wipes her wet cheeks against my chest.

"You know what a great cure for crying is?" I ask.

"No, what?"

"More make-up sex." I tickle her.

"Ky," she screeches, attempting to fight me off. But I'm too big and powerful for her little frame. She doesn't stand a chance. I roll on top of her, trapping her body beneath me. I smother her with a consuming kiss, pouring out as much affection, heat, and emotion as I can.

"Let's go to bed." I flick my tongue against her lips. "I want to show you exactly where my love lies."

"I think I know." She widens her legs, touches my mouth, and then my heart.

This woman.

After her, I'll never be the same.

19

Kira

WE'RE BACK at The Lion's Den.

I'll admit, I'm not a fan. I stick out like a blinding light. Everyone stares at me. Whispers behind my back or throws daggers in my direction. The women, especially. They don't like someone like me with someone like Ky. I'm encroaching on their territory. But Ky insisted we needed to get out of the house. We'd been holed up since last night. And he feels his bar is the safest place to be. For him, maybe. I'm beginning to understand why Gerard never mixed his two worlds. This is sorely uncomfortable. I surmise he wanted to spare my mother exactly what I'm experiencing right now. Pure discrimination.

"Another, princess?" the older bartender they call Popeye asks.

"Sure." I push my empty glass forward. I've thrown back two rum and Diet Cokes since we've been here, and I don't foresee myself stopping anytime soon.

Ky is having a pow-wow with a bunch of guys in the corner of the bar. I recognize most of them. Hawk, of course. He's shoved so far up

Ky's ass, I'm amazed he can breathe. Vet and Breaker, Agent Orange from the first day I was here, and his good friend, Panty Peeker.

The group looks thicker than thieves, and I know they're definitely as sly as them.

"One, rum and Diet for the pretty lady." Popeye places the glass in front of me, and I look at it forlornly. "Buck up. A beautiful face like that shouldn't look so sad. Ky will figure out who's bothering ya, then it'll be lights out for him." He winks with his one good eye.

"I don't want Ky . . . snuffing anyone's lights out." I make that clear. I want to be left alone, but not at the expense of my boyfriend going to jail for murder. "And it's not just that . . ." I let the sentence linger.

"Oh?"

I lean in a little closer so only Popeye can hear. For some reason, he's easy to confide in. He may look like a real, live pirate, but he's sweet as can be. "Everyone hates me."

He laughs. "Nonsense. You're just new. And our Prez has taken a liking to you. You're the second most important person in this bar right now."

"Me?"

"You're Slashes ol' lady, so yeah."

"I'm not old. I hate that term." I heard Vet use it when he was talking about Dahlia.

"It's a term of endearment. Half the women in this bar would kill to be Slash's ol' lady."

I look over my shoulder. There are still plenty of women giving me the stink eye. "I'm aware of that."

"Just wear his cut with pride, and don't worry about the rest." Popeye taps on the bar top.

"I'll try. What's a cut?" Ky hasn't explained a damn thing to me. This world is completely new. And confusing. And I'm definitely Alice navigating through Wonderland.

Popeye laughs at my expense some more. "Let me get a drink and then we'll have a chat." He hobbles around the back of the bar with his walking stick and one good leg. I peek around the room some more as he gathers his items. I read the neon beer logos on the wall and the outlandish roadhouse wall signs. One says 'A pair of balls beats everything.' But it's the knife that's stabbed into the wood at the end of the bar which is the most curious.

Popeye pulls up a stool in front of me and props his empty glass and bottle of scotch between us.

"What's with the Crocodile Dundee knife?" I ask.

"Fallen brother. Deacon," Popeye explains as he pours himself a hefty glass. "May God have mercy on his soul." He toasts then drinks.

"Oh, I'm sorry. I didn't realize—"

"No bother," Popeye waves me off. "It's just there as a reminder. So no one ever forgets."

"A memorial of sorts. That's . . . *nice.*"

"Sure." He takes another sip. *"Nice.* Now, what else do you want to know? What's a cut, right?"

"To start." I suck down my own sugary cocktail. Popeye can sure mix them. *Whoa.*

Popeye begins to explain what a cut is when I hear someone call my name over the hum of the crowd.

"Is there a Kira Kendrick here?" A loud voice yells. The entire places zeroes in on the strange man standing in the middle of the room holding a Tiffany-blue box.

"Who the fuck wants to know?" I recognize Ky's low timbre immediately.

"Nobody in particular. I just have a delivery for her."

Ky emerges from the back of the bar, flanked by all his men. He peers menacingly at the man dressed in a black hoodie and baseball cap.

"Who's it from?" He crosses his arms, his biceps bulging, strangling the cotton of his short-sleeve shirt.

"No idea. Some guy gave me fifty bucks to walk it in here."

"What'd the guy look like?" Hawk steps forward and takes the perfectly wrapped box.

"Some African-American dude. Real nice, actually. Said please and everything."

"Did he now?" Panty Peeker snarls. He's definitely the most intimidating of the bunch. There is just something so dark and ominous about him with his leather jacket, gages in his earlobes, and slicked-back hair.

"Take it in the back," Ky instructs Hawk. "You, get the fuck outta here. And the next time someone asks you to deliver a package, say no."

"Or go get a job with FedEx," Breaker tosses in.

Vet, Breaker, and Panty Peeker stand shoulder to shoulder like a wall of muscle in front of Ky until the man leaves.

"Follow him," Ky barks an order, and all three of them stride to the door. My anxiety has spiked tenfold in four short minutes.

"Snow." Ky takes my hand and leads me away from the bar. There's a private card room in the back of the bar Several poker tables are scattered around the space, and a full bar is situated in the corner.

"You guys take cards seriously."

"It was bred into us. Courtesy of your stepfather." Ky glares down at the box sitting on one of the tables.

"It looks just like the other one," Hawk makes an observation.

"Other one?" I look at Ky.

He rubs the back of his neck restlessly. "Show her."

Hawk retrieves a similar-looking box from the back of the bar. He opens it so I can see the contents.

"Holy shit." I cover my mouth with both hands, then reach in and pull out a lock of hair with a white ribbon tied around it. "This is mine." A chill races down my spine.

"It was delivered to Ky yesterday morning," Hawk explains.

"I got it just a few minutes before you called."

"Someone sent you my hair? What kind of sick maniac are we dealing with here?" I brush my thumb over the stolen strands.

"Not sure. But 'maniac' seems to be an accurate description," Ky considers. "Open it." He nods to Hawk.

Hawk removes the white envelope and hands it to Ky. He slips out the cardstock and reads the note:

Slashes are so pretty in the Snow.

. . .

Every hair follicle on my body stands at attention. "Same note." Ky crushes it in his hand. Those familiar feelings of isolation and fear begin to creep in on me. They know where I am. They know who I'm with. I'm suddenly so cold I shiver.

Ky draws me under his arm protectively as Hawk opens the box.

I'm actually terrified to see what's inside.

Hawk inspects the contents first before he pulls each of them out. First, he places a pink silk dress on the table, which I recognize immediately.

"That's mine. I wore it to our parents' wedding." I hold it up and display the huge gash right down the center of the neckline. *Why?*

"There's more," Hawk continues, pulling out the beaded headband and sparkly shoes that complete the outfit. The thought of someone in my house, in my room, fills me with absolute dread. How many times has he been there? While I was gone? While I was sleeping? I feel sick.

"I need to sit down." I reach for a chair.

"Get her some water," Ky snaps as he kneels down beside me. "Kira, just breathe."

"They know where I am. They've been in my house. In my room. Mutilating my things. Who knows how many times?" I glance over at the dress. "What does it mean? What do they want?" Panic ensues.

"Calm down." Ky rubs my leg as Agent Orange hands me a bottle of water.

"We need to go to the police, Ky. It's time. My mother and Gerard will be home eventually. I don't want to put them in danger. They have to know what's going on."

"They aren't coming back anytime soon, so there's no need to alarm them right now." Ky looks up at Hawk, who nods conspiratorially. "But maybe you're right and we should get the police involved. Hawk will take care of that. He's got the connections. I would just rather have it be low-key. I don't want to spook whoever it is. Is that fair?" He compromises with me.

I nod. "Yes, as long we're taking precautions." I open the water bottle and chug it. I'm so fucking stressed out.

"I will take every precaution possible when it comes to you." He pledges.

I breathe shallowly, believing him.

"Can we go? I just want to go," I plead with Ky.

"Of course." He stands, and I pull my legs up onto the chair, tightening into a ball.

"Hawk, do what you gotta do. Check in with Tempest about our delivery man friend, too. Keep me posted on everything. I'll be home with Kira until this shit blows over."

"You got it, man." I hear them clasp hands and snap, but I don't look up.

"C'mon, Snow, we can go out the back." Ky helps lift me to my feet. I'm like a feather in his grasp, barely any weight at all.

"Which one is Tempest?" I ask as he leads me out a back door.

"Plugs in his ears."

"Ah, him. One of these days you're going to have to formally introduce me to all your friends."

"Sure, I'll throw a barbecue when this is all over." He's blatantly sarcastic.

"Sounds like a plan. Popeye can bartend."

"All he's good for is drinking the scotch."

"He was nice to me," I explain to him as he places my helmet on my head.

"Yeah, Popeye is a good guy. Known him my whole life. He rode with my dad before the diabetes took his leg."

"Do you miss him?"

"Miss who?"

"Gerard. Do you miss him?"

Ky chews the inside of his cheek. "He's my Pops. Of course I miss him. I've just been so angry at him I didn't want to admit it. Hurts too much."

"He misses you. A lot." I take his hand. "He would say it all the time. And you could see it on his face at every holiday. He would ask to leave a seat open for you."

"Shit, Snow." Emotion bubbles in his voice. "How did this suddenly become about me and my dad?"

"I don't know. I'm just starting to realize life is short. And so fragile. Fix things with him," I urge.

"I'm going to," he promises. "I just need to fix things with you first."

"I'll be hiding under the covers until that happens."

"Naked, I hope." Ky straddles his bike.

"If that's how you prefer me." I slide both my arms around him.

"Always, Snow. Always."

20

Ky

KIRA WASN'T KIDDING when she said she wanted to hide under the covers. I haven't been able to get her out of bed all day. Not that I have a problem with that, because she's also been naked all day. I don't want the situation messing with her mind. I know she told me she hasn't had an episode in years, and that she's in a better place, but I can't help but wonder with everything that's happening if she'll digress. After she went to sleep last night, I googled psychosis and memorized what it is, how it feels, causes, treatments, and therapies. I barely slept a wink, but that doesn't matter. All I care about is that Kira slept safe and sound. And that she keeps sleeping safe and sound. That she stays safe, period. Mentally and physically. From the moment I met her, this intrinsic desire to protect Kira developed. It just cropped up like a spring flower. I've come to learn she's so fragile. So very fragile. Maybe not on the outside, but inside, her core is delicate. It's beautiful, like a piece of cut glass, and equally as breakable.

How do you protect something so precious? Do you hide it away from the world? Do you put it in a glass case to look at but never touch? Do you allow it to roam free and hope for the best while expecting the worst?

I just want to do right by her, whatever that may be. Maybe I should just worship her as she walks through life, a sworn disciple. A vowed protector. A pledged soldier. I have the experience for that, at least.

I let the hot water run over my shoulders, washing away the soap as I ponder life. Kira was with me only minutes ago, pinned up against the wall while I fucked her senseless. It's impossible to keep my hands off her. She's my sweetest addiction, a love born out of lust. A storm of desire that rises beneath my skin. I want her now, again, even after I just finished having her.

"Ky." Kira rushes back into the bathroom. Her hair is still wet, but she's dressed in black leggings and a crop top that shows off her midriff. "Look what I found. Is that you?" She holds up a picture of me from the third grade with a goofy, gap-toothed grin, and the worst bowl cut known to man. I swear my mom was out to make me a virgin for life.

"Where on God's green Earth did you find that?" I wipe away the water from my eyes.

"The back of your closet. I was looking for my bag. There's a whole box of stuff."

"Oh, yeah. I forgot that was there." I sorta had a moment after my dad left and I tore down every picture and memento that reminded me of him.

"You were so cute." She beams.

"I was a total geek until my dad got his hands on me."

"There's pictures of him, too. Get out of the shower. Let's look."

"A trip down memory lane. Awesome," I hum dryly, turning the shower head off. Kira hands me a towel and then bounces out of the bathroom. Someone is way too excited to dig into my past.

"Oh, my God, look at Gerard. What is up with that mustache?" She holds up another picture.

"It was the eighties. Who knows?" I sit down on the edge of the bed as Kira pulls apart the box.

"Who is that?" She shows me a picture of a young blonde woman with a crown of flowers on her head.

"My mom."

"She's beautiful. You look like her."

"Yeah." I take the picture from her. "Too bad she's a head case."

"That's not nice to say about your mother."

"It's the truth. Her mind is stuck in the clouds. She is definitely not in touch with reality."

"She's a free spirit."

"That's putting it nicely."

"Look at you on Gerard's bike." Kira becomes excited again. "How old were you there, three?" She hands me yet another photo.

"About that? Yeah." The image makes me smile. "My dad had me on a Harley with a deck of cards in my hands before I could walk."

"Sounds like Gerard. The first week I met him, he had me on the back of his chopper explaining strategies of poker." She laughs. "He was such a badass." She inspects yet another photograph. "Is that a gun in his waistband?"

"Probably." I take the picture to look. The image is just how I remember him as a kid. Dressed in a leather cut, blue bandana, and ripped-up jeans. He was nobody to fuck with back then. Hell, he's still nobody to fuck with, but during those days, the club was like a band of wild outlaws. My grandfather, Alfred, was a crazy motherfucker, which makes me wonder if that's why my mom is a little off her rocker. Growing up with a hard-ass like him had to have some kind of effect. Losing her mom at a young age I'm sure didn't help either.

"Huh." Kira scrutinizes one picture a little more closely.

"What is it?" I rub my hand across my hair to dry it.

"Who is that?" She flips the picture over and points.

I curl my lip. "Deacon. Old member of the club."

"Deacon? Is he dead?"

"Not that I know of. He was doing some real shady shit back in the day, so my dad blackballed him. Kicked him out of the club in front of everyone."

"Ky, I know him." Kira is convinced.

"From where?" It's preposterous. No one has heard from Deacon in over ten years.

"He's the alarm tech who came to the house. The one who was supposed to fix it before I came to you for help."

My heart drops into my stomach. "Kira, are you absolutely sure?"

"I'm positive. We had a whole conversation. I made him coffee. I remember his face."

"Jesus fucking Christ." I spring off the bed. "This was never about you." I scramble to find my phone when the doorbell rings. Kira and I both freeze like ice sculptures. Who the fuck could that be?

"Stay here." I walk out of my room and downstairs, tightening the towel around my waist. I spy out the side window of the front door to find a man I don't know, but he's holding a small box I recognize well.

Not this shit again.

I open the door and stand guard. "Whatever it is, I don't want it. You can tell Deacon to go fuck himself. His secret is out, and I'm comin' for him."

The scrawny man on my front stoop looks like he is about to shit. He's swaying back and forth on his skinny legs looking over at the courtyard. I take my eyes off him for one stupid second, and it's my biggest mistake, because when I looked back at him, his crazy expression spells out doom. Fast as a cat, he removes the top and hits me in the face with a dusty substance. As soon as it makes contact with my eyes, it burns and steals my breath as I inhale it. Whatever was in that little fucking box was lethal.

I cough and choke, falling to my knees, unable to see a fucking thing.

"Kira, run." I fight to holler, but someone kicks me square in the gut, and the little air I have left in my diaphragm evaporates.

"Get her," I hear a voice say. A deep voice. An ominous voice.

"Deacon." I battle to my knees, throwing punches into the air. I can't see, I can barely breathe, but I can still fucking fight.

"Little Ky, all grown up." He snaps my head back by my hair.

"Stay away from her." I punch upward, but my attempts are futile. I miss every fucking time.

"She's mine now," he laughs sinisterly.

"I will fucking kill you if you hurt her," my voice strains.

"That's cute, kid. How ya gonna do that when you can't even see me?" He digs his fingertip into my eye, and the sting intensifies.

"*Ahhh!*" I howl like the wounded fucking dog I am, still trying to gain my bearings, but my eyes burn so fucking bad I'm completely blind.

"Good ol' concentrated capsaicin powder. Gets 'em every time.

"Ky!" I hear Kira shriek somewhere close to me, and I dive in the direction of her terrified sound.

"So long, kid." He kicks me right in the face. "Tell your Pops I said hi."

"Fuck off," I growl, crawling down my concrete walkway, scraping my bare knees to shreds as I go.

"No!" Kira screams again, and my entire body breaks out in prickling goosebumps.

"Kira!" I bellow, sluggish from the toxic powder affecting my senses.

I hear car doors slam and tires screech, and I know she's gone. I fucking failed her. Ambushed by my father's oldest enemy.

"He has her. He fucking has her." I lose my mind as Fender treats my eyes with some homemade cleaning solution.

"Sit fucking still, man, I need to flush all this shit out." There are definitely perks to having a paramedic as one of your best friends. No hospital visits.

"I can't sit still. I'm gonna kill him. I'm going to shove the barrel of a shotgun down his fucking throat and pull the trigger."

"You aren't gonna do shit if you can't see. Hold him down." What feels like a dozen sets of hands pin me to the chair as Fender performs Chinese water torture. Everyone is here. Hawk, Fender, Vet, Breaker, Bone, and Tempest. All my closest accessories to trouble and the people I trust most in the world. "At least he was stupid enough to tell you what he hit you with." Fender places two soaked cotton balls on each eye. "He's good. You can let him go. Hold those there." He guides my hands to my face.

"The question is, what the fuck do we do now?" Hawk asks.

"We fucking find him," I rumble.

"Well, no shit, Sherlock, but he could be anywhere. He's got some deep connections."

"So do we. *Use them.*"

"We don't even know what kind of car they drove away in. I could at least track them on the traffic cams that way."

"Deacon knew what he was doing. Knew exactly when to strike. None of the neighbors saw anything?" I'm T-minus two seconds away from blast off.

"Only your willy," Bone grunts. "You gave your elderly neighbor quite a fright. You need a conceal and carry for that thing."

"I'm glad you've got a crush on my dick, but I'm not in the mood for fucking jokes right now. A psychopath has my fuckin' girl, and I can't do shit about it at the moment," I erupt like fucking Mount Vesuvius on her period.

"We will find her," Hawk tries to reassure me.

"*How?*"

"I'm working on that."

"The question is, what does he want?" Tempest voices his thoughts. "He messed with her, took her, but why? What's his endgame?"

I am not at all surprised at this train of thought from him. He's a paranoid motherfucker who questions everything. He's a lethal mix of scary as shit and smart as a whip.

"Money?" Vet throws out a suggestion. "I mean, she's got loads of it. Maybe he's going to hold her for ransom?"

"Fuck." I nearly bust a blood vessel in my brain knowing Kira is alone and helpless and most definitely terrified.

This is all my fucking fault, I fall down into a black pit of despair. If anything happens—

"Hello?" There's a knock at my front door, and I pop out of my kitchen chair. "Ky?"

I recognize the voice immediately.

"Dad?" I rip the cotton balls off my eyes and squint through my blurry vision.

"What the fuck happened?" He strides through the house, the egotistical asshole he is, until he's right in front of me. I'm already a shitstorm of emotions, and him randomly appearing out of thin air sends me into a tailspin.

"This is your fucking fault!" I attack him. A blind fucking fury possesses me. A burst of aggression I can't control commands me, and chaos ensues. "You did this! All of it!" I throw sightless punch after sightless punch, a brawl breaking out right in the middle of my kitchen.

"Chill the fuck out, man," someone barks as I'm ripped away from my father.

I feel him slip through my fingers as Bone pulls me down into a submission hold.

"What the fuck has come over you, boy?"

My only response to his question is heaving breaths and mental middle finger while I'm subdued like a wild animal on the kitchen floor.

"Where is Kira? What happened?" my father demands answers.

"That fuckface Deacon took her!" I detonate with my cheek squished to the hardwood.

"Deacon?" I hear my father's blatant surprise. Yeah, I sounded the same way when she figured out who was messing with her.

"Um, not that it's not great to see you, Gambit," Breaker addresses him. "But what are you doing here? We thought you were in Paris?"

"I was, but I got a message from Ky saying Kira was in trouble. So I booked a private flight as quickly as I could and got my ass back here."

"Of course you did," I complain. "Can you let me up now? I'm fucking calm."

"Yeah, you sound it," my Pops patronizes me.

Bone scoops me up off the floor like I'm a ragdoll. The six-foot-five beast can toss all of us around at once like stuffed playthings if he wanted.

"Jesus, kid, what the fuck happened to your face?"

I touch my eyelids gently. They must look as red and swollen as they feel.

"Pepper bomb to the kisser," Fender explains. "Leave these on." He presses the cold cotton balls back in place. "Everyone's safer when you're blind."

"Except, Kira," I bite. "And I never left you a message. It was Deacon. He must have spliced my voice somehow. He plotted all of this. He's been spying on Kira for over a month. Been lurking around your house, too. Kira knew something was up, so she came to me."

"You? How did she even know where to find you?"

"She's got a brain in her head. She put two and two together. Said you used to talk about me. Made her feel like she could trust me."

"She trusted you, all right. You charmed your way right into her damn bed." My Pops sounds none too pleased. Too fucking bad.

"It wasn't paradise island right off the bat, if that makes you feel any better."

"Not a fucking lick."

I pull the cotton balls off my eyes. "She's my fuckin' girl now, and you're just gonna have to deal with that." Fender's remedy is finally working, cause my vision is starting to improve. I can see the room and everyone in it a bit more clearly.

"Right now, I'm not worried about who she belongs to, I'm just worried about getting her back." My father begins to pace. He looks so different and exactly the same. Still commanding, still assertive, still in control, except now he's looks like he's been photoshopped like those models you see on the Harley Davidson website. Put together cleanly, not a hair out of place. Refined and rugged all at the same time. Before Kristen, he constantly had motor oil smudged on his clothes or on his face and couldn't care less who it bothered. Now, there isn't a speck of dust on him.

"At least we can agree about that," I mumble.

"It's a start," Breaker interjects. The tension is running sky high in the house.

A suffering silence descends upon all of us. We're left with no options and no clues. I've never felt so helpless, not even when my MRAP rolled over an IED in Afghanistan and all seemed lost. Men were wounded all around me, but even then, there was an exit strategy. Procedures in place. This situation feels like guerilla warfare. There's no rhyme or reason, just ambush, sabotage, and raids.

And all that's left to do now is sit in the jungle and wait.

Wait for the enemy to make his next move.

Wait for an opportunity to strike back.

Wait. Wait. Wait. Wait . . .

21

Kira

I COME to in a strange room.

My head hurts, and I feel a little woozy, but the zip ties biting into my wrists are what's alarming me the most.

I'm tied to a chair, alone, confused, and most definitely terrified.

I gaze out the huge, double glass doors directly in front of me, trying to figure out where I am, but all I see are trees. Trees everywhere, with no inkling of civilization in sight.

Bits and pieces of the whirlwind that happened earlier come back to me slowly. I remember hearing Ky scream to run. A man blocking me by the stairs. I tried to fight him off, but he overpowered me. The image of Ky helpless on the ground. Being hauled away into a strange car. Then something was put over my nose and mouth, and that's the last thing I remember. My heart is hammering so hard from the recollection I could be an abandoned pet on death row.

I need to escape. Survive and escape. Trying to free myself from the binds, I pull as hard as I can, a miserable attempt to slip my wrists out of the ties.

"C'mon, c'mon." I yank and jerk until my skin is rubbed raw. "Fuck." This is not working. They're way too tight. I begin to panic. I need to get out.

In the midst of my very unsuccessful attempt at escape, I hear footsteps. Heavy, horrid, harrowing footsteps.

The room I'm being held captive in seems to be the heart of the house. Stashed in the living room of what I think is a log cabin.

"She's conscious," a deep voice rumbles from behind me. The hairs on the back of my neck stand straight up. I hate whoever he is already.

He comes into view, and I recognize him. An older man with greying brown hair, a thick beard, and slim figure. He actually looks more sickly now than I remember from a month ago. His skin is saggy and pale, and there are purple bags under his eyes.

"Hey, princess." He leans on the arms of the chair, his face disgustingly close to mine.

I jerk my head back, wanting to get as far away from him as possible.

"You are a pretty one." He touches my cheek, and I fight with my digestive tract not to vomit. "I thoroughly enjoyed the little chat we had. You were quite the hospitable host." He stands upright and crosses his faded tattooed arms.

"I was trying to be polite. What a mistake."

"Being nice usually is. It's a weakness. Makes you vulnerable. And then you end up in situations like these." He motions to our surroundings. Our highly secluded surroundings. "I was nice once, you know. Generous with my connections and my money. You know where it got me?" His eyes darken sinisterly.

I shake my head.

"Ostracized. Kicked out of the only family I ever knew. They turned their backs on me. Blackballed me because I was different. Because they didn't agree with my methods."

Do I dare even ask what methods those were?

"So, you brought me here why?"

"Why else? Revenge."

"What do I have to with any of it?" I'm trying to understand his motives. *Why me?*

"At first? Nothing. Your mother was the intended target."

My heart sinks as soon as I hear that. Fucking bastard.

"I needed to get inside the house so I could tap into your alarm system and spy."

"You were watching me through the cameras?" I feel violated. Disgusting. They're all over the house. The only small consolation in finding all this out is the fact that I'm not crazy. Up yours, Hawk. I wasn't making it up in my head. I knew someone was watching me. I could feel it. And here he is, bragging about it. Holding it over my head. Proud of every despicable thing he accomplished.

"Pretty much."

"You know the code, too."

"Yup. Once I was connected, I could control everything from my laptop. I could come and go as I pleased. Manipulate what I wanted. I was in and out of your house so many times. I watched you sleep. Shower. Eat . . ." Something else lingers at the end of his sentence. A perverted inclination.

"You watched Ky and me." I'm nauseated. We had a fucking audience the whole time.

"Now that was a plot twist I didn't see coming. You two were entertainment for sure. Watching your little soap opera unfold. When he fell in love with you, I realized you were the key."

"Key to what?"

"Everyone's suffering. It's a chain reaction, and you are at the center of it. You're the switch. Hurt you, hurt them all."

I don't like the sound of that one bit.

"Hurt them how?" I probe.

"Emotionally, of course. Killing Gerard would be too easy. Too fast. There would be no satisfaction in it. But" — he points his index finger up — "kill someone he loves, and he suffers for the rest of his life." Deacon begins to cough fitfully. His body shakes so hard he spits blood right at my feet.

Ewww.

He walks off behind me, and I hear water run. I also hear the sound of his short breaths and uncomfortable moans. He's sick. And I believe terminally so.

"How much time do you have left?" I ask.

"More than you," he heaves.

My blood runs cold from his callous response.

"You don't have to do this," I try to appeal to his human side. "You don't want to leave this world with blood on your hands."

Deacon creeps around me, startling me half to death. "That's what confession is for."

"I don't even think a priest can absolve you of that sin," I argue.

"I guess one day I'll find out." He wraps his hand around my throat and squeezes. I try to pry myself from his grip, but his hold is too tight. Hysteria rolls over me as my windpipe is crushed and all the air is stolen from my lungs.

I plead with him, "Don't, please, stop." Tears streaming down my cheeks as I see stars. Deacon laughs in my face while I gasp for precious oxygen. My muscles strain and spasm in the chair, my fingers go numb from pulling at the restraints, and all the life drains from my body at a debilitating speed, like water being wrung from a rag.

Just as my vision colors over with black, Deacon let's go. I cough and spit automatically as I instinctively suck air back into my lungs.

I break down and cry right in front of him, a terrified little girl at the hands of a monster.

"Your pain is just beginning, princess." He pulls a strand of my short hair through his fingers, enjoying my agony. "Sit back and relax," he mocks. "I'll be back."

God, I hope not.

I hang my head and ignore him. Sniffling softly, scared of my situation and ashamed of my susceptibility.

An image of my mother creeps into my mind. Crawling out of her bathroom after my father had finished doing whatever horrible thing it was. I was too young to understand, but she was bruised and weak and crying. She didn't know I was there. Not until I wormed my way out from under her bed. I hated when she cried. I wiped her face and hugged her neck, and I remember vividly what she told me. "Tears may fall, but strength can rise."

For some reason, those words resonate.
They bring me comfort.
They make me feel less alone.
She walked through hell and survived.
Maybe I can, too.

22

Ky

POPEYE REFILLS my shot glass for the fifth time.

I don't know what's making me crazier, knowing Deacon has Kira and I can't do a fucking thing about it, or that my dad is playing Mr. Social, catching up with everyone in the Den.

This is not a happy reunion, goddamn it. His stepdaughter is out there. The love of my fucking life. And he's surrounded by smiling fucking faces, all wanting to know how life is fucking treating him.

"Gimme the bottle." I slam my hand on the bar.

Popeye places the Jack in front of me, and I grab it by the neck. If it was Deacon, I'd squeeze the shit out of it.

I head into the back room to wallow alone in the dark. All I can think about is Kira. All I can hear is her voice. Is her terrified screams. I'm falling apart. I slide my hands into my hair and pull, welcoming the pain. My eyes water. I'm so lost. Just like she said I was. She knew. She's known me from the very start. Saw everything I was trying to hide.

The only thing I was guilty of was caring about you. Her words destroy me. Tear me apart piece by piece.

A renegade tear rolls down my cheek.

How did this happen? How did everything just fly off the rails? And how can I fix it? That's the question that's eating me alive. How do I fix it? How do I find him? Find her?

"Ky?"

I wipe my wet face as fast as I can at the sound of my name.

"You okay, son?"

"No, I'm not fucking okay." What's the point in hiding it?

My father puts his hand on my shoulder.

"You really love her, huh?"

"More than you could ever understand," I admit.

"Oh, I think I understand more than you realize when it comes to a Kendrick woman's power."

I huff. "They're like fucking witches, right? They possess you."

My Pops laughs. "That's definitely one way to put it." He sits down at the poker table next to me.

"How can you be so calm?" I ask, lost. "Just out there socializing? Aren't you pissed off? Don't you want to rip someone's head off?" I clench my jaw, my hands shaking.

"Yeah, I fucking do, and much worse. And I will. But expending all that energy now isn't going to get us to Kira any faster. When the time comes, I'm going to use all that bottled-up rage to raise hell. Summon the Devil himself." He sits back and crosses his arms, and for the first time since we walked into the Den, I see the wrath in his eyes. It brings a sense of relief. I want the killer to come out. I want the man I heard stories about by my side. The one who would shoot first and ask questions later. The one who was ruthless. The one my crazy-ass grandfather named his predecessor.

My father has definitely undergone a metamorphosis in his life. He said having me changed a lot of his perspective. It made him want to be a better role model. A man I could be proud of. I know he has demons, way more than any one man should have. But he succeeded in turning his life, and this club, around. The Baum Squad Mafia may not be perfect. It may still have some shady corners, but for the most part, the men who are a part of it can ride with their heads held high. Can be proud to wear the patch and still be a functioning member of society. That's all he ever wanted.

"Dad, I'm sorry," I apologize earnestly.

The surprise from my declaration is blatant on his face. Yeah, I wasn't expecting it either, but it feels like the right time to say it. "I'm sorry I turned my back on you. I'm sorry I shut you out." I rest my weary head in my hands. I have blamed him this whole time. Accused him of walking out on me when, in reality, I walked away from him. I was so angry. Angry that he wanted something different. That a woman was influencing his decision. I manifested a person I could hate so my resentment could grow. It was wrong. I didn't understand. I didn't know a person could feel like this. That love could take such a strong hold. Being apart from Kira is literally suffocating me. It's difficult to breathe. Difficult to think. Difficult to function. I'm shriveling inside like a rotting piece of fruit.

And now I know how my father feels about Kristen. How he could walk away from the life he knew and still be perfectly content. Looking at him now, I see how good she is for him. Equally as good as Kira is for me. She's opened my eyes and my heart to so much and paved a way back to my father. Kira has given me everything, and all I have given her is grief and heartache and failure.

I failed her.

"It's okay, son." He rubs my shoulder.

"Kira made me promise to fix things with you."

"Looks like you're taking her advice. She's a smart one."

"Yeah, she is. Too smart for me. Too good for me. Did you really leave an empty seat for me during the holidays?" I recall her telling me that, and how much it affected me.

He nods. "Every one. Birthdays, too. I just wanted you there. With us somehow."

"I really fucked up, huh? Lost all that time with you." Regret moves in like an uninvited house guest.

"We've all made our mistakes. But what've I always told you about them?"

"Learn from them." He drilled it into my head.

"It's all any of us can do."

"I'm learning, fast."

"I know you are." He places his hand on my neck and presses his forehead to mine. "You're my boy. You'll find your way."

"I want to find Kira." I close my eyes and wish hard.

"We will." He taps my cheek reassuringly.

"What did you tell Kristen? Does she know?"

"I just told her you needed me, and I had to come back. She understood. I didn't want to alarm her if I didn't have to."

"You're gonna have to tell her something, eventually."

"I'll deal with that when the time comes." He rubs his hands together, clearly concerned about that conversation.

"They've been through a lot, huh?"

"Too much. I'm not sure how much Kira told you, but I don't think even she knows how bad it was. How deep it went. How deprived her father really was." A dark flash of malice blackens my father's eyes. "If I were to ever come out of retirement, he'd be the first person I park a bullet in."

"She didn't tell me everything, but what she did tell me was pretty bad. She tried to commit suicide?"

"She was pretty fucked up over it, yeah."

"And now she's dealing with this. How much can one person take?"

"I'm not sure, but if she's anything like her mother, she can survive a lot."

"I hope so." I pray so.

My father's phone rings. "Crap, that's probably Kristen. Wish me luck."

"I'm here for you, Pops." I slap his leg.

When he looks at the screen, though, his expression is perplexed.

"Who is it?"

He shakes his head and slides to answer it.

"Gambit. Long time, brother."

I shoot out of my seat at the sound of Deacon's voice. My father motions for me to circle behind him so I can see the screen; it's a FaceTime call.

"Kira," I exclaim. Deacon has her hands bound behind her back, sitting on the edge of a full bathtub, shivering and soaking wet. "If you fucking hurt her, Deacon, I swear to fucking God, I will kill you!" I roar.

He laughs at me. "Kira and I have been having so much fun. Want to see?"

Kira shakes her head and begins to cry as Deacon wraps a hand around her throat and pushes her back into the water. He holds her under as she helplessly kicks and fights, deprived of air.

I lose my fucking mind watching her tortured. "Deacon, I will bury you!" I scream so loud everyone in the bar rushes into the poker room.

"What the fuck do you want?" my father demands.

"I want you to come find me."

"Tell me where you are, and that won't be a problem," my pops threatens.

"Let her up!" All I can concentrate on is Kira's suffering.

"Your little mermaid likes the water." He continues to hold her under, and I continue to race down the road of insanity.

"Deacon." My father utters his name in a tone so chilling it gives everyone in the room hypothermia. "Your fucking beef is with me. Let's finish it."

"I plan on finishing it." He finally lets Kira up, and she gasps and coughs so hard it sounds like she has bronchitis.

"Ky," she cries, and I nearly fall to my knees.

"You know where to find me." Deacon dunks Kira back under the water, then hangs up.

"No!" I grab the phone and almost crush it in my hands. "What is he talking about? Where is he?" I grill my father.

"I have no idea. I haven't had any contact with Deacon in ten years."

"A place from the past, maybe?" Tempest suggests.

"Give me the phone." Hawk grabs at my hand. "Maybe I can trace the number."

Just as he takes it, it beeps with a text message. He opens it, and we all look. It's an image of an A-frame cabin with a double glass door outlined in red.

"Dad?"

My father inspects the image. "He's in Arrowhead. That's his family's cabin. We used to go party up there. It's remote. And a decent drive away."

"Well, let's fucking go." I'm ready for this to go down.

"It's a trap," Hawk states the obvious.

"Of course it is. But I don't care if the fucking tree-lined drive is covered in landmines, we need to go. You saw what he was doing to her."

"Ky is right. We need to go now. No more waiting," my father thankfully agrees.

"There's shit behind the bar," Tempest announces. "Enough for all of us."

The "shit" he's referring to is guns and ammo. "Hawk made us stock up after the whole hair situation."

"Hair situation?" my Pops repeats.

"I'll explain everything later." I burst back into the bar. "Pull everything out."

Hawk and Tempest unveil what looks like a mini arsenal onto the bar top. They weren't playing around.

"We need some kind of plan," Breaker voices as he locks and loads a 9mm.

"Kill that motherfucker." I aim a Glock at a green gin bottle displayed behind the bar.

"That goes without saying." Bone ties his long red hair up into a bun, then flips two handguns around on his fingers.

"I can send a drone in to canvas the area," Hawk suggests.

"I don't think you'll see much. The cabin is small and hidden in some dense woods," my dad informs us.

"Sometimes you don't need a plan." I pull the trigger, exploding the bottle. "Just some big balls."

"Jesus Christ, kid. Save it for Deacon." My dad grabs for the gun and lowers my hands.

"I needed to fucking destroy something."

"Feel better?" he asks.

"No." I holster the gun in the waistband of my jeans. Then I shove another in my boot. "The ace in the hole." I wink at him. He taught me that.

"So, are we going in there all *Young Guns* then?" Tempest poses like a gun slinger. The man is a West Coast version of an urban cowboy. Leather, denim, and hardnose attitude.

"We're rollin' seven deep. Unless he has a fucking army up there, we have the advantage on our side," Breaker rationalizes.

"We don't know what the fuck he has up there, but we can't waste any more time talkin'. We proceed with caution and evaluate the situation when we get there," my father makes the final call.

"I'm good with that." I head straight for the door.

"Hey." He grabs my arm, pulling me aside. "Your sole concern is Kira. Got me? I'll handle Deacon."

"Pops, I'm not gonna let you do anything stupid."

"When have you ever known me to do anything stupid, kid?" He slaps me in the face.

Just like old times.

The ride out to the Arrowhead cabin takes a little over two hours. I am an antsy mix of emotions the whole way there. I want this to be done and over with fast. Bullet in the brain and be gone. Riding off into the sunset with Kira safe and sound on the back of my bike. The end. But a gnawing feeling inside me is anticipating it to be much worse.

My dad gives the signal to turn off while on the back of Breaker's bike. I think it's the first time I've ever seen him sit bitch.

He wasn't kidding when he said the cabin was remote and hidden in dense trees. The dirt pathway through the forest slows us down considerably. Four-wheel drive would have been a much better choice.

Once we see the little structure come into view, we fall back to a crawl.

"Tempest, Vet, head around the back, canvas it, then catch up," my father instructs.

Like nothing has changed, they immediately do as he says.

We roll up to the light grey front deck where a muddy Ford pickup is parked off to the side. All four bikes completely surround the wooden structure.

The environment is so peaceful, so quiet. A true picture of nature, with the smell of pine potent in the air, and the sound of birds chirping in the trees.

"This just seems too easy," Hawk shares his concerns as we all dismount our bikes.

"My thoughts exactly." My dad surveys the woods.

"Let's just get this over with." I pull the gun from the back of my waistband. "Deacon! Show your fucking face! Let's see how tough you are now!"

Nothing. No response, not even a peep.

"He's inside," Bone rumbles, staring straight through the glass front door. I look harder, and sure enough, there he is, sitting right in front of us in a chair.

"This is some whacked-out shit. Anyone else think this is whacked-out shit?" Breaker asks.

"Deacon always was a little odd." My Pops steps up onto the deck, and we all follow.

Our guard raised for anything, he slowly opens the door.

"Don't be such a fucking pussy, Gambit. Walk the fuck in," Deacon snaps.

My father steps inside first, and my heart palpitates. I'm suddenly feeling as protective over him as I do over Kira.

"Been a long time, old man," Deacon address my father as all five of us invade the small living room. He doesn't move a muscle in his chair, a 9mm resting on his knee.

"You ain't kiddin'. You look like shit."

"Cancer will do that to you." He breaks out into a long fit of dry coughs.

Time feels like it's in fast forward. I need to know where Kira is, and I need to know right now.

"Sorry to hear about the diagnosis, but where the fuck is Kira?" I point my gun right at him.

"I wouldn't be so rash. Shoot me, and you'll never find her."

"What is this all about, Deacon? Revenge? Are you just so petty and miserable, you need to get back at me?"

"You took everything from me, Gerard. I just wanted to return the favor. One last, friendly gesture."

"Friendly gesture, huh? Stalking, stealing, and kidnapping is not usually how I treat my friends. Ky asked you once, I'll ask you a second time. There won't be a third chance. Where the fuck is my stepdaughter?"

Deacon smiles perversely. "She's gone."

Something in my stomach twists in nauseating knots from his response.

"Search the place," I order, and Hawk, Fender, and Breaker tear through the house as Bone, my father, and I keep Deacon company.

"Look all you like; she isn't here." He clears his phlegmy throat.

"Then where the fuck is she?" I tighten my grip on the gun pointed right at Deacon's head.

"I told you, gone. Gerard, your son has to have his hearing checked."

My rage is rising faster than high tide. He's wasting our time. I take two threatening steps toward him, and he holds the barrel up under his jaw. "One more step, and I pull the trigger."

We are all left flabbergasted. "Like I said, kill me, and you'll never find out where your little mermaid is."

What kind of sick joke is he playing?

I start to breathe harder, my body searching for an outlet for the building stress.

"Nothing," Breaker reports back. "She isn't in the house. We looked everywhere, even pulled up squeaky floor boards."

"A basement? Storm cellar?" I demand.

"No," he sounds confident.

Fuck.

"What do you want, Deacon? What will fix this?" my father appeals to him.

"Seeing you suffer will be the only thing that fixes anything. And like I told Kira, she was a plot twist I didn't see coming. I was just going to kill your wife, but your stepdaughter? So much sweeter. Her death causes a domino effect. You, your wife, your son. Everyone hurts. One continuous, vicious cycle."

"*Death.*" I lunge at Deacon but am restrained by Bone and Breaker. "You tell me where the fuck she is, old man, or I will beat you within an inch of your pathetic life and dangle you there."

"No place I haven't been before, kid." He squeezes the trigger, and a shot of adrenaline has me speeding toward him like a bullet from a Semi. I knock him off the chair, and we wrestle on the floor. We grapple around for the gun, both grabbing it at the same time. Several shots pop off, and blood suddenly pools beneath our bodies. It all happened so fast, my mind is having difficulty catching up to my body. I'm ripped off the floor and hauled to my feet by Bone and Breaker.

"Ky, you're shot." Hawk lunges toward me, pressing his bare hands to the wound.

"So is Deacon." Fender inspects his injury, feeling for a pulse. I see him shake his head.

My father falls to his knees. "John," he calls him by his God-given name. "Where is Kira? Where the fuck is she?" He shakes him violently, but there's nothing, no response. He's dead.

"No, no, no," I slip into denial. "That can't be it. We didn't find her."

My father looks up at me with a gallon of tears in his blue eyes. *My father,* the strongest man I know. Crying.

"Slash, we gotta get you to a hospital, man, before you're the next one to meet the Reaper." Hawk begins to push me to the door.

"I'm not going anywhere. We have to find her!" Woozy on my feet, I fight to stand on my own.

"She's gone." Hawk puts his hands on my shoulders and looks me square in the eyes.

"No," I break down. My legs turning to jelly.

Bone and Breaker support me as Fender presses a kitchen towel to my side. "Keep pressure on it."

My father rummages around the small kitchen until he finds what he's looking for. "Keys. To the truck outside. Get him in the flatbed."

"No!" I scream in pain. And not the pain from the gunshot wound. The pain from my heart being pulverized into dust.

"Ky." My father grabs hold of my neck and presses his forehead to mine. "We have to go. I can't lose you, too. Listen to Fender, or we will drag your unconscious ass out of here. Time is not on our side."

I bawl like a baby in my father's grasp. "She can't be gone."

"It looks that way." Two streams of tears race so fast down his face, you could name them like rivers.

"Yo," Vet's voice suddenly cuts through the chaos. "We found a shovel with fresh earth on the side of the house. Looks like there's a grave about twenty yards out into the woods."

I perk up at his sudden announcement. I push my way forward as we all haul ass out of the house.

"Ky, you need to get to a hospital," Fender argues with me as I stumble into the woods, holding the cloth against my side.

"I'm not leaving her."

"Son—" my father tries to reason.

"No," I snarl. "I'm the Prez. It's my fucking call."

Everyone shuts the fuck up after that.

When Tempest comes into view, he's stripped down to his undershirt, sweaty, dirty, and digging like a maniac. "Hurry up." His blackened, ink-covered arms flex hard with each hearty scoop of dirt.

We all fall to our knees and dig, the tension so sharp it could slit each one of our throats clean.

"Kira," I yell, light-headed and weak. "Kira!" I gouge handful after handful of cool earth, believing if anyone can survive this, she can. I rake away the soil until my biceps burn and my fingertips scrape something hard.

My emotions implode as we discover the long wooden box, and I nearly puke at the thought of what could be inside.

If I can't trust you, it's over before it even began. Her words wash over me like acid. They broke me then, and they're breaking me now. It can't be over. We had so little time. Barely any at all.

My father, Vet, Tempest, and Breaker open the box, and we find Kira bound and unconscious inside.

"Get her out." Fender jumps into action. Lifting her limp body up, they lie her on the ground. Tempest cuts her hands and feet lose with his pocket knife as Fender checks her vitals at rapid speed. "No pulse, but she's still warm." He starts compressions, and all I can do is crawl next to her and beg. Beg her, beg the Lord, beg any god who will listen to let her live. To bring her back.

"Five, six, seven, eight, nine, ten . . ." Fender's voice is like a far-away echo. "Twenty-seven, twenty-eight, twenty-nine, thirty."

No response, so he gives her two solid breaths and starts again. "Five, six, seven, eight, nine, ten . . ." And then once more. My vision comes and goes as I lie next to Kira just holding her hand. Bone keeps pressure on my wound, but I've gone completely numb. I don't feel a fucking thing except despair. I start to drift off, it becoming nearly impossible to keep my eyes open.

"Ky, don't you fucking give up, boy." My dad shakes me. "Stay awake."

I flutter my eyes open, but they're so heavy. I just want to go to sleep.

Then I'm startled by a jerk of my hand and sharp gasp. Kira coughs, gulping in air, and I'm suddenly thrust back into consciousness.

"Oh, thank Christ." Fender collapses from exhaustion as I haul Kira weakly into my arms.

"Ky?" she cries disoriented, hugging my tightly.

"You're okay now, Snow. I've got you. We've got you." I cradle her in my arms and clutch her face. The angelic face that caused me to fall madly in love the moment I laid eyes on her. But it was her soul that kept me coming back. A soul that is too precious to take from this world. To take from me.

"You came for me." Her voice is shaky and small, but it's still the most magnificent sound I have ever heard.

"Always." I try to hold on, but the pull of the darkness is too strong. Black inky spots cloud my vision, stealing the sight of Kira away from me.

Then, in a snap, everything just disappears.

23

Kira

"Ky?" I scream as he just passes out right in my arms.

"Fuck, get 'em up and into the truck." Fender scurries to his feet.

Everything is happening so fast. I'm confused. There's too much movement.

"Sorry to break up the reunion, princess. But we gotta get Slash the fuck outta here." Bone lifts his unconscious form off the ground, and he's hauled away by three of the other guys.

What the hell is happening? I'm left alone once again, an exhumed grave right at my feet. My grave. I shudder, recalling Deacon dragging the wooden casket through the woods. Recall the paralyzing fear as he kicked me into it and closed the top.

"You're not alone, Little Darlin'." I look up to find Gerard standing beside me. His hand held out.

I don't know how or when he got here, but I reach for him desperately. He hauls me up, securing me in a bear hug and I completely break down.

"It's okay," he coos. "It's okay."

"Gambit, we gotta go!" Breaker yells through the trees.

"We'll talk more." Gerard pulls me in the direction of the house.

I yank at my hand. "Where's Deacon?"

"Gone. Dead. Ky killed him."

"What?" I step forward in a daze.

"Like I said, Darlin'. We'll talk more. Right now, we need to worry about Ky."

Gerard and I run through the woods to where everyone is waiting. We hop into the back of the pickup, and Tempest peels away.

"How far to the nearest hospital?" I sidle up next to Ky's unconscious body, placing his head on my lap. There's blood everywhere. It's seeping through his clothes, on his hands, and all over the truck.

"A few miles out. Vet already called ahead. They know we're coming." Fender and Bone keep continuous pressure on the wound, and I feel completely helpless.

"Why didn't you take him to the hospital sooner?" I viciously snap. Out of anger, out of fear, out of worry, out of uncertainty. So much is circulating so fast my thoughts are a muddled mess of brain cells.

"We tried." Fender looks directly into my eyes. "But he wouldn't leave you."

I gaze down at Ky. His cheeks are pale and cool to the touch. I can't stop the onslaught of tears. They've been falling since the moment I opened my eyes.

I kiss his forehead, his nose, and length of his scar, then I pray.

I also beg Ky to fight. I whisper how strong he is. I whisper how much I love him. How much I trust him. Then I plead, "Don't let it all be for nothing."

My heart squeezes painfully in my chest from the lack of response.

When I look up at Gerard, he's as pale as Ky, his eyes bloodshot but missing tears. He's holding them back. He's holding it all back. The devastation right at our fingertips. Knocking at our front door. If Ky dies, Deacon wins, and it really will have all been for nothing.

When the hospital comes into view, Tempest seems to take this as a cure to drive more like a maniac, hitting the gas and fishtailing through the intersection.

"Hey!" Breaker bangs on the glass. "Let's not put anyone else in the hospital!"

Tempest stops short at the emergency room entrance where there are already people waiting. They're dressed in scrubs and paper aprons, with masks on their faces and a gurney all ready.

There's so much commotion once we stop, it's hard to keep track of it all.

Ky is slid out of the flatbed and rushed away before I even have a chance to say goodbye.

"Kira, let's go," Gerard calls to me. I crawl next to Ky's pooled blood, the image now burned into my memory.

Gerard lifts me up and out of the truck. Then he stashes me under his arm protectively, exactly the way Ky used to.

I find myself in the waiting room. It's like reality is setting back in. I'm aware of my surroundings. I see everything clearer and feel everything more distinctly. Like my emotions are magnified. They're too big for my little body. It's feels like I'm going to explode.

I sit next to Gerard just holding his hand. The room isn't very large, but there's enough space for all the rugged, tattooed men covered in dirt to pace about.

These are all the people Ky loves. Every single one of them is here. Even Gerard. The father who's been absent from his life for over three years.

"Kira?" Gerard squeezes my hand.

"Yeah?" I turn my head in his direction vacantly.

"What'd you do to your hair?"

I touch my messy bob. "Deacon snuck into the house while I was sleeping and cut it," I explain shamefully. "And then he sent it to Ky."

"Piece of shit." Gerard runs his palms over his face with an exasperated huff.

"Ky likes it." I recall what he said after Dahlia fixed it.

It's sexy as fuck.

I would give anything to hear him say that to me again. I'd keep my hair short for the rest of my life if that's what he wanted. Just as long as he's with me, I'd do almost anything.

I lean on Gerard's shoulder, just watching the time tick by. Waiting is agony. It's amazing how long a minute lasts when you stare directly at the clock.

"You know he apologized to me," Gerard shares randomly.

"Oh?" I lift my head to look at him.

"He said you told him to do it. That if the two of you were going to be together, we needed to fix things."

"It's the truth. How could our relationship work if the two of you hated each other?"

"I never hated Ky."

"I know. I think deep down he didn't hate you either. He was just hurt and didn't know how to deal with all those feelings." I place my tiny hand over his. It's so much bigger and covered with tattoos. The combination an illustration of our two worlds merging together.

He smiles weakly. "It felt good getting him back." He looks straight ahead and his voice cracks at the end of his sentence. He doesn't need to finish his thought. I already know what he's thinking. It was good to get him back . . . *even if it was for just a little while.*

"Should we get you checked out, Little Darlin'? I'm sittin' here worrying about Ky, I completely spaced on you."

"I'm fine, Gerard. Shaken up. Totally in shock, but fine. I don't want to be anywhere but here with you."

"You know your mother is going to cut my balls off when she finds out about all this."

"I know. You're screwed." I offer no consolation.

Gerard's jaw drops, then his lips curl up into an appreciative smile. "I love you way too much, little girl." He wraps his arm around me.

"It's hard not to." I snuggle against him.

"Ky never stood a chance," he grunts.

"Nope," I agree.

"Kira." Hawk clears his throat off to the side of Gerard and me. "I thought you could use some coffee."

"Thank you." I accept it graciously, even if he is one of my least favorite people on the planet right now.

"Can I sit?"

I look at the empty chair next to me. "Sure." I shrug.

Hawk takes a seat and rests his elbows on his knees. "I just wanted to say I'm sorry for causing trouble with you and Ky. I was just trying to protect him. It's my job, ya know." He looks over at me so solemnly. His apology is sincere. "Ky is one of my best friends. My brother, my leader. I just wanted him to have his eyes open."

Through Hawk's explanation, I come to realize just how important Ky is to the men in this room. I observe each and every one of them, and they all have the same worried, misplaced look on their faces. They're a band of brothers, lost boys, and Ky is their Peter Pan.

"I appreciate your apology. And I accept it. Let's just start fresh, okay?"

Hawk nods forcefully. "And just so you know, no matter what happens with Ky," he speaks with so much anguish on his face, "you'll always have someone to turn to. Anyone of us, all of us. We'll be here if you need us."

It's the most heartwarming and heartbreaking sentiment I have ever been offered.

"Thank you." I fight to smile.

Hawk leans back in his seat looking like a weight has been lifted off his shoulders.

Gerard sneaks his arm behind me and flicks Hawk in the ear.

"Ouch! What'd ya do that for, Gambit?" He covers the side of his head.

"You're always causing trouble," Gerard scolds.

A doctor enters the waiting room, cutting away any small distraction from the dire situation.

"I'm looking for the family of Ky Parish." A tall woman with a low bun and glasses announces, and she is rushed by half the room. She looks a little overwhelmed by all the men crowding around her. I know that feeling. That was me a month ago.

"Back off." Gerard moves through the throng. "Let the doctor breathe, you bunch of animals." He stands face to face with the doctor. "I'm his father."

I creep up behind Gerard, peeking out behind his broad body.

"It was touch and go there for a while. He lost a lot of blood and needed a transfusion," she explains clinically. "It is a miracle the bullet didn't hit any major organs."

"So he's okay?" Gerard asks hopefully.

"He's stable, and resting, but he'll need to stay here a few days for observation. There's still a concern for internal bleeding."

I breathe a small, thankful sigh of relief. Truthfully, I breathe for the first time since Ky passed out.

"Can we see him?" Breaker asks.

"Only immediate family while he's in the ICU."

"Well, that's horseshit," Bone communicates his dissatisfaction with that response.

"Sorry. Hospital rules." She pushes her glasses up her nose matter-of-factly.

"You can follow me if you'd like, Mr. Parish."

"C'mon, Kira." Gerard places his hand behind my back.

"And she is?" the doctor inquires.

"She's his stepsister. They're very close," Gerard informs her, keeping a straight face.

The whole room breaks out into a fit of laughter, even Gerard and me. The doctor clearly doesn't get the inside joke, but it's obvious something's up. She eyes Gerard and me speculatively, then turns on her heel. "This way."

As we follow the doctor through several sets of double doors and past the inner workings of the hospital, I begin to feel lighter and lighter. All the worry and stress from the past twenty-four hours lessens with each step closer I get to Ky.

"Stay as long as you'd like, just please keep your voices down for the other patients." She stops in front of a closed curtain. The ICU does not provide much privacy. There are lines of beds down several corridors off a main hallway with machines, glowing and beeping everywhere, and nurses coming and going in every direction.

"Thank you." Gerard clears away his emotions. He's a professional at keeping it together. "We appreciate everything you've done."

She nods. "It's what I'm here for. If you need anything, ring the bell."

"We'll do that." Gerard pushes the curtain aside, and I get my first glimpse of Ky. My knees go weak from the sight of him. He's bandaged and sleeping, with an IV in his hand and monitors stuck all over his chest.

"Do you think he's cold?" The blanket only reaches his lower torso.

"He's so out of it he probably doesn't even know what cold is." Gerard pulls the curtain back, concealing us, and circles around the bed. I yank the blanket up a little farther, just wanting to make him feel as comfortable as possible. Wanting to do anything that will make him feel better.

Gerard takes Ky's hand, and the gentle gesture nearly brings tears to my eyes.

Seeing Ky lying here is excruciating for me, but I can't imagine the depths of pain it's causing Gerard to see his son this way.

"I still remember the day Ky got that scar. He was such a scrawny little shit," Gerard reminisces. "He hated being so small. Wanted to be tough, just like his dad. I remember sitting in the emergency room, terrified he was going to lose his eye. There was so much blood; the wound was so deep. And here was this little guy who couldn't put an ounce of weight on him if he tried, being so brave, not a lick like his father. 'Dad, do you think I'll have a scar?' 'It'll look so cool' 'Can my nickname be Scar?'" Gerard laughs darkly. "I told him Slash sounded cooler. I was such an enabler, but I hated seeing him in that bed. It killed me. But he was a fighter. Just like his old man. More than his old man. His heart was so big for that little body. And now, here we are again." Gerard gazes at Ky.

"And he's going to be fine. Just like before." I make my way around the bed to hug Gerard. I hate seeing him in so much pain. I hate seeing them both in pain.

"Next to Ky, you and your mom are the most important people on Earth to me. I don't know what I'd do if I lost any of you." He holds me tightly.

"Well, hopefully, you won't have to worry about losing any of us for a long time. And now you and Ky can make up for the time you've lost."

"I'm hoping beyond all hope, Little Darlin'."

"It'll happen if I have anything to say about it."

"Got him wrapped around your little finger, huh? Just like his old man?"

"Maybe."

"Definitely. The way he fought for you. He wouldn't leave your side. For a second, a terrifying second, I thought if you lost your life, he was going to give up his, too."

That revelation shocks me. I stare down at Ky. Pissed at his stupidity and maybe a little more in love with him for it, too.

Ky whimpers, trying to shift his body on the bed.

"Hey." I rush to his side. "Don't try to move too much." He flutters his eyelashes, attempting to open his eyes. Once he does, his attention seems far away. "How are you feeling?"

"Like I got fucking shot," he complains.

"You did get shot, numb nuts."

"Hey, Dad." Ky closes his eyes again and breathes deeply. He seems to drift back off, but he surprises me by startling awake. "Kira?"

"I'm right here." I touch his face.

"Are you okay?" He suddenly seems to be mentally alert.

"I'm traumatized, exhausted, and in shock, but I am trying to keep it together," I answer honestly. "I also may never go back into the water again."

Ky frowns at that admission. "Kira—"

"Ky, don't." If we open that flood gate of emotion, the entire hospital will get washed away. If there is one thing I've learned how to do, and do well, it's compartmentalize. I'm a teetering fishbowl of frazzled nerves at the moment, and soon I will tip. I just need to hold it together long enough to know everyone I love is okay.

"We'll fix it," he promises. "We'll fix all of it."

"I know we will." I try to smile, but it's becoming increasingly harder to suppress the stress. I'm falling back into that blank space where the line between reality and delusion blurs. Where anxiety takes over and holds my life hostage. And now, the place that is supposed to help me escape, help me heal, terrifies me. It's associated with chaos instead of calm. It's been transformed, leaving me in the middle of nowhere. Alone, but not scared, protected but still confused, even with all the answers laid out right there before me. "Rest." I kiss him on the forehead, the cheek, the lips, finding immense relief that we're both alive.

We're together, we're safe, and though tears have fallen, strength did rise.

EPILOGUE - GERARD

Gerard

I SPY on my wife as she watches Ky and Kira from the kitchen. She is the most beautiful woman I have ever laid eyes on, and somehow, some way, by the grace of God, she's mine.

"Penny for your thoughts, Darlin'."

Kristen shakes her head thoughtfully. "He's good with her."

"He has definitely come a long way," I agree. Ky is standing with Kira by the edge of the pool. They look cozy, facing each other and holding hands, but looks can be deceiving.

Kristen pays little attention to me. It's been that way for a few days now. She's cycling through emotions just like the rest of us. But Kristen's scars, like Kira's, run deep.

I place my hand on her hips and rest my chest against her back. Here we are in our big, beautiful house, financially stable, our children with us, and the picture that is supposed to be perfect is broken. There's a crack, and I am doing everything in my power to fix it.

"She's been through so much," Kristen thinks out loud. I'll take whatever thoughts she wants to give me. Even the bad ones. She's been so quiet and distant, I was beginning to go crazy. "What if she can't bounce back from this?"

"She will." I wrap my arms around her and place my chin on her shoulder. "She has you, and me, and Ky in her corner. And she's strong. Just like her mother."

It's been a week since Ky has been out of the hospital. He's bouncing back just fine. It's Kira we're all concerned about. She's been having a rough time of it. Not sleeping, barely eating, and deathly afraid of the water. She went through a traumatizing experience. We all acknowledge that. And unfortunately, it wasn't her only one. She and Kristen have traveled down this road before. I have only ever known Kira to be a sweet, beautiful, happy girl. A loving, loyal, woman any man would be proud to call his daughter. Stepdaughter or daughter-in-law.

Kristen's body language is so stiff. She has never felt like this in my arms. Not even after I told her about my past, about the awful things I had done all in the name of being a rebel without a cause. When you're young, you want to be tough. You want to be taken seriously, especially in the arena I grew up in. But then events happen in life that make you see things differently. You have a child. You hold this defenseless little being in your hands, and you suddenly want to be better. Do things better. Do things differently. I didn't want Ky to grow up and follow my path. When his grandfather Alfred passed down the presidency to me, I knew I wanted to make a change. So, I did, gradually. And to my surprise, the majority was behind me. Turns out a simpler life was what most of us were after. Just riding free, enjoying our family, and having a little fun. Deacon was part of the minority. He was my right-hand man for a long time. He loved the life. Loved hurting, stealing, and killing. So, when things started to change, he did everything in his power to keep them the same. He got in bed with some bad people, tried to use the club to launder money and push drugs. Had the 5-0 turning eyes on us. It got to be too much, so I gave him an ultimatum. Quit it or get the fuck out. He didn't appreciate my bluntness, so he tried to kill me with the knife currently stabbed into the bar top at the Den. Things obviously didn't turn out in his favor. He left that day, bloody and bruised, and was never heard from again.

"What if it happens again?" Kristen turns to look at me, wrath in her beautiful blue eyes.

"I want to say this was a fluke thing, Darlin', but there's no guarantee in life. I've done a lot of bad things, but most of the people I crossed are in the ground." Put there by yours truly.

Kristen frowns, her forehead wrinkling. I don't like that expression one bit on my beautiful girl.

"I'm scared, Gerard. And I'm angry. And I'm worried, and all I can think is that it's my fault."

"Your fault?"

"Yes. Maybe we moved too fast. Maybe I didn't give it enough time. I put my daughter in jeopardy again—"

"Kristen, stop." I fluster, taking her face in my hands. This conversation is taking a hard left down a road I don't like. "I will do everything in my power to prevent anything like this from happening again."

"It shouldn't have happened in the first place." Tears spring to her eyes.

"No, it shouldn't have," I agree. "But it did, and we all came out okay."

"Did we?" She's referring to Kira.

"She will be fine. I will not rest until she's as happy and confident and secure as she was before, and Ky won't either. You are not alone, Darlin'. Not anymore."

That has always been one of Kristen's biggest weaknesses, taking everything on herself. By herself. She's as strong as they come wrapped in one gorgeous, feminine package.

"I want to believe you."

"Don't just believe me, believe *in* me." I clutch her face sternly. Kristen visibly relaxes, and I think I have finally gotten through to her. Kristen begins to cry, and it's the first time I have witnessed real emotion pour out of her since she got home from Paris.

She buries her face into my neck and lets the tears loose. I hug her tightly, allowing her to just let it all go.

Ky can see everything that's happening inside, but luckily Kira's back is turned. He stealthily shoots me a knowing look. He'll keep Kira distracted. We both know seeing her mother break down will not be conducive to her healing process.

"Why don't we go upstairs, Darlin'? For a little more privacy."

"Okay," Kristen sniffles, with no indication of detaching herself from me.

"Do you want me to carry you?"

"No," she blubbers adorably, wiping her wet cheek on my shirt.

"Better?" I gaze down at her as she rests her head on my shoulder. She looks exhausted, and stressed, and in need of some decent rest.

"A little."

"Feels good to get it all out?" I tuck some of her dark hair behind her ear.

"There's way more."

"Hmmm, I can think of a few ways to help you relieve some of that stress. I've been missing you these last few days."

"Have you?" She tilts her face up to look at me.

"So much." I drop my head and skim my lips across hers. "I'm here for you. Better or worse."

"I know you are." She regards me with warmth and love returning in her eyes. The way she's looked at me for the last three years. The way it's intended to be. "Now take me upstairs and fuck me slow, and make it mean something." She reiterates what she said to me on our first date.

It makes me as hot and bothered now as it did then. We're finally rekindling the embers that have been left smoking the last few days, and I couldn't be more thankful for it.

Kristen, Ky, and Kira are my life. They're my family and my reason to be.

Nothing is ever going to jeopardize that again.

I trap Kristen in my arms and plant a slow, hot, possessive kiss on her lips before I drag her upstairs.

If she wants it to mean something, it will.

I'm going to make it mean more than just something. I'm going to make it mean everything.

KY

I hold Kira's hands up against mine as I watch my father drag Kristen from the kitchen. They look like they're working things out. I don't know Kristen well, but from what my father has told me about her, she's very much like Kira, happy and loving and loyal, but lately some of those sentiments have been distant in this house.

"C'mon, Snow, just a short swim. We'll stay in the shallow end."

"I don't want to, Ky," Kira fights me, squeezing my fingers with hers. "You're never going to get over your fear if you don't try." Kira hasn't gone near the water since we've been home. Even showers have been difficult for her.

She glances down at the crystal blue H_2O and shivers. "I'm not ready."

"What if I gave you a little incentive?" I bait her.

"What kind of incentive?" She raises an eyebrow.

"Not that kind of incentive. Not yet anyway." I lick my lips salaciously. Kira rolls her eyes, and it's comforting to see her sense of humor retuning little by little. For a minute there, it was touch and go. When she finally broke down, there was a moment when we thought more professional accommodations were needed – i.e., twenty-four-hour observation in an institution — but luckily Kira persevered. She's been seeing her psychologist daily, and I think it's really helping. Her therapist gave her a journal to write in, too, to jot her feelings down so she can pinpoint the triggers, but all she keeps writing is "tears may have fallen, but strength has risen." She says the saying soothes her, so far be it for me to interfere in her healing process. I'm just here, for whatever she needs. Hopefully for life.

Letting go of one of her hands, I pull something out of the pocket of my shorts and hold it up.

Kira stares at it. "Is that what I think it is?"

"Yup. An engagement ring." The jeweler called it a Stargazer ring because of the "stardust" like diamonds on each side of the square center stone. I just liked it because it screamed Kira — elegant, delicate, and feminine. It made a statement, just like she does.

"Don't you think it's a little fast to get engaged?"

"No," I state matter-of-factly. "Our parents got married after three months."

"They're a special case."

"And we're not?" I argue.

"You have a point."

"It doesn't really matter anyway. I'm not officially proposing."

"You're not?"

"Nope." I toss the ring into the pool. "Not until you go get it."

"Ky, I can't believe you just did that." Kira peers down into the water.

"Incentive." I cross my arms. I'm a devious bastard.

"Well, maybe I don't want to marry you." She mirrors my stance. I love it when she tries to act tough.

"Well, maybe that's bullshit, because I know you do. Anyway, I told you, I'm not proposing until you get that ring. So, we don't have to worry about whether or not we're getting married right now." I lean in close, so my lips are an inch away from her ear, and whisper, "It's all up to you, Snow."

The ball is in her court. I'm just the spectator.

"Ky," she hums my name so seductively.

"Yeah?"

"You know I love you, right?" Kira runs a fingertip down my

jugular vein, tracing the letters of my tattoo across my clavicle, then teases her way south to my hip. That single touch has my hormones racing. It's the Indy 500 inside my pants.

"Yeah, I do," I growl like the rambunctious puppy she reduces me to.

"Good." She pushes me right into the pool. "Enjoy your swim," she sings as she struts off, flipping her short hair and everything. Now there is the girl I know and love.

I do believe there's hope for us yet.

KIRA

It's been two days since Ky tossed my engagement ring into the pool.

It's been on my mind nonstop.

I won't deny I want it, or that I want him to propose.

I barely even got a good look at it. It glistened in the sun for the half of a second he held it up, and then it was gone.

Tossing it was such a Ky thing to do.

This is the third night I've sat poolside while everyone sleeps, contemplating going in. But I just can't bring myself to do it, no matter how much I want to. I just keep flashing back to Deacon, holding me under in the bathtub, over and over, until I was barely conscious. He knew the water was my safe place, and he shattered that escape for me.

I run my thumb over the delicate wave tattoo on my wrist. Where do I go if not the water? Where do I find my peace?

The lights below the surface of the pool tempt me to search again for my ring. Retrieving it would mean so much more than just a piece of jewelry on my finger. It would mean Ky and me together for life, and that is an enticing idea.

I touch my palm to the surface of the water. It's warm and tranquil, inviting like always.

Staring at my reflection, the memories stir. The fear, the pain, the agony, it all sharply tingles under my skin, but so does want, and perseverance. Tears rise like the sea, and I let them fall. I let them rain out of me hard and fast and torturous. They hurt, but they also heal. *Though tears may fall, strength can rise. Though tears may fall, strength can rise. Though tears may fall, strength can rise.*

I inhale a deep breath and fall head first into the water.

It's terrifying at first. Immediately, I want to swim to the surface and escape, but I don't. I fight, because as frightening as it is, it's also magnetic. The water calls to me. It cleanses me. It offers me a second chance.

I swim to the bottom of the pool and feel around for the ring. A tiny glint catches my eye, and I know I've found it.

Picking it up, I slide it on my finger and admire my hand under the shadows of the lights. It's beautiful, and special, and perfect.

I push off the pool floor and break through the surface, gasping for air. I feel reborn. I feel alive.

"'Bout time you went down and got that thing." Ky's voice startles me. I spin around in the pool, and there he stands, watching me.

"How long have you been spying on me?" I swim to the edge, right beneath him.

"Every second of every day."

"Stalker," I accuse.

"Yup." He wears the name with pride.

"So, I think we had a deal." I hold up my hand and him over the fire.

"I believe we did." He crouches down. He's shirtless, and sinful, and way too sexy for his own damn good. "I like you all wet."

"I like you wet, too." I pull him into the pool.

When he pops his head out of the water, he heads straight for me, pinning me against the wall and sliding his tongue all the way into my mouth, eating me slowly with kisses. I moan instantly, my body succumbing.

"I've missed you." I wrap my arms around him and kiss him back with full force.

"I've always been right here." He licks my neck, up and down, tasting, craving, consuming. Shifting us over to where we can stand better, Ky crushes me back against the wall. I get lost in the feel of him. In his strong hands groping me, in his powerful body pinning me in place, in the feel of his erection digging in right between my legs.

"Kira." The intensity in his eyes and his voice tells me everything I need to know. He wants me. Right here and now, no matter what, and I want him, too. I need him, too.

"Yes, God, please. Fuck, yes." I'm desperate for him. There's so much inside me that needs to come out, and Ky is the only one who can release it.

"You have to be quiet, Snow." He spins me around so I can grip the ledge of the pool. I can barely stand on my tiptoes, but he locks me in a hold so tight I'm not going anywhere.

He groans against my neck as he massages one of my breasts. The need pouring out from him insatiable. I love the way he overtakes me. The way he dominates me. The way he makes me feel safe even in his ravenous state.

"Please touch me," I rasp as his hand moves south down my torso. He traps my mouth with his as he sensually uses all four of his fingers to massage my clit. "This is mine," he growls, and I nearly see stars, the pressure is so perfect. "And this." He pushes a finger inside me and pumps sternly. "You're all fucking mine, Kira."

"Yes," I huff, arching in his iron hold. "Ky, I need you." My voice is breathy, and he's barely even begun.

"Need me where?" he goads.

"Inside me, please." I'm achy and anxious and just want him to dive in so deep the stars and solar system blend into one.

"Mmm." He nips at my flesh, liking my response. He shifts slightly behind be, and then I feel it, the blissful head of his erection nudging at my entrance. We're both barely clothed, him in just basketball shorts and me in a tight tank top and panties, but it's as if we're completely bare. Nothing is stopping us or coming between us.

Ky sinks into me so deliberately slow I experience every single inch of him on a heightened level. I moan out into the blackness of night, smothered by a haze of lust.

"Shh, baby." Ky covers my mouth as he flexes his hips provokingly. But it's so good, and I'm so over-sensitized, I just want to release it all. There is so much I need to let out. I don't hold a damn thing back, using his hand as my sound barrier. My sighs intensify with every powerful, measured thrust. My body permanently tense, my pussy permanently constricted. "Jesus, Kira." Ky feels it, too. We don't break eye contact as we fuck, as we make love, as we reconnect in a way we so desperately needed to. "You're so tight I can barely take it," he pants, labored. He doesn't realize I'm riding the same maddening wavelength. He's so thick and hard and long I'm disintegrating right in his grasp. I'm battling for breath when something suddenly shifts, a snap of sparring desire. We both instinctually need the release, our bodies assuming control as nature intended. Ky drives harder, faster, deeper, possessed by a surge of ecstasy. The fiber-splitting rhythm is our undoing.

There's no holding back the orgasm rushing to engulf my body. I tremble and fight against Ky's hold, needing an outlet for the moment of impact, but he keeps me restrained, forcing all the pressure to concentrate right smack in the center of my thighs. I scream behind his hand when I come from the hysteria of pleasure. It's one of the hottest, most forbidden orgasms of my life. It explodes right out of me, releasing tension buried so deep inside it was residual from my past.

Ky comes seconds after me, the water splashing around us as his violent thrusts rattle us both.

His hand slides from my mouth when the convulsions subside, and he rests his worn, heaving body against mine. Pressing sensual kisses down my neck, he continues to hold me tight. "You drive me crazy, and you make me sane. How is that possible?" he murmurs.

I laugh in a sex-induced daze. "I could ask the same thing about you."

Loosening his hold, he spins me in his arms so we are face to face and stares at me like I am the most beautiful thing he's ever seen. "I am so stupidly in love with you," he declares. "I can't wait to make you my wife."

"I don't recall you actually proposing. That was the deal, right? I get the ring, you pop the question?"

"I do recall such a conversation. Yes. That seems like such a long time ago, though." He pretends to ponder.

"I know how to keep a guy waiting." I steal a kiss from him.

"You also know how to teach him a few things."

"Oh, yeah, like what?" I ask dreamily.

"Let it hurt then let it go."

I regard Ky thoughtfully. "I taught you that?"

He nods. "You've taught me so much. You've helped me fix so much. You brought my family back together and made me own so many of my mistakes."

I blink blankly. "*I* did all that?"

"You are a pretty remarkable woman." We drift through the calm water together, tangled in each other's arms. "You've made me realize every single mistake I have ever made has brought me to this moment. To you. To us."

"I don't feel remarkable."

"Well, that's the thing about remarkable people. They never know they're remarkable. But everyone else can see it." He tucks a strand of wet hair behind my ear. "And I want to spend the rest of my life with someone remarkable."

"No pressure."

"None." Ky plants his hands on my ass and squeezes. "So, what do you say? Will you marry me and be my remarkable person for as long as we both shall live?"

I slide my hand down Ky's shoulder to his chest. We both look at the sparkling ring sitting on my finger. "I think I already said yes."

Ky smiles brightly. Happily, freely. "I think I love you." He leans in to kiss me.

"How did that happen?" I echo a question he once asked me.

Ky glances upwards, then whispers, "Only the stars know."

THE END.

AFTERWORD

I hope you enjoyed Ky and Kira's story! They were so much fun to write! If you would like to know more about Kristen and Gerard, you can download Snowfall now, the prequel to Slashes in the Snow! You can also listen to the audiobook for FREE on the Read Me Romance podcast!

Do you want more Baum Squad Mafia? Be on the lookout for Aces High, Breaker's book coming late 2019!

SNEAK PEEK AT ACES HIGH

Breaker

SOMETIMES LIFE DEALS you a shitty hand, and sometimes it deals you a sweet one.

Four years ago, my father died and left me with a steaming pile of horse shit. That pile? Two hundred fifty thousand dollars in gambling debts. The man sure loved the ponies. Luckily for me, my dad's bookie was one of his closest friends, so he allowed me to pay off the debt little by little. For years, I've lived meagerly under the radar of my Baum Squad Mafia brothers who were unaware I was financially drowning.

I had everything under control until the turn on the river went bust and The Bowman passed away. Now, I'm fucked, cause the arrangement he made with the men I owe died the day he did, and now they're here to collect. I have two measly weeks to cough up the money, or it's lights out Breaker. The only silver lining about having two weeks left to live? The Bowman's death brought Liv, his daughter, back into my life. We grew up together. She's practically my sister —

and hates me with the same ferocity of an estranged sibling, too. But time apart and grief do strange things to people. They bring them together in unexpected ways. Like drunk and horny and naked in your bed.

Life, I tell ya. It can sure deal one hell of a motherfuckin' hand.

ABOUT THE AUTHOR

M. Never is a USA Today bestselling author of dark and contemporary romance. Her females are fierce and her alphas are magnetizing, just like the romance she provokes between them. She casts a spell, weaving one wonderous word at a time. A native of new Jersey, she is now a Maryland transplant juggling life the way one would juggle knives —carefully reckless. She has a dependence on sushi, a fetish for boots, and is stalked by a clingy pit bull named Apache. Writing is her passion, but readers are her love.

ALSO BY M NEVER

Owned (Decadence After Dark Book 1)

Claimed (Decadence After Dark Book 2)

Ruined (A Decadence After Dark Epilogue)

The Decadence After Dark Box Set (Books 1–3)

Lie With Me (Decadence After Dark Book 4)

Elicit (Decadence After Dark Book 5)

Moto: A MFM Ménage Romance

Trinity: A MMF Ménage Romance

Ghostface Killer

The Southern Nights Series

Stripped From You (Stripped Duet #1)

Strip Me Bare (Stripped Duet #2)

A.C.H.E.

Snowfall: A Slashes in the Snow Prequel

www.mneverauthor.com

#ProvocativeRomance

Printed in Great Britain
by Amazon